Dedication

This book is dedicated to my parents. Thank you for believing that I could do this and never making me feel like pursuing my dream wasn't important. Thank you for reading my terrible early drafts of each book, for the hour long phone calls to chat storylines and plot holes, and for all the times you've talked business strategy with me as I navigate this new career. I love you both. This one is for you, Mum and Dad.

Stuck On You

HEATHER THURMEIER

CRIMSON
ROMANCE

F+W Media, Inc.

Published by
Crimson Romance
an imprint of F+W Media, Inc.
10151 Carver Road, Suite 200
Blue Ash, Ohio 45242

www.crimsonromance.com

Chapter One

Paige Anderson stood on the outskirts of the staging area under a clear blue sky trying her best not to hurl on her new hiking boots. She'd made a mistake. She didn't stand a chance against teams like Mr. Muscles and Friend—Team Everest, according to the official game team names—or any of the others for that matter.

Speaking of Mr. Muscles, every time she glanced his way—which seemed to be more and more often—she'd catch him staring at her when he was supposed to be engaging in conversation with his teammate. This time when her eyes caught his, she noted his subtle eyebrow raise and a tiny smirk pulling up the corners of his mouth. Combine that with his light brown hair and sun-kissed skin, and it was hard to look away. Not to mention a little twinkle of something interesting in his dark chocolate eyes she couldn't quite pinpoint but found incredibly intriguing nonetheless. She tried to look away but it was difficult when Mr. Muscles stood there with his arms folded across his chest, biceps bulging against his thin cotton t-shirt.

Poor material doesn't stand a chance.

She swallowed the sudden urge to comfort the pathetic t-shirt that looked as if it were a single pushup away from tearing and forced her eyes to keep moving. She couldn't enjoy the man-candy competition fully while her own teammate was still MIA.

Where the hell was Cassidy? She should have arrived yesterday or the day before like everyone else, and yet Paige hadn't heard from her. Nor had Cassidy answered any of the texts or voicemails she'd left before the show's producer Chip had confiscated her phone. How were they supposed to survive on an adventure show if they couldn't even communicate their whereabouts before the show started?

Cassidy and Paige had become fast friends the year before while on a different reality show—one where they'd both vied for a bachelor's attention, along with eight other women. Out of all the women on the show, Cassidy was the nicest and most beautiful and it came as no surprise to Paige when not only the bachelor, but also a cameraman, had fallen in love with Cassidy during the show.

Of course, Paige hadn't made it anywhere near the finale with bachelor Brad. Nope. She'd been sent packing at the third elimination—humiliated and crushed.

Thank God this wasn't another dating show. No chance of major televised rejection to tarnish the experience. No sexy bachelor to distract her and Cassidy from winning the money and prizes.

Her eyes flickered back to Mr. Muscles again as if to prove her theory wrong right from the start. Damn. He was built to climb mountains. She'd like to climb his mountain.

Yeah, right. In my dreams.

Paige let out the breath she hadn't realized she'd been holding when she spotted Evan, Cassidy's new fiancé, chatting with a few other cameramen. If Evan was here, that had to mean Cassidy was here too. And when Paige finally found her, Cassidy would get a solid reminder about how you're supposed to tell your friend and teammate that you've arrived in one piece so said teammate doesn't worry.

"Gather around everyone," Chip Cormack, the show's producer said, waving the contestants over. "In a few moments we'll start filming. After a brief introduction by our host, Spencer Daley, the competition will begin. Now is your last chance to ask any questions you might have after reading the information packet you were provided."

He paused and looked around the group as if he expected an immediate outburst of questioning to begin. No one said a thing. The packet of information had been very thorough. A list of dos and don'ts for the show, legal obligations and warnings, and health waivers had basically covered everything you could imagine.

Except for one thing still weighing on Paige's mind: What to do if your partner is a no-show.

The main reason Paige stood here to begin with was to spend time with Cassidy doing something fun. Well, that and she really wanted a little time away from the chaos awaiting her back home. Seemed every single guy in a fifty-mile radius of her house had seen her get kicked off *The One* and each claimed to be her perfect man. How could she have a perfect man when she felt like a walking rejection? The bachelor Brad on *The One* hadn't wanted her, so why would any of these other guys?

Cassidy always knew the right thing to say to cheer her up, make her feel more confident, and send her on the right path again—exactly what she needed right now.

Of course, she needed Cassidy to actually show up before any of that could happen.

She cautiously raised her hand, reverting back to her Catholic school days of ornery nuns who didn't take kindly to children who spoke out of turn.

"Yes, Paige." Chip smiled one of his famous smiles that could make any woman agree to just about anything, including being on another reality show when she'd sworn she wouldn't be caught dead on television again. Ever.

"Um." She swallowed, her throat feeling dry as all eyes turned toward her. "My partner hasn't shown up yet. Is that a problem?"

"We'll get to that soon."

Not quite the response she expected considering he'd said they would start filming in a few minutes. Maybe he'd seen Cassidy and knew she was on her way here. That had to be it.

"If there are no other questions, then I think it's time we get started. I'd like to see each of the teams standing together in their groups of two." Chip turned his attention to the camera crew. "Guys, you can take your places with your team now."

Paige glanced around feeling her nervousness escalate. All

around her, teams formed, looking eager to get started. She stood alone, quivering in her hiking boots and cursing Cassidy. Her gaze landed on Evan as he took his place a few feet to the left, pointing his camera at her.

"Where the hell is your fiancée?" she asked in a stern whisper as she applied a fresh coat of mint lip balm. In about five seconds she was really going to lose her calm façade and start to panic.

"She'll be here. Don't worry," he said, a silly grin breaking his otherwise calm demeanor.

Great. Evan was laughing at her and the show hadn't even started yet. Awesome.

She turned away from his stupid grin and focused instead on Chip who was now standing with Spencer Daley, the host of the show, talking in a hushed voice. Just behind them, movement from one of the production trailers caught her attention. The door to the trailer opened and out stepped Cassidy.

The butterflies in Paige's stomach calmed to a flutter instead of a full on frenzy at the sight of her friend walking toward her. Finally, she wouldn't be standing alone like a chump anymore. She'd have a partner by her side like everyone else.

She waved Cassidy over. Cassidy returned a weak smile, but instead of coming to stand beside Paige, she joined Chip.

Maybe she needs to explain why she's so late to the filming.

Cassidy chatted with Chip for a few minutes, darting tiny glances back at Paige and Evan. Although a spark of nervousness flashed across Cassidy's face, she looked calm and happy. In fact, she looked radiant. Her hair fell down her back in giant waves; her light tunic-style blouse flowed loosely over her body, except for where she held her hand to her stomach.

I hope she's not ill. Starting a competition like this—one promising to be high-energy with tests of endurance—would be difficult if sick with a stomach bug.

Come to think of it. Cassidy's outfit, complete with leggings and ballet flats, didn't look at all like what the other competitors were wearing. Certainly she didn't go with Paige's Lycra yoga tank top, slim-fit jeans with just the right amount of stretch in them to make it possible to actually do more than stand still and look cute, and pristine hiking boots, fresh out of the box and laced tightly up to her ankles.

Paige stepped toward Cassidy to find out what exactly was going on, but before she could, Chip held up his hand to quiet the bit of talking that had started amongst the teams.

"If I can have your attention again, please. We're ready to begin. Camera crew, it's time to start recording. So without further ado, here is your host for the show, Spencer Daley." Chip clapped as Spencer turned on his television-worthy smile and waved at everyone to stop fussing over him even though he clearly enjoyed every second.

"Welcome, everyone, to the first season of *Treasure Trekkers*, the show that will have you racing for treasures in caches hidden around the New York metropolitan area as well as the lower Hudson Valley." He paused to smile for the camera a moment before continuing on. "You never know what surprise you'll find in the next cache. Perhaps you'll find money, or a fantastic trip for two. Maybe you'll even find the keys to a new car!"

The contestants cheered. Even Paige who was normally pretty quiet and reserved cheered at the idea of being able to win really awesome prizes along the way without having to win the whole show. Even with Cassidy as her teammate, the chances of winning the adventure show were pretty slim for two girls who weren't exactly athletic or outdoorsy. Winning a few prizes could go a long way to making Paige more comfortable in life. Her salary as a freelance graphic artist covered the bills, but little else. But at least she could take time off whenever she wanted.

"Speaking of surprises, we're starting off the show with a big one." Spencer motioned for Cassidy to come and stand beside him instead of off to the side where she had been next to Chip. "I'm sure most of you have already noticed that one of our teams of two is currently a team of one. But not for long."

Paige felt her insecurity creeping up into her cheeks. She hated being the center of attention. Why had she ever agreed to come on this new show? Was a free trip, an interesting experience, and time spent with her good friend really worth all this?

Spencer gestured to her. "Paige has been patiently waiting for her teammate to show up and here she is with me. Cassidy, why don't you tell everyone why you're here with me instead of over there with your teammate."

Cassidy glanced around the small gathering, smiling as she found the spot where Evan stood filming. Then her eyes met Paige's quickly before settling back on Spencer. "Well, um, there's been a little change of plans."

What change of plans? No one spoke to me about any changes and I've been here all day.

"I was supposed to run the race with Paige." Cassidy caught Paige's gaze again, her expression clearly apologetic for what she was about to say. "But I'm sorry. I can't run the race with you."

Can't run the race? I can't run it alone.

"And why is that?" Spencer asked even though he absolutely had to already know the answer. But America didn't and neither did Paige.

How? Why? What could possibly make it okay for Cassidy to think she could abandon Paige at the last minute like this? Her chest tightened at the thought of having to run it alone. Or drop out before they even started.

Damn. Getting voted out in the third round on *The One* was bad enough, but now she was about to be kicked off in the first episode of a show where everyone was supposed to compete until the end. This wasn't fair.

Cassidy looked away from Paige and back to Evan, a smile coming to her lips. "Because I'm pregnant."

Tears instantly pricked Paige's eyes. Pregnant? Okay, that was a pretty damn good reason not to run a possibly dangerous race. Without thinking, Paige took the few steps separating her from her friend and wrapped Cassidy in a hug.

"A baby? And you didn't tell me," she teased.

Cassidy nodded. "We just found out. I'm so sorry, Paige. I was really looking forward to running the race with you."

Paige stepped back from Cassidy. "Don't be silly. We can't have you putting a tiny Cassidy/Evan baby in danger for some stupid show."

"Hey now." Spencer laughed. "The show is anything but stupid."

"You know what I mean," Paige said, brushing off Spencer's comment and focusing only on her friend—her pregnant and engaged friend. Tears blurred her vision. "I'm just so happy for you both."

"I wanted to tell you right away, but once I told Chip I couldn't do the show anymore, he forced me to wait to announce it here."

"And now that you have made this wonderful announcement, the show must go on," Spencer said, nudging Paige back to her spot. He gave a huge smile to Cassidy. "On behalf of the production company, congratulations and we wish you well with everything." And with that, he motioned for Cassidy to step out of frame.

"The show must go on and go on it will. But not with Paige as a solo team."

Paige felt her pulse race again. So this was it. The moment she was asked to join Cassidy on the sidelines where she could watch the show with the rest of America. Kicked off on day one. And she thought getting rejected by Brad was bad. This was a new low point for her life.

Yippy.

"Paige, we can't let you race alone. It wouldn't be fair to you or the other teams and honestly, it would be dangerous considering some of the caches we have hidden for you." Spencer paused, his hands clasped, fingers intertwined as if he were going to pray for help.

She swallowed the lump in her throat and prepared to take her exit with as much grace as she could. She didn't want to run the race alone anyway. It would be too hard. Too lonely. Too embarrassing. She'd much rather sit this whole game out and be able to keep Cassidy company while Evan was filming the show. They could talk about baby names and buy little tiny clothes and have an excuse to eat outrageous amounts of ice cream.

"So, we've made a decision," Spencer spoke, capturing her attention again. "And we've picked a new partner for you."

Say what now?

Just then, someone stepped out from behind the production trailer. The moment Paige glimpsed platform stilettos and long golden hair, she knew she'd died and somehow gone to hell because there was no way this was really happening.

No. Fricken'. Way.

Chapter Two

"I'm sure you all remember Zoe Oliver from *The One* and from her appearance on the game show she almost won before that," Spencer continued without waiting for a response. "Zoe, please join your new partner. Zoe has graciously accepted our invitation to be a part of the show on such last minute notice and we're thrilled to have her here."

Jack Miles eyed the petite brunette now standing next to Zoe and wondered if he would have to catch her before she hit the floor since she suddenly looked as if she might faint. He wouldn't mind catching her. She was tiny, tight, and hot—just the way he liked his women. Add to that her porcelain skin in contrast to her long brown hair and her dark eyes, and it was enough to make him take a second look.

Of course, he also liked his women to be confident, which by the sheepish look on her face, she was anything but. She didn't seem too happy to be in the spotlight for this interesting turn of events. Maybe her lack of confidences was just nervousness from starting the game with a twist like a new teammate.

He couldn't imagine losing his teammate Ben either. Ben had been his hiking buddy since college and they'd seen some of the most amazing places in the world together. He couldn't imagine having him bail last minute and being stuck with a new partner with no notice or prep time before the show started.

And to end up with Zoe Oliver as your partner, well, that might just be too much for the most even-keeled person to handle. Zoe wasn't exactly known to be a nice girl. Or a team player. Interesting choice on Chip's part to put her on the show.

But from the amount of nodding from the other teams, everyone else knew Zoe as well. It was hard not to. It had been

Zoe who'd stood beside Cassidy in the finale of *The One*. It was Zoe who had ended up on the cover of tabloid magazines for months after the finale aired.

And it had been Zoe who'd played the part of villain and had made it her mission on the show to make the other girls' lives miserable. No one—who'd seen the show or tabloid news—would want to be forced into a partnership with Zoe after how she'd acted on that show.

"Now that everything is settled with the teams," Spencer said, "it's time to kick off our show. At the sound of my whistles, these ten teams will race down the hill behind me to the marked vehicles with your names on the windshield. Inside each vehicle you'll find your backpacks, a cooler of cold water and energy snacks, and a state of the art hand-held GPS unit, which has been specially equipped with a camera and internal server for our game. You'll use your new GPS to find the five hundred treasure boxes—or caches, as we like to call them—we have hidden around the area."

Miles smiled, feeling sure of himself and his partner. With all the supplies they gave them, this challenge would be a breeze. And with a vehicle to get around in, it would be easier for Ben— because of his limitations with his leg, physical fatigue and long- term mobility were probably going to be their team's biggest personal challenges.

"Each day you will get to race from eight in the morning until eight at night, during which time you are free to find as many caches as you can. But be warned. You will be turned away from some caches if you arrive too late to complete them before the end of the day. By eight p.m. sharp, every team will be expected to have checked in at the base camp where you'll all be staying. If a team fails to check in at base camp before time is up, they will receive a two-hour time penalty for the next day's hours."

The rules didn't sound too tricky, but it may be a lot to think about once the game got rolling and adrenaline started pumping.

Although, Miles didn't expect adrenaline to be a problem for himself or Ben. They lived for the rush. Always had.

"The game is simple," Spencer continued. "Find as many hidden caches as you can in the next twenty-eight days. Be the first to find the cache and you may find more than just game points. Many caches have prizes to collect but only for the first team to find them. At the end of the race, we'll tally the points you've collected with each cache you've found, and the team with the most cumulative points will win the grand prize of… half a million dollars!"

The teams cheered. Even Miles couldn't help but cheer for that kind of money. He'd do whatever it took to win. Then he'd give his portion to Ben to help right his wrongs.

"Oh, and I'd expect a few surprises along the way too." Spencer winked. As if sensing a growing concern among the teammates, he raised his arms over his head to get them to quiet down so he could finish his speech. "Okay, everyone. I'll see you at base camp for our first check in. Teams, start searching!" With that, he dropped his arms as if he were starting a drag race.

Teams on every side of Miles bolted past Spencer and down the hill. Two of the bigger guys—Team Firefighters from New York City, if he remembered correctly—were the first to find their vehicle. Not surprising since guys like them were trained to be fast. And efficient. He made a mental note to keep them in his sights.

A cluster of three or four teams reached the vehicles next. The team of sisters was fast, but Kent and Kyla, the dating underwear models, were even faster. They had sprinted the entire way. They were definitely faster than he'd expected. For being incredibly thin, they were also in amazing shape. Team Models might actually be more of a threat than he thought at first glance.

Miles and Ben ran too, but at a slower pace. Still, they made it down the hill and to the vehicles only moments later than the rest of the teams. Well, not including Paige and Zoe's team. It appeared those girls were in no real hurry with Zoe in her four-inch heels and Paige still looking shell-shocked from the early twist in the game.

But Miles couldn't sit around wondering how the girls would do in the race. It was their business, not his. His priority number one was getting Ben to the end of the game with the most points and prizes in hand. And proving to him they could still take on any challenge together. And succeed.

Miles and Ben found their SUV easily since there were only two left. A quick glance at the name on the windshield and they pulled open the doors. Miles hopped into the driver's seat while Ben jumped into the backseat behind him. Their cameraman rode shotgun where he could film facial expressions of both men.

He handed the GPS unit to Ben and ripped open the folder of information they'd been given to start the race. Inside he found a logbook with a series of numbered GPS coordinates listed. Pages and pages of longitudes and latitudes stared back at him. Even for an experienced hiker, it was overwhelming.

"Wow. Look at this." Miles showed the logbook to Ben. "The other teams aren't going to know where to start."

"Good. Because I think we've fallen behind already," Ben said, looking out the side window instead of at the logbook.

"No worries. This is a long race and where we lack on speed, we'll make up for by being able to use the GPS better than the others. Let's just pick one in the middle and get started."

Ben shook his head. "I hope you're right. But I'm pretty sure we're due for last place."

"Well, I think you're wrong and it's about time you started believing in yourself again. You're just as able as any of the other teams here." He glanced down at Ben's leg, already stretched out along the backbench seat, unable to stop himself from reliving the injury again as if it were his own.

"Well, I'm definitely as able as that team. Can you believe they only just now reached their vehicle?" Ben said, sounding marginally disgusted.

Miles couldn't really blame him. It was pretty sad that two able-bodied girls couldn't even beat them in a footrace to the trucks. "Probably don't want to break a nail."

"That's most likely true for Zoe, but I'm not so sure about that Paige girl. That's a team of polar opposites if I ever saw one. Glamorous and high-maintenance paired with functional plain Jane."

Miles eyed the girls. Ben was right about Zoe, but what about Paige? Functional? Sure. That tight top and those sensible hiking boots were definitely functional in this game. But plain Jane? No way. She might be understated but she certainly wasn't plain.

"Well, we can beat one team for sure," Miles said, looking away from Paige's tiny hourglass figure and delicately curved lips. He didn't have time to take in the scenery right now. But later, at base camp, well, there'd be plenty of time for sightseeing then. "And I know we can beat the others too."

"Whatever. Let's go already," Ben said.

Miles had heard the dismissal in Ben's tone more times than he cared to remember. Somehow, some way, he had to prove to Ben that he was still capable of everything they'd ever wanted to achieve. And maybe this show would finally be the thing that got through to him.

But there was no sense pushing things with Ben now. Not right at the beginning of what would be a long and challenging race.

Together they skimmed through the logbook, trying to decide where to start their search. Finally they picked cache 252—just a couple off from the middle to be one step ahead of all the teams who started exactly in the middle. Perfect.

Ben effortlessly punched in the latitude and longitude listed beside the cache number into the GPS unit. A moment later, the screen flashed to life and an arrow pointed the direction they needed to go.

As Miles drove through the parking lot toward the highway, he could already make out a couple of other SUVs up ahead on the side of the road. They didn't look to be in any distress, unless you counted not knowing how to even turn on a GPS unit.

He smiled at his friend, feeling triumphant already. "See, I told you we'd be okay. Game on." They bumped fists as they did at the peak of every mountain they'd ever climbed. And it felt great. Two years had been way too long to be without his best friend by his side. Now that he had Ben back, he had to make sure to keep him. And the best way to do that was prove to Ben they could win.

*

Paige pulled their name card off the windshield of the truck and climbed into the backseat on the driver's side behind Zoe who was busy scowling at her fingernails.

"Damn it. I broke a nail on the stupid door handle. That's a great way to start our race. Now we'll have to stop at the nail salon to get it fixed."

Paige's mouth dropped open. "You can't be serious."

"Serious like a Manolo Blahnik sale."

"Wow. We're almost the last team still sitting in the parking lot and all you can think about is getting your nail fixed. You remember we're in a competition right?"

Zoe rolled her eyes. "Of course I remember. But I also remembered that we're being followed by cameras." She turned in her seat to face Evan who'd climbed into the SUV and filmed from the front passenger seat. "Long time no see, Evan. Good thing you got that girl of yours knocked up. Now she won't be around and we can really have some fun at base camp each night."

"Zoe! Cassidy is going to see that on TV, you know."

Zoe smiled. "Good. She needs a reminder of the temptations facing her man everyday while she's at home eating ice cream and getting fat."

"Oh my God. Stop talking." Paige couldn't have felt more uncomfortable in front of the camera at that moment even if she'd been buck-naked. Well, maybe that wasn't totally true. Naked in front of the national viewing audience would definitely be worse. But she wasn't crazy about Zoe's behavior. Especially not at Cassidy's expense.

Evan caught her eye from behind the camera and shrugged. If he was unconcerned about Zoe, then there was no reason for Paige to waste any more time worrying about her either. Nope. She had bigger worries right now, like how to catch up in a race they were already way behind on.

"Can we focus on the competition we're supposed to actually be competing in and you can worry about getting your precious nail fixed later? Like maybe after we check in at base camp for the night." Paige glanced out the window as Team Everest pulled out of the parking lot. It seemed strange that they hadn't been faster getting to their vehicle since they both looked so fit. Maybe they were just muscled without actually being athletic. "Great, now we really are the last team to leave."

Zoe glanced up from the packet of information and watched as the team drove off. If Paige wasn't mistaken, she could have sworn Zoe stiffened at the sight of the other team, her back straightening and her eyes narrowing a little. Weird. It was way too early to have enemies here. Unless you had a history with someone like Paige had with Zoe. Then it made perfect sense to be enemies already. Too bad she had to now be partners with hers.

Zoe handed over the GPS unit, which Paige then tried unsuccessfully to turn on. Damn it. Why did everything have to turn to shit today? Seriously, today was supposed to be the start of a fun adventure with her best friend. She and Cassidy should be zipping along the highway on the way to their first cache now, laughing and joking around. Getting caught up on all the things that had happened in their lives since agreeing to do another reality show for Chip.

Instead she was stuck in a car with bitchy Zoe in an empty parking lot without a sniff of an idea what to do first. Already at the back of the pack and it was only day one of twenty-eight.

If there was a hell, this was the front gate.

And Zoe was the hostess with the mostest.

Suddenly, being sent home before the show had even started didn't sound like such a bad idea. Too bad they'd dragged Zoe out of whatever rich man's bed she'd been in so she could come and harass Paige.

Zoe took the GPS unit back and expertly switched it on. "They just had to stick me with the girl who can't even work a simple piece of technology. Switch with me. I don't have time to teach you how to use this thing right now."

Paige ignored Zoe's rude comment and climbed into the driver's seat while Zoe settled herself in the back. She wasn't a great driver either, but as long as they stayed on the highway, out in the country, she should be fine. "What cache should we look for first? Maybe start at number one and work our way through them?"

"Sure, if we want to be following half the other teams around. And the other half is probably split between starting in the exact middle and starting at the end. No, we need to pick a random spot and hope for the best."

Good thinking. Maybe Zoe was smarter than she looked.

Paige flipped through a few pages but it did little good. All the coordinates blurred together with no possible way to discern what might be the best one to start with. "How about number 303? Random enough for you?"

"Perfect. I'll punch in the coordinates while you start driving. Looks like there's really only one way out of here right now and it will take us to a major interstate. By then I should have this up and running and I'll tell you were to go."

Why can't I be the one to tell her where to go? I have so many creative ideas.

Zoe leaned back in the seat and put her feet up on the middle console between the driver and passenger's seats. Paige couldn't help but notice the bright red sole beneath the sparkling heel.

"Nice shoes," Paige teased as she pulled out of the parking lot. "Let's hope the first cache isn't anywhere without a sidewalk."

"Christian Louboutins are perfect for any occasion."

"Even hiking?"

"You'd be amazed at what I can do in these shoes." The tone of Zoe's voice turned flirtatious as she peered into Evan's camera.

"I'm going to pretend you didn't imply something I'd really rather not think about you doing."

"I'm sorry, prude. Are your panties in a twist all of a sudden? I've heard that's painful but I wouldn't know since I don't wear any."

"TMI, Zoe. Seriously. I may be your partner in this competition but I really don't need to know your panty preferences."

"Just because you're comfortable in combat boots and a turtleneck—"

"Hiking boots and a yoga top," Paige interrupted.

"Whatever." Zoe waived her hand at her dismissively. "Make a left onto the interstate. Looks like we're headed into New York City."

Chapter Three

Paige panicked at the thought of having to drive into a city with millions of other people on the road. It wasn't bad enough that she was stuck with Zoe. Now she also had to drive, which she didn't really care for unless the road was straight and empty. Nope. Now she was headed into one of the busiest cities in the world being navigated by the biggest bitch in the world.

Maybe if she pretended she wasn't nervous, she wouldn't be. Or maybe she'd still get them killed in a multi-car pile up on the Henry Hudson.

"Now which way?" Paige asked, gripping the steering wheel.

"Straight. I'll tell you when we have to take an exit."

"Oh, okay," she mumbled. She didn't like this at all. Cars surrounded her on every side. Zoe muttered from the backseat repeatedly about how she needed to drive faster. Easy for her to say when she wasn't the one who had to avoid hitting obstacles moving seventy miles an hour.

"You are competent enough to drive a vehicle, right? You do have a license?"

Paige rolled her eyes then quickly focused back on the highway again, swallowing hard. Note to self: No eye rolling while driving.

"Of course I have a license."

"Then why do I get the overwhelming feeling that I'm at driving school again and you're one panic attack away from getting us all killed?"

"I just, um, don't like driving in so much traffic. That's all."

Paige heard Zoe whispering to herself but couldn't make out what she said. Did she really want to know? Probably not. And yet she felt compelled to ask. They were teammates after all. "Everything okay back there?"

"Great." Zoe's voice deadpan and very much reflective of Paige's mood.

Don't ask. Just move on.

She sighed. If they were going to be together for weeks and work as a team, they needed to be able to talk about everything. Even if she didn't really want to, she needed to be nice to Zoe. Maybe if she treated her with respect, Zoe would do the same.

"If we're going to work together, we should talk about things that are bothering us. It's not going to help to keep everything bottled up inside."

"Well, therapist Paige. I was thinking to myself that when we check in at base camp, I'm going to find Chip and rip him a new one for pairing me with a girl who's not only technology impaired, but also can't drive. What else are you lacking that I should be aware of? Because maybe I should know that now. I may as well be running this race alone for all the help you've provided so far."

So much for nice and respectful.

"When you're done with Chip, send him my way so I can thank him for partnering me with Cruella de Vil. Do you kill puppies in your spare time? Because I think you've got the right personality for that line of work."

"We need to take that exit up ahead."

Paige felt her head spin for a second. "What?" She shoulder-checked quickly before gunning it and swerving into the right lane, narrowly pulling ahead of a minivan. "I told you I needed notice for exits."

"That was notice. The GPS only gives me so much advance warning."

Paige took the exit too fast. She pressed hard on the brake to slow the SUV down quickly before they flipped going around the tight corner. The car behind her honked. But they could honk all they wanted. If they had Zoe in the backseat, they'd be frazzled behind the wheel too.

"Ouch," Zoe called from the back where she'd banged her shoulder into the door as they'd come out of the sharp corner.

If only Zoe's door had flung open at the time. Then Paige would have one less headache.

"You have no one to blame for your injury but yourself. Maybe next time you'll give me more warning if you want me to drive."

"Maybe there won't be a next time with the way you drive."

A yellow cab came out of nowhere, laid on the horn, and flipped Paige the finger as she hit the brake so hard the tires squealed. Zoe shrieked in the back as she slammed face first into the back of Paige's seat.

With her knuckles white on the steering wheel, Paige took a couple of deep breaths and tried to stop her sudden urge to throw up. From beside her, Evan chuckled as he pointed his camera toward Zoe.

"I blame you for all of this," Paige said, narrowing her eyes at Evan. "You just had to go and get Cassidy all knocked up so she couldn't be my partner. You better name that baby after me if it's a girl."

He shrugged and smiled in response.

Refocusing, she asked, "Where to now, Zoe?"

For the next few minutes—that felt more like eternity—they made their way through the busy city streets with Zoe telling her where to turn. Paige did her best not to get them into any more close calls with taxis.

"It's somewhere in there," Zoe said as they pulled alongside Central Park.

"Okay, where can I turn in?"

"I don't know. It says we're pretty close. I think we're going to have to park and do the rest on foot."

"Park where?"

Zoe leaned in between the two front seats and pointed a little way down the street. "There. That big P is a parking garage. We can drop the car off then double back into the park."

"Did they give us any money in the information packet?"

Zoe opened it and pulled out a handful of bills. "Looks like more than enough for parking."

"But what if we need it for other things?" Paige asked. They should be careful with their money since no one had told them yet if they were going to get any more along the way. What if this was the only money they got and then didn't have enough for another one of the caches later on?

"Unless you want to drive around for an hour looking for street parking and wasting even more time, then I suggest we pull into the garage and tell them to keep it somewhere close since we'll be back in a few minutes."

Paige didn't answer. There was no point. Zoe was right and arguing with her or strategizing other options was only going to waste precious time. They'd already lost enough of that at the beginning of the race.

After dropping off the SUV, they crossed into the park at the light then sprinted in the direction the arrow pointed. Now that they were close, only a quarter of a mile away according to the GPS, Paige felt her pulse quicken. And it wasn't just because of the jogging. The thought that they were going to find their first cache was so exciting.

What if there was a prize inside? What if they had to do something crazy to get the cache once they found it?

That made her feel marginally sick so she forced it out of her mind and instead focused on running without falling. They wove through a pathway that was as close to following the arrow as they could. It was either that or run through trees, which didn't sound like any fun. Countless confused looking dog-walkers later, the path opened up, leading directly to a castle.

A castle in Central Park.

"That has to be where it's hidden," Zoe said, sprinting in her heels.

Paige raced behind her, barely managing to keep up. Zoe wasn't kidding when she said she could do anything in those heels. As was proven again when she bolted up the stone staircase taking two stairs at a time. They looked along the stone wall and balcony for any kind of spot where a cache could be hidden. Too bad Paige hadn't a sniff of an idea about what a cache actually looked like.

Paige glanced down to the GPS unit in Zoe's hand. "It must be up here somewhere. We're really close."

They followed the arrow, watching as the distance on the screen shrank. As they came to the far edge of the outdoor balcony, they glanced around, finding only a covered area left to check. Finally after a few minutes searching, they found a small container, no bigger that a pill bottle with the show's purple TT logo stuck to the lid, tucked up into a nook in the decorative facade.

Paige held her breath as she dumped out the contents into her hand. A small laminated note tumbled out, followed by… nothing. Paige sighed. Oh well. Not every cache would have an extra prize inside. At least they'd found one and now she knew they could do it.

She unfolded the note. A large 303 was written inside.

"What are we supposed to do now? How do they know we've been here and found this one?"

"We take a picture with it on the GPS and it will upload to their main tracking server."

"How do you know that?"

"I read the information packet while you tried to kill us on the road. I had to do something to distract myself from the crazy woman behind the wheel holding my life in her hands."

Paige rolled her eyes. "Just take the picture." She held up the note with the cache number card in front of her and smiled with a thumbs up for the camera, trying to look cute and giving in to her happiness at finding their first cache. She hadn't mentioned it to Zoe, but she'd secretly been scared she'd come on this show only to be a part of the team who never finds a single cache. Ever. Thankfully, they seemed to work well enough together that it wouldn't be the case.

Zoe snapped the picture then lowered the GPS. "That was perfectly dorky in every way. And you wonder why Brad didn't keep you around."

Bitch. Her good mood dissolved instantly.

Paige kept her thoughts to herself and shoved the note back into the canister, securing it into its originally spot. Of course, shoving it up Zoe's ass might make her feel better. Maybe she'd drive to their next cache and see if she couldn't find a few more corners to take too quickly. Maybe then Zoe would be too busy to throw out any more unsolicited comments.

She grabbed the logbook from Zoe and quickly jotted down the location of this cache and the day and time they found it. Moving to the next one on the list, she read the coordinates to Zoe who entered them in.

"Looks like this one is a long drive—fifty miles from here."

"Isn't there anything closer to where we are now?" Paige asked.

"Maybe, but with five hundred coordinates to read through, it would take a while to find them."

"Then I guess we better get a move on." Paige turned on her heel not waiting for Zoe to lead the way with the GPS. First things first, they had to get their SUV out of the parking garage and Paige didn't need Zoe's help for that. Hell, she didn't want Zoe's help for anything anymore. Maybe she should ask Chip to let her run this race alone after all.

*

Paige and Zoe ran for the line drawn in white spray paint across the lawn in front of a gorgeous lodge. Other teams were already standing to the side as they crossed the line and stopped running.

Paige moved to the side near the others, then doubled over, trying to catch her breath.

At five minutes until eight, they'd snuck in under the cutoff time for check in that night and with only a couple of caches to their credit. Not exactly the first day she'd been hoping for.

The last team—Team Grandparents—finished just behind Paige and Zoe.

"We might be last, but we made it," they cheered, less out of breath than Paige was. She really should have worked out more before coming on a show like this.

Spencer moved from the sidelines to stand directly on the line and faced the teams. "Welcome, teams, to the beautiful Cascade Lodge. This is where you'll be staying for the month while we film." He paused while the teams looked at the lodge. "Each morning you'll leave from this line at eight for check-out and every evening, you'll check back in at eight. That gives you twelve solid hours of racing time. Use it wisely. And remember, checking in after eight will earn you a two-hour penalty the following day."

The teams cheered, but it wasn't as enthusiastic as it had been in the morning. Apparently Paige wasn't the only one feeling like the day had taken it all out of her. Now that she'd finally caught her breath, she noticed other teams looked as tired as she felt.

"I know you've had an exciting day and I'm sure you're all ready for a hot meal and a warm bed. So without making you wait any longer, here are the keys to your rooms." Spencer handed each team an envelope with their names and a room number written across the front of it. "Go find your rooms, relax, eat, and rest. After every check in, you'll be given a time slot for your daily wrap-up interview. The first one is tonight. You'll find a filming schedule posted in the common room each evening.

"Oh, and one more thing, there are cameras mounted in the common room to catch all the after hours action since the cameramen are only filming out in the field with you during the day. However, there are no cameras mounted in any of the bedrooms. Rest assured, the privacy of your rooms will not be compromised by the show in any way. So if you need a place to talk strategy with your team, remember that. If there are no questions, let's wrap this up. Goodnight!"

Paige yawned and followed Zoe into the lodge. Looked like she wouldn't only be racing with Zoe each day, but sharing a room with her each night too.

The show kept getting better and better.

*

Miles threw his bag down on to his bed. It wasn't the ritziest of hotels or the largest room, but it was clean and looked comfortable enough. And best of all, it was quiet after a grueling day of racing.

Ben had already flaked out on his bed, his leg elevated on a pillow, snoring gently. Miles would wake him in an hour for a late dinner.

Miles lay back on his own bed, folding his arms under his head as he stared up at the ceiling. The day had been harder than he'd expected and he was a seasoned traveler and climber. He could only imagine how hard it had been for Ben.

He tried not to look at Ben's leg.

Damn it.

What he wouldn't give to take that moment back. That one stupid moment that had made a mess of everything.

And every day Ben had to live with the reminder of everything that had gone wrong.

His friend rolled over in his sleep, his leg twisting on the pillow and his pant leg creeping up around his calf. The hard plastic of his prosthetic leg peeked out from beneath the material; forcing Miles to move his gaze back to the ceiling.

Miles went over their race day in his mind. The caches they'd found today hadn't been that challenging which meant they'd been easier for Ben to reach, but also meant that they hadn't been hard enough to deserve any extra reward for finding them. He'd really hoped they'd get lucky right off the bat and find a few caches with money in them. Money he could then help Ben pay off his medical bills with.

Even with good insurance, suffering an injury like Ben's came with a big price tag. As if the pain and suffering wasn't enough to bear on its own.

Or the money could be used to buy a fancier prosthesis for Ben. One that would make rock climbing again a real possibility.

And Miles would do whatever he had to in order to make sure that Ben and his family were taken care of. That his children could go to college. That Ben could have some money in the bank to ease the burden of everyday life. It was the least he could do.

If Miles could even help Ben realize that he still loved hiking and climbing, and that he could still do it even with his injury, well, then that would make coming on some silly reality show all the more worth it, especially after having to pull every trick in the book to get Ben here to begin with. The man was stubborn and convinced he couldn't race. It was only when Miles begged him, claiming he had no other partner to run with, that Ben had finally caved and agreed to try and run the race. When Miles added that he missed having someone to climb with, adventure with… well, that was the final push Ben needed to sign up for the show.

Now they were here and Miles had to make sure Ben didn't push it too hard. He wanted him to realize he could still do this stuff, but he didn't want him to take any unnecessary risks that could result in another injury. Not on his watch. Not this time.

Chapter Four

Paige settled herself into one of the wooden rocking chairs on the covered patio of the lodge, her back to the beautiful lake behind them. The room was more like a sunroom than a patio with twinkling lights strung from the beamed ceiling and screened walls separating them from the elements and bugs.

The sun would set any minute, but the twinkling lights above them as well as the crew lights would make it possible to do the daily wrap-up segment regardless of how late of a time slot they got. Luckily, they'd gotten the first fifteen-minute time slot this evening. After which, they would be free for the rest of the night to eat dinner and relax.

In the rocking chair beside her, Zoe sat looking more annoyed. "Are we ready to go yet? I really don't want to waste my entire evening doing a silly interview."

"I think we're good. One more second," Evan said, fiddling with some papers on the little table next to him.

Paige watched as he finished getting everything ready. It was strange to be sitting here in front of Evan since he'd always been the one to interview Cassidy on *The One*. And it made her a little sad, wishing for the hundredth time that Cassidy was here with her instead of Zoe.

"Okay, let's get started. Paige how did you feel when you found out Cassidy wouldn't be on the show?" Evan asked.

"I was shocked. And totally terrified that I'd be kicked off the show before it even started." She glanced up to Evan who had that silly half-dazed smile on his face again like he had when he'd seen Cassidy at the start of the show. "And I was thrilled for Cassidy's good news too, of course," she added quickly.

"How did you feel when you learned you'd be paired with Zoe for the race?"

"I was terrified again. And annoyed that Chip would give me a new partner without even asking for my opinion."

"Well, would you have agreed to be my partner if he had asked?" Zoe questioned, looking even more annoyed.

Paige shook her head. "No way. No offense."

"Oh, none taken. I wouldn't have said yes either."

"Wait, you didn't know who you were teamed up with before you got to the show?" Paige asked. How was that possible?

"Nope. And if I had, I would have thought a lot more about it before saying yes. I'm the one who has to put up with you long enough to do the whole show."

"Gee, thanks."

"You're welcome."

Paige motioned for Evan to move on with the interview.

He cleared his throat. "Back to the provided questions. How do you think you did today after your first full day of racing?"

"I think I would have done a hell of a lot better with a partner who could work a GPS or drive," Zoe said. "I can't do everything myself."

Bitch.

Paige closed her mouth, which had fallen open at the rudeness of her partner's words. "You're no prize partner either, you know. You're the one who wanted to stop at the salon to get your nail fixed while we're running a race. I wish Chip had given me a partner who was less superficial."

"There's nothing wrong with wanting to look my best. If I look my best, I perform my best."

Paige sighed. "Sure, 'cause having perfect nails really helps us find caches faster."

Zoe narrowed her eyes.

"Anything you'd like to add to that, Zoe?" Evan asked.

Zoe folded her arms across her chest and leveled her gaze at the camera. "No."

Good. There wasn't anything she could say to justify a salon stop during a race and she knew it. Maybe tomorrow she wouldn't make another stupid request to stop for something else ridiculous and unnecessary.

"Last question before our time runs out for tonight. What do you think of the other teams you're racing against?"

"I think we have our work cut out for us. Some of the other teams seem way more prepared to do these kinds of challenges. But I still think that if we work hard together we'll be able to hold our own." Paige smiled, hoping she looked confident in her answer because she certainly didn't feel it.

She was pretty sure they would lose. Horribly.

*

Paige eased into one of the cushy oversized chairs in the common area and curled up, cuddling her cup of hot chocolate in her hands, the three giant marshmallows in it slowly melting. The large stone fireplace threw enough heat to make her feel warm and cozy without feeling cooked. Perfect for relaxing at night after competing all day.

If only Zoe would wander off and find somewhere else to hang out for the night. Like the snake hole she'd slithered out of for the show.

Currently, Zoe sipped a glass of wine and glared at Mr. Muscles where he sat in another armchair opposite Paige. If only she could figure out why Zoe was acting like that. They hadn't even exchanged names yet and already she seemed to have a rather large chip on her shoulder whenever she spotted him.

His partner carried a drink in his hand as he wandered over to the couch, hobbling a tiny bit, almost as if one of his legs was stiff or sore, then settled himself onto the couch near Zoe. Perhaps he'd gotten hurt at one of the caches.

"How did you girls do today for caches?" the friend asked. "I'm taking a tally of everyone's progress."

"Ben, you can't ask people that kind of thing," Mr. Muscles interrupted.

"Why not? I'm not asking where the caches were, just how many they found. Relax, Miles. We're all friends here."

Miles shot a glare at Zoe. "No, we aren't."

Zoe responded with an equally disgusted look right back at him, but said nothing. She turned to Ben and spoke directly at him. "We found a couple. But our first was pretty far away so we spent a lot of time driving instead of searching."

"How many did you guys get, Miles?" Paige asked, hoping that directing the question at him would release some of the tension that had built up around them so quickly.

Miles. Interesting name. Maybe because he has miles and miles of lean muscle.

When her gaze traveled back up his chest to settle on his face again instead of all those wonderfully sculpted muscles she could see under his fitted T-shirt, she found him staring back at her. And if she wasn't mistaken, he knew exactly where her eyes had just been too. Her stomach fluttered.

"Four. Not as good as I would have liked." Miles shrugged.

Paige was relieved he didn't look at her with the same look of loathing as he did Zoe. So it wasn't because Zoe was on another team. There seemed to be something about her that rubbed Miles the wrong way. Not really surprising. Zoe rubbed everyone the wrong way.

Except for the producer Chip. He seemed to be able to handle Zoe without much trouble at all. That was probably part of the reason he kept putting her on shows when all of the other contestants were always annoyed with her. He wasn't annoyed at all.

"Four is better than our two. How many did the other teams get?" Paige asked.

Ben pointed to a team in the far corner of the room watching TV. They looked like a father daughter team. "They got four too." Then he pointed to the other teams in the room. "Team Firefighters got six, the show offs. Team Married found five and five hundred dollars. I still can't believe someone found money on day one."

Paige followed his pointing around the room as he listed off all of the teams and how many caches they found. How he kept everything straight, she wasn't sure. She could barely remember who everyone was. She always had trouble remembering names.

The other team with two girls was pretty easy to remember since they were both gorgeous enough to compete against Zoe in a beauty pageant. She'd been introduced to them a little earlier, Eve and Rayne, Team Sisters. Currently they sat in the big armchairs by the window that looked out into the Catskills. The view was beautiful, but Paige preferred the warmth of the fireplace.

As she watched, Eve glanced up from her spot and caught Paige's gaze. Even from across the room, Paige could see the girl's eyes narrow, her jaw set. Why Eve looked at her as if she hated her, she had no idea. She'd have to watch out for her. Good thing she'd had lots of practice with girls like Eve since she'd had to deal with Zoe for so long. Eve would be easy in comparison.

She glanced over to Zoe. "I think we're going to have to step up our game tomorrow. We're so far behind already."

"We'll be fine," Zoe said with way more confidence than Paige felt. Then she turned back to Ben, asking him questions about the caches they'd found and how far they'd had to drive.

While they chatted, Paige had trouble keeping her mind on the conversation. Hopefully if he said anything important, Zoe would remember it and tell her later.

How could Paige possibly concentrate on boring cache details when Miles sat across from her looking all beefy and delicious?

And when he smiled, she melted. She peeked up at him as he joined in to the conversation. The light from the fireplace danced across his skin highlighting the stubble that had grown along his jaw during the day. He looked like he really needed a shower.

A hot shower with lots of slippery soap. And a loofa. A loofa she could navigate over his chest, scrubbing every contour, and down what was most likely a six-pack of abs. All the way to…

A cough startled her, making her jump like she'd been caught sneaking around somewhere she shouldn't be. She glanced up from Miles's lap only to find a silly grin on his face and a cocked eyebrow. Oh, yes. She'd been caught. But he didn't seem at all bothered by it.

Let the melting commence.

"So," Paige started, trying to force her thoughts into some semblance of small talk. "How did you find the first day of racing?"

Miles shrugged. "It was good—fun, exhausting. I think it's going to be an interesting few weeks. What about you? How did you find it today?"

"Exhausting, annoying, frustrating. You know, a typical day with Zoe." Paige laughed, hoping to lighten the moment despite her rather large, inappropriate complaint about her teammate.

Miles's gaze found Zoe again, his jaw twitching as he appeared to clench it before he looked back to Paige. "Life is never dull with Zoe around, is it?"

Why did it feel as if Miles and Zoe had a history together when they'd only just met on the show? Was it all the media Zoe had done? It wasn't exactly uncommon for regular people to feel like they "knew" celebrities in a personal way because the media did a great job of sharing their intimate moments with the world. Was that what it was with Miles and Zoe too?

"What do you do when you're not on a reality TV show?" Paige asked, eager to learn more about Miles. It wasn't just his looks that intrigued her. There was also something about his calm demeanor, his laidback attitude, and the confidence pouring out of him that drew her to him.

"This is my first show. I'm usually off climbing mountains, or I'm teaching climbing to kids at The Rocks."

"You teach kids? That's awesome. How old are they?" A hot guy who also liked working with kids? Yes, please.

"All ages. Whoever wants to learn can, I don't discriminate by age. I adjust the program accordingly to fit their skill level."

"So what made you decide to come on the show, if you don't mind my asking? Was it for the adventure of it, since that seems to be your thing?"

"That was part of it." Miles stopped talking. His gaze flickered to where Ben sat, then back to catch Paige's eyes again. She got the distinct impression there was more to Miles than he let on. He'd come on the show for more than the adventure and the reason had to do with Ben, but what it was, she couldn't figure out without more information. It probably wasn't any of her business anyway.

"I think the only ones here who've been on a show before are you and Zoe. Are you girls all head over heels for cameramen like that Cassidy girl was? Is that why you both agreed to be on another show?" Miles asked with a smirk, his expression softening and his voice taking on a distinctly teasing quality. The combination made her breathing falter.

"I came on the show for the experience. Not the hot guys."

He cocked an eyebrow at her as if he was insulted.

"Not that the guys here aren't hot. You're all very hot." Paige felt her cheeks grow warm. This conversation had taken a sudden turn into embarrassing territory. How had she managed to put her foot in her mouth during a perfectly normal conversation?

A little chuckle escaped Miles as her face grew warmer, no doubt also growing redder by the second.

"I'm calling it a night," Paige said, getting up from the chair, completely forgetting the hot chocolate in her hand. It sloshed over the rim of the mug and down the front of her shirt. Great. Just what she needed on night one at base camp—to look like the clumsy girl she normally wasn't. Now they'd all think the reason she and Cassidy were such fast friends was because of their affinity for accidents—clumsy girls united.

Not to mention, now Miles would realize she could be flustered with a simple smile from him. Awesome. One of the many reasons guys as sexy and confident as Miles didn't go for girls like her… why Brad hadn't gone for her either. Because no guy who could make you forget yourself with a smile or a nod—or hell, by sitting in a chair in a fitted tee—could ever find an ordinary girl like her worth his time or interest.

At least now she wouldn't have to worry about how she acted around him since there was no possible way he'd ever look at her as anything other than the girl who spilled hot chocolate on herself.

Paige let herself back into the room she shared with Zoe. It would be a long, long month sharing a room with her, but there was nothing she could do about it. Better to suck it up and make the best of things as always.

She grabbed the tank top and shorts she wore for pajamas and quickly changed, thankful that on this show she didn't have to change in the bathroom every day like she'd had to on *The One*. This time, Chip hadn't been allowed to put cameras and microphones in every corner of every room in the hotel. Only the common areas had cameras. She'd heard something about privacy laws since parts of the hotel were still open to regular guests.

Paige didn't mind at all. She'd hated feeling like a caged mouse in some giant lab experiment on the other show. At least here she could escape to her room for privacy as needed.

Zoe strolled into the room just as Paige pulled her tank top down to cover herself. So much for privacy.

"Could you knock next time?" Paige asked. "I don't really want to flash my chest to everyone walking by the room when you barge in unannounced."

"Go change in the bathroom if you're a prude. It's not like anyone would see anything anyways."

"Gee, thanks." Paige climbed into bed and propped herself against the wall so she could relax with her book for a while before falling asleep. Reading always helped her unwind and de-stress after a busy day. "I'm not a prude. I just don't believe in showing off my assets to anyone and everyone."

"First you'd have to figure out what your assets are to show them off. When you're ready for your big girl boobies, you just let me know. Until then, I wouldn't worry about anyone noticing you—naked or not." Zoe laughed and disappeared into the bathroom.

Paige gritted her teeth and forced herself to focus on the words in front of her. What she needed tonight was to get lost in her book and forget that Zoe even existed for a while. Just as she felt her shoulders relaxing, sounds of Zoe singing filtered out of the bathroom.

Sighing, Paige put her book aside, clicked off her light, and rolled away from the bathroom and the noise Zoe called singing. No chance of forgetting she existed when her squawking made it impossible to read.

Nope. Better to just go to sleep and let today end. Finally.

Chapter Five

Miles pulled off the winding dirt road and into a small deserted parking lot at the beginning of the trail. This was their third cache of the day and they still had yet to find a prize in one. He'd hoped this one was remote enough that they'd be the first to find it and maybe there'd even be some money inside.

They grabbed their logbook, GPS, and a couple of water bottles and started down the trail. The GPS said they had half a mile to go. A long hike made longer by Ben having to trek on the uneven terrain of the dirt trail. So who knew how long it could take them. If the trail got rougher or steeper, it could take them the better part of the day. Best to be prepared with the waters even if it sucked having to carry them.

"It looks like it's straight ahead," Miles said.

"I hope it's right beside the trail in a big easy box to find. It's too hot to be traipsing through the underbrush looking for another pill bottle sized cache."

"Whatever it is, we'll find it."

"What do you think about the other teams? I think Team Firefighters are our biggest competition for sure. Possibly Team Frat Boys will give us a good race too, if they can keep the beer pong tournaments to a minimum." Ben stumbled, but caught himself, shooting a glance at Miles. "I'm fine."

Miles nodded. No sense in arguing with Ben. And he was fine. Just the trail was rough. Anyone could trip. "I think you're right but I don't know what we can do about it. It's not like we can sabotage the other teams or anything."

"True, but there has to be a way to get a little advantage over them. I just have to think of how." Ben was quiet for a moment. "Maybe an alliance with another strong team?"

"It's worth considering. We'd have to be very careful about who we chose to ally with."

They trudged on in silence for a few more minutes. Miles racked his brain trying to find a way they could beat Team Firefighters. How could you beat the team that was stronger than yours, faster than yours, and who was from the area? It was a massive task to conquer.

But that hadn't stopped them from climbing Everest a few years ago.

If they could climb Everest together, surely they could find a way to find more caches than any of the other teams. They just needed to figure out a winning strategy.

For now, the best they could do was to get each cache as quickly as they could. And this one was proving to be a total pain in the ass and complete time suck. The sooner they got there the better.

They wandered on. Miles watched the GPS screen and tried his best not to accidentally pick up his pace faster than what was comfortable for Ben. After coming up with no good strategies, he decided to worry about it later and let his mind drift. And drift it did.

Right over to Paige and the wet shirt clinging to her chest. He wasn't really a hot chocolate kind of guy, but he would have helped her clean up if she'd asked. She was cute when she got all flustered around him. What he wouldn't give for just a little taste of chocolate flavored Paige.

"What was that?" Ben asked suddenly.

"What? I didn't hear anything." Maybe his thoughts were too loud.

"I thought I heard voices behind us. Girls."

They stopped and listened for a moment. Sure enough, the sound of Zoe's sharp voice cut through the air. Bitching about hiking in the heat, of course. Like she should only have to find caches hidden in an air conditioned mall or poolside, and not have to tough out the heat for these other ones like everyone else had to.

That girl was something else. Poor Paige. She should get a bonus prize just for enduring Zoe's company for the duration of the show.

"Let's go. It looks like we're only seven hundred feet away now. If we hurry, we can get there before the girls and I know we can find it before them." Miles started down the path again, faster now that he knew they were only moments away from the other team catching up. This was the first time they'd met another team while looking for a cache and he didn't want to lose out on a possible prize because of it.

Ben caught up and did his best not to fall behind as the girls' voices grew louder. At four hundred feet, they broke into a jog, but only for a minute or two before they heard the girls spot them on the trail.

"Run, Zoe!" Paige yelled. "There's another team ahead of us. We can't let them get there first."

Miles heard the fall of footsteps growing closer and closer. He knew it would only be another moment or two before the girls caught up and passed them. But Ben obviously struggled at their current pace. He couldn't ask him to push it any faster.

The girls and their cameraman rushed passed them on the trail, leaving behind a cloud of dust that caught in Miles's throat, making him cough. "Shit." He meant to curse under his breath but he knew Ben had heard when he stopped running.

"I'm sorry," Ben said, his breath uneven. "I tried, but I'm not that good in this stupid prosthetic yet."

Miles turned to him, all thoughts of the girls gone. Ben should never have to apologize to him or anyone else about his challenges with his lower leg amputation. Hell, it couldn't be easy to adjust to wearing a prosthetic leg.

If anyone should apologize, it should be Miles—again.

"Never be sorry. You're doing great. This competition is challenging for all of us."

"Not the girls. They'll probably pass us on their way back at this point."

"No way. It's only a little further. I bet when we get around that next bend, they'll still be trying to figure out which way is north and nowhere near the cache."

They jogged again and sure enough, when they came around the bend in the trail, the girls were up ahead still searching. And it didn't seem quite like they knew where they were searching. Paige was on one side of the trail with her head down and her foot kicking the soft grasses around, while Zoe peered around a few large rocks. Neither looked at the GPS unit sitting on the trail where they'd abandoned it.

The boys slowed as they came up to the girls. "Let's stick together and watch the GPS. I bet we can find it first." Miles held his hand out between them so they could both see the little screen.

"Nice of you to finally join us," Zoe said from her spot near the boulders alongside the trail. "Took you long enough."

"Zoe, don't be so rude." Paige glared at her from across the path.

"Well, I ran in stilettos. What's your excuse, boys? Aren't you at all concerned that two girls beat you in a foot race?" Zoe laughed.

"Considering I only have one foot still attached to my body, I think that's a pretty good excuse, don't you?" Ben said, raising his pant leg to show off his prosthetic leg.

Zoe held her ground, barely acknowledging her error in judging Ben too quickly. "I didn't know. How'd you earn that trophy?"

"I'm not sure I'd call it a trophy."

"Better than being stuck with a scar," Zoe mumbled. She sat on the rock and folded her arms across her chest. "Scars are something you regret, but a trophy is something to be proud of because it helped make you who you are. So which is it?"

"Then I guess I earned this trophy with Miles on the side of a mountain. Not that I feel like reliving the incident play-by-play. Let's just say I climbed up fine, but getting back down wasn't so easy."

A silence fell over the two teams while they took in the seriousness of his words. The only sound was the cameramen as they circled the group for better angles. Miles wanted to be pissed at Zoe for bringing up a painful past that he and Ben were working so hard to overcome. But when he went to send her a warning look, her eyes were rimmed in red as she blinked away tears.

Her gaze flickered up to his and for a moment he wanted to go to her. To comfort her. Thank goodness she took that moment to pull her back up straight and put her bitch mask on again, quickly reminding him why it wasn't worth giving her the time of day.

"So, you girls still looking for the cache box or have you already found it and you're just having a little siesta out here on the trail?" Miles said, finally breaking the silence.

"We looked, but can't find it anywhere. I've double-checked our coordinates and everything looks right. I don't know what we did wrong." Paige walked back on to the trail and peered down at her GPS unit still sitting on the ground. "It says it's right here. I guess it's an invisible cache or something because the thing doesn't exist."

Miles joined Paige, his shoulder brushing lightly against hers as he compared his screen to hers. His earlier thoughts of her and her chocolate flavored breasts filled his brain again and he instantly forgot what he was doing standing beside her in the first place. Was he supposed to lick her? Because standing so close to her, peering down at her as her chest heaved with the exertion of hiking in this heat, licking her was really the only thing he could think of doing.

She turned her head, peering back at him. His gaze fell past her gorgeous dark eyes, past her soft pink lips, and landed on the patch of ivory skin peeking out of her top—the skin reddened and glistening in the intense summer sun.

She opened her mouth a couple of times, but did little more than lick her lips before closing her mouth again. Finally, on her third attempt to speak—not that he was any better at finding words himself—she managed a simple sentence. "Can I see yours?"

Yes. Yes, you can.

"Your screen," she squeaked. "Your GPS screen, I meant."

He smiled. He couldn't help it. She was too damned sexy. "Of course you can see my GPS screen. What else would you refer to, Paige?" Her name rolled across his tongue like a ripe berry—sweet, fresh, and leaving him wanting more.

She blushed. His smiled widened. He loved causing a reaction in her so easily.

Moving his arm so she could see too, they compared their units. And both looked the same. The cache was here. But who would find it first?

*

Paige took one last deep breath, hoping that after she moved away, Miles's scent would somehow stay with her. He smelled… manly. And yummy.

And the second she'd looked up to see him staring at her cleavage, his scent had hit her. She'd thought her knees might give out right then. They probably would have if she hadn't made an ass of herself asking if she could see his GPS in a way that made it sound like she'd asked to see his penis.

Not that she wouldn't like to see his penis. She could imagine that it was just as gorgeous as the rest of him. But they were in the middle of a trail, under a blazing sun, with their teammates and cameramen standing around. Not exactly the time to check out anyone's goods. Not even Miles's.

With her lungs full of his aroma, and her belly a pool of molten lava, she stepped away from Miles. "So, um, I guess we should keep looking then, huh?"

"Yep," Zoe said, springing up from her spot on the rocks. "Well, if you two can stop eye-banging."

Paige choked, her throat feeling like it had closed. *Eye-banging? Is she implying what I think she's implying?*

"I—" Paige started.

"Save it for someone stupid. Neither one of you are fooling me."

"As witty and sharp as ever, aren't you, Zoe?" Miles asked. His jaw looked more set than it had a moment ago. Apparently Zoe annoyed everyone she came in contact with—that wasn't a privilege saved for Paige.

"I don't believe it," Ben said. He walked in between Paige and Miles and looked up into the tree hanging over the trail. "They are really sneaky."

Ben reached up and plucked something from the branch, directly above the GPS unit on the ground. Whatever it was, it was tiny. Literally the size of an acorn.

"What is it?" Paige asked, stepping closer to get a better look.

"A nano-cache. I read about these online on the geocaching websites, but I've never seen one in real life."

"That's what we were trying to find?" Zoe sneered at the acorn as if it had purposefully wronged her.

"Yep. It was exactly where it was supposed to be." Ben beamed triumphantly.

Zoe held out her hand. "Awesome. I'll take that now, thanks."

"The hell you will," Miles said, stepping in front of her as if Ben needed some kind of protection. "We found it. And if we're the first ones to open it, the prize inside is ours."

"Like hell it is," she fired back. "We were here first. It's ours."

Miles laughed then turned his back on her. "Sure, you may

have gotten here first but that's not what the rules say. It's the team who *finds* the cache that gets the prize."

Paige moved closer, watching as Ben twisted off the miniature acorn top. He pulled out a tiny piece of paper and unfolded it at least six or seven times before it was large enough to read. The cache number card was easy to spot, but there was another paper with it. A smile grew on Ben's face.

"Ten thousand dollars." Ben voice wavered as if he fought back tears. "Each."

Miles let out a loud cheer and fist pumped the air. "I knew there'd be something great in such a difficult cache."

"Wow. Congratulations," Paige said. Seeing how happy they both were, it was hard to be too disappointed that she'd missed out on the money. Sure, she could have used it like anyone else, but somehow, seeing a grown man fight back tears made her think that Ben needed the money more than she did.

"You're congratulating them?" Zoe sneered. "They took our money and you pat them on the back for it."

"Hey now. It's our money. We won it fair and square." Ben puffed his chest, defending himself. "You may be able to beat us in a foot race, but I'll beat you in an intelligence test any day."

His challenge was directed at Zoe for her harsh comments, and Paige couldn't help but agree. After all the time she'd known Zoe, intellect wouldn't be the first character trait that came to mind to describe her. Bitchy, yes. Materialistic, yes. Giant high-maintenance pain in the ass? Oh, you betcha.

As Ben and Zoe threw words at each other, Paige held her GPS unit out to Miles. "Can you take a picture of me with the cache card so I can get Zoe out of here?" she asked, sliding her lip balm quickly against her dry lips. A little glistening minty lip balm never hurt a photo op.

He quickly snapped a picture of her holding the number then she snapped one of him, although she wasn't quite as speedy about it as he was. Seeing him standing there, smiling at her with the same dorky thumbs up she'd done at her first cache—which Zoe had made fun of—made her feel slightly less dorky. If a hunk like Miles could do it, why couldn't she? Of course, a hunk like Miles could probably do whatever he wanted and still look amazing. That was the difference, wasn't it?

She took one last glance at his picture on the screen before giving it back, and wished she'd thought to make the mistake of using her GPS instead of his so that she'd have the picture to look at whenever she wanted. Oh well. Maybe she could sneak a picture another time. It wasn't like they'd been told not to take pictures of the scenery and such along the way. And Miles certainly was good scenery.

Pulling Zoe away from Ben as they continued to shoot insults at each other, they made their way back down the trail toward the car. The only thing that got Zoe to focus on the game again was to remind her there were still other caches to find and arguing with Ben on the trail wasn't going to help them find them before the other teams.

As Zoe peeled out of the parking lot, Paige glanced back. She couldn't help but remember the feeling she'd had with Miles standing so close. Or how the smell of him had made her head feel a little woozy.

Not that it mattered anyway. A guy like Miles would never go for a girl like Paige. No. He was more likely to go for a girl like Zoe. Minus the bitchy confrontational part, because really, who would want to put up with that for a lifetime of matrimony?

But no matter how annoyed Miles appeared to get with Zoe, surely not even he could resist her good looks for long—no guy could resist a body like hers, even it was home to a girl with attitude.

If only there was a way for Paige to be herself but have a fraction of Zoe's feminine style and total confidence. Then maybe a guy like Miles—smart, self-assured, and totally sexy—would give her the chance to show him how awesome she was on the inside too.

Chapter Six

Miles and Ben stood by one of the window screens looking out at the lake as the moon glimmered across the calm surface. It would be truly romantic if he weren't standing with a dude. Now, if he were here with Paige, then it might be a different story.

There was something about that girl that made him lose focus of everything else every time he was near her. It wasn't just her looks, although they were distracting enough on their own merits. It was something else. Maybe it was the shy embarrassment she seemed so prone to that made her come off as dainty and demure, even though he knew there was a passionate fire burning inside her. Or maybe it was the way she seemed to give everyone the benefit of the doubt, even Zoe who didn't deserve the benefit of anything from anyone.

Mostly, it was the way she looked at him, a twinkle in her eye that hinted at her innermost thoughts…the thoughts she kept to herself. He couldn't help but feel that some of those thoughts were directed at him and he was curious to find out exactly what they were.

If only Zoe wasn't standing in his way just by being Zoe. He had to figure out a way to deal with her so he had a hope of getting to know Paige better.

"You boys ready to start?" their cameraman, Bill, asked from behind them.

"Hell, yes," Ben said with the same sentiment that Miles felt. The sooner they got the daily wrap-up over with, the better. Already these interviews were getting very tiresome to do at the end of each day when all he wanted to do was relax in the common room.

"Absolutely," Miles agreed, as he and Ben took seats in front of the camera.

"How did you feel today when you were overtaken on a cache?" Bill asked.

"Wow. Just jumping right in there tonight, aren't ya? No gentle lead in to the hot topic. That's kinda cold, man." The show's producer came up with some of the most heated questions and they never failed to turn his stomach.

"It's okay, Miles," Ben said, not appearing bothered by the question at all. "It totally sucked to get beaten in a foot race against the girls, especially when we had such a big lead on them to begin with. But they're faster than us. Nothing I can do about it."

"Does it suck more being out raced by a team of women?"

Miles shook his head and forced his temper to stay at bay. "Should it matter that they're women? I don't really think so. Judging someone's expected performance because of their gender is just about as low as judging them by whether or not they still have all their natural limbs or wear glasses or because of their hair color. Zoe and Paige beat us because they were faster runners. *We* won the cache prize because we were better thinkers today. Well, I wasn't. But Ben certainly was. He's the one who found the cache even though the other team got there first."

"That's right. I may be slower than the rest because of my leg, but I'm still a big threat to the other teams."

"Speaking of the prize," Bill said from behind his camera, "you each won ten thousand dollars today. What are you going to do with the money?"

Miles motioned for Ben to answer first.

"I'm going to stick it in the bank, pay off some stuff that still needs paying off. Nothing too special or fun, but the money is a welcome surprise."

"And you, Miles? Trips? Down payment on a car, maybe? What do you have planned for your money?"

"I plan to write a check." Miles cleared his throat, which suddenly felt tight. "I'm making it out to Ben and his wife to help cover their medical expenses from his injury."

Ben turned to him, eyes bright with moisture that hopefully the camera would never notice. "You are not. You're going to use that money on something for yourself. Something fun."

"My mind was made up the second you agreed to come on this show with me, so nothing you say is going to change my mind. It's my money and I'll do what I want with it."

"I don't know what to say…" Ben's voice cracked.

"I think we'll end the interview for today. Our time slot is up. See you guys tomorrow." Bill packed up his stuff and wandered out of the room. Ben and Miles followed behind him, leaving the room for the next group.

"I can't believe you're really doing that for me, for us," Ben said, shaking his head.

"It's the least I can do. Now I don't want another word about it, okay?"

Ben nodded. "I can't wait to tell Tammy. This is going to make a big dent in our remaining bills."

"I'm happy to hear that. Let's see if we can win you the rest before the show is over."

*

Miles took a swig of his third beer and scanned the room. The other teams were either mingling or huddled together, no doubt talking strategy. He and Ben probably should've been doing that too, but it was hard to think about the game after another long day driving, hiking, and searching. All he wanted to do was relax with a cold beer and some good food, and enjoy a night just hanging out with his best friend.

The game could wait until morning. Or at the very least, it

could wait until they went back to their room for the night. He didn't think the other teams were being especially smart talking game out in the open like that anyways. Not when their hotel rooms were private and camera free.

In the corner of the room, he spied Zoe, talking with one of the other teams. Cosmetic surgery doctors, if he remembered right.

Ben appeared to have started a game of chess with the father portion of Team Father Daughter. Sam, he thought he remembered the man saying on their first night here. Seemed like a nice guy. But chess was a two-person game and he didn't feel like being a third wheel.

In the far corner he spotted Eve sitting alone. Normally Rayne was with her. Eve waved him over and smiled. He didn't really have any desire to spend the night chatting with her since he didn't find her the least bit entertaining. She did though, and enjoyed laughing at her own jokes. With a laugh that got on his nerves. But he didn't want to be rude.

Walking over to where she sat, he tried to think of a way to get out of joining her. Luckily, before he got there, her sister came out of the kitchen and sat in the free chair. Perfect. Now he wouldn't be able to stay long. If he wasn't mistaken, Eve glared at her sister.

"How's it going, ladies?" he asked, trying to sound friendly. He wasn't here to make enemies.

"Better now that you're here," Eve said. "Care to pull over a chair and join us?"

He scanned the room looking for his escape. His gaze landed on the one person sitting alone, staring into the fireplace as if the world around her didn't exist. "Actually, I was on my way to talk to Paige, but I thought I'd say a hello since you were so sweet to wave me over. But it looks like you two are ready to do some strategizing. I'd hate to interrupt."

"Thanks, Miles," said Rayne. "Not all of the other teams seem to get this is a game, not a vacation. And we definitely need to plan our next move."

"Rayne," Eve said with annoyance clear in her voice. "Don't be so rude to Miles. We can talk about the game later. If he wants to join us now, I think we should be more gracious, don't you?"

"I—" Rayne started.

"No worries. Really, I was on my way to talk to Paige. I'll catch up with you some other time. Have a good night."

Without waiting for Eve to put up another fight, he wandered over and took a seat on the couch beside Paige even though both armchairs were empty. For whatever reason, he wanted to be near her.

She glanced over to him and smiled as he settled himself in beside her. The sight of her in the glowing firelight with a smile on her face for him, made an indescribable warmth pass through him. And it had nothing to do with the heat coming from the giant fireplace.

"All alone tonight, Paige?" He twisted in his seat so he could lay his arm along the back of the couch and have a better view of her. She looked tired. And in need of a shower. And absolutely gorgeous.

She nodded. "Seems that way. Not that I mind a break from Zoe. It's nice to get a little peace and quiet for a change."

He took a swig of his beer. "I didn't mean to disturb you."

"No, that's not how I meant it." She put her hand on his leg, just above the knee, then quickly removed it as if she was embarrassed. "You're welcome to stay."

"Good," he said simply. He focused on the fireplace, trying his best not to concentrate on the heat that radiated through his leg from where she'd just touched him.

Say something.

He wasn't used to being at a loss for words around women, but something about Paige made him forget all his best one-liners. Maybe because he wasn't trying to pick her up on a lonely night in a hotel bar while he killed time until sunrise when he could go climbing again. Not that he'd mind spending that kind of time with her.

"Sorry about Zoe today. She was very mean to both of you, but Ben especially."

Miles glanced down at Paige's hand now sitting in her lap while he silently wished she'd touch his leg again. And leave it there this time.

"You don't have to apologize for her. You're not her keeper."

"I know. But with Ben… I guess I felt bad about how it all went down. That's all."

"Ben can take care of himself." His beer empty, he set the bottle on the coffee table in front of the couch.

"Of course he can. I didn't mean to imply he couldn't." Paige twisted her hands in her lap.

"I know it's easy to think he might be more fragile than the other people here, but I assure you, he's one of the strongest people I know, and he's more than capable of taking on Zoe."

Paige met his gaze. "You seem like a really good friend to him. He's lucky to have you as a partner."

"Thanks." It was nice to hear even if he didn't fully believe it himself.

She stared at him, her hair falling forward to frame her face now that it wasn't pulled back into a ponytail like it had been earlier. He fought the overwhelming urge to run his fingers through her hair, tangle his hand at the nape of her neck. She was just as sweet as she was beautiful. A distracting combination if he wasn't more careful. And yet he couldn't move away. "Zoe's lucky to have you too, she just doesn't know it."

"I'm pretty sure she'd disagree with you. But it's nice of you to say so."

"Zoe can have a one track mind when she sets her mind on a goal." Zoe might not be the nicest person or the most intelligent person Miles had ever met, but she was definitely the most determined. When she set her goal, no one and nothing would cause her to deviate from it.

Paige tilted her head to the side slightly. It was the motion he could imagine her doing if they were about to kiss. That feeling of wanting to run his fingers through her hair returned even stronger than it had been a few moments ago.

If he leaned forward and tilted his head a bit to the other side, he could capture her mouth with his. He could kiss those sweet lips of hers that had just parted slightly. Would she prefer soft kisses or firm? Would he even have enough sense to experiment with his kisses like he usually did to see what she responded to most? Or would his mind become completely undone when his lips pressed to hers, his body taking what he wanted, how he wanted?

"Miles?" Paige's voice filtered into his thoughts. Yes, he'd like to hear her say his name again and again.

Say it again.

"Miles, are you okay?" she asked again, her mouth forming the words with the cutest little pucker of her lips as she waited for his response.

He was better than okay. In one more second he'd be perfect. In one more second, his mouth would be on hers and all would be right in his world.

The feel of her breath caressing his lips caused him to blink. Why could he feel her breath on his lips? He pulled his gaze from her gorgeous inviting mouth to stare her in the eyes. Eyes which were all together closer to his than they should have been, and a mouth that was only a fraction of an inch away from touching his.

Holy shit.

His heart pounded in his chest as he realized how close his little fantasy had taken him to almost kissing Paige. Not good.

He sat back against the couch, putting much needed distance between them. "I'm sorry. My mind wandered away for a second. Did you ask me something?" That sounded casual enough.

"I was asking why you seem to know so much about Zoe, but maybe you have other things on your mind you'd rather discuss."

Like how I almost kissed you.

He rubbed his eyes and yawned, buying a minute to think. "Doesn't everyone know Zoe after how much she's been in the tabloids since that show?"

"Sure. I guess that makes sense."

He rested his head back against the couch and looked at Paige, hoping she bought his story more than her voice led him to believe. He really didn't feel like explaining tonight, or any night. Ever. As far as he was concerned, he didn't know Zoe any better than anyone else and he wanted to keep it that way.

And he couldn't ignore the simple truth that Paige and Zoe were not friends. Enemies was more accurate. If his past with Zoe became public knowledge, Paige might look at him like an enemy too. That was the last thing he wanted.

Paige shrugged, clearly suspicious of his answer but appearing to let it go at least for now. "Seems like there's maybe something else on your mind tonight too," she said, leaning toward him. She licked her lips. "Anything else you want to... discuss?"

It was an invitation if he'd ever seen one but he couldn't RSVP to that party. Far too distracting when he needed to focus on the competition.

No. As tempting as Paige was, he couldn't risk it. He might not want Paige to become his enemy if she learned about his past with Zoe, but he also didn't want Paige to become a distraction and end up getting in the way of his goals for Ben.

Another time, another place, and he'd have given in to that kiss a moment ago. But not here, not during the game he desperately needed to prove to Ben they could win.

"I'm tired. I'll see you around, Paige." He couldn't miss the disappointed expression on her face as he climbed up from the couch. Somehow seeing the expression of hurt and disappointment on her face made the climb off the couch harder than the one to the summit of K2.

Chapter Seven

Paige drank the last few drops from her water bottle and tossed it onto her bed beside her. The last thing she wanted to do was wander around the hotel in her pajamas but unless she wanted to drink water out of the bathroom faucet, or go thirsty until breakfast, she didn't have many other choices. The only other water in the room was Zoe's coveted Perrier and she would kill Paige if she drank any. Not that it mattered since Paige couldn't stand the bubbles. Regardless of what Zoe said, water should not have bubbles.

Nope. She needed water from the kitchen. And since she'd been in her room at base camp every evening for the last few days, she was really running low on munchies and soda too.

It wasn't that she was hiding exactly. More like avoiding.

Avoiding Miles.

In the days since their almost kiss on the couch in front of the fireplace—or what she thought was an almost kiss, at least—she'd tried her best not to run into Miles again. Certainly she didn't want to be anything resembling alone with him. No way. Not when he'd made it perfectly clear after the almost-whatever-it-was-or-wasn't happened that he wasn't interested in her that way.

She'd been so foolish to lick her lips in a pathetic attempt to solicit a kiss from him. But when he'd gone into some sort of trance like state a few minutes before that and ended up with his lips a breath away from hers, she'd really believed that's what he'd been going for. A kiss. And yet her attempt to show that she was willing had been shot down by his supposed tiredness.

Really? Tired? No.

No matter how tired a man is, if he's interested in a kiss, he's going to go for it. Men don't think in terms of tired. They think in terms of how quickly they can get it in and how long they can stay in for.

When Miles turned her down, he'd made it perfectly clear he wasn't interested in her. And since she couldn't be sure what stupid thing she'd do if she saw him again, she'd done the only thing she could do. Hide.

Until now. Now her tummy grumbled, since dinner never seemed to fill her up with all the exercise they were doing hunting for these stupid caches for twelve hours a day. What she should do is go to bed and get a good night's sleep so she'd have energy for tomorrow. But no way would she ever fall asleep with her stomach yelling at her for food and water.

She glanced at the clock on the bedside table. It was just after midnight. Surely almost everyone must be in their rooms by now. Everyone except Zoe, who was missing from her side of the room. But Zoe was out late every evening. Doing what, she didn't know. Or care, actually. What Zoe did on her off time was her business and Paige didn't want to get involved.

But at least at this hour, she should be safe to wander to the common room and slip into the kitchen unnoticed for long enough to grab a couple of granola bars and refill her water without anyone seeing her in her pajamas.

Although, she could take a moment and change into her regular clothes just in case, but that would mean changing back into pajamas again in a few minutes. Best to save time and go quickly. Stealthily, if possible.

She peeked out into the hallway. Everything seemed pretty quiet. Usually from here she could hear noises from the common room at the end of the hall. But tonight, not even the TV played. Perfect.

Padding down the hallway as quickly as she could, tiptoeing in bare feet, she made it to the corner without being seen. She tugged down the lace edging of her pajama shorts, which suddenly felt a few inches too short, and peeked around the corner into the common area. Empty.

Relaxing now that she was alone, she walked normally into the kitchen and scrounged in the cabinet until she found a selection of snacks then filled her water bottle with ice and fresh water. She grabbed an apple from the fridge and washed it quickly before taking a bite.

Hopping up onto the counter, she took a few more bites of her apple, her stomach finally quieting. No sense in taking the apple to her room just to throw the core into the garbage. It would get stinky by morning in the little room. She was better off eating it here and throwing it away before she went back.

A few minutes later as she chewed another bite, she could have sworn she heard talking out in the common area. She stopped chewing and listened. Nothing. She swallowed then listened again. Still nothing.

She was biting off another chunk of apple when the kitchen door swung open. She paused mid-bite as Zoe and Miles walked in. Their voices hushed as they discussed something, their tone anything but pleasant.

"She can't find out. If she does, then I don't stand a chance. And I'm not about to lose out on her because of you," Miles said, his voice laced with annoyance and frustration. Not surprising since he was talking to Zoe after all. But who were they talking about? What couldn't someone find out?

"You can't hide it forever. She's bound to find out sooner or later," Zoe retorted, her tone sounding equally as annoyed.

Paige held her breath with the apple still poised in her mouth like a stuffed pig on a platter, not even moving when the juices from the apple dripped down her chin.

She felt as if she were spying on a very private conversation. But they were the ones who'd come to her. She was merely a bystander and couldn't help it if she was now privy to their... intimate sounding conversation.

And why were they together anyway?

"Later would be better," Miles stated as if it was fact.

"Fine," Zoe grumbled, shoving past Miles into the kitchen. "But if you strike out, don't blame it on me."

Suddenly realizing they weren't alone, Zoe and Miles froze, mouths open, fingers pointing at the other as if in the middle of an accusation party instead of a conversation.

Interesting.

Zoe was annoying, but annoying enough to fight with after hours when everyone else was already sleeping?

Slowly, their heads swiveled to stare at Paige.

"I'm tired. Goodnight," Zoe said, disappearing out the kitchen door before either of them could say anything to stop her. Not that Paige could have found her voice to stop her anyway.

Nor could she find her voice to say anything to Miles who still stood frozen, staring at her. The annoyance she'd seen on his face as he'd walked in with Zoe had already dissolved, replaced by a twinkle of mischief in his eyes.

And she suddenly felt as if she were perched on the edge of a doctor's exam table instead of a kitchen counter. A cold kitchen counter.

Come to think of it, the entire kitchen was pretty damn chilly. So chilly in fact, the thin material of her camisole didn't seem to do much to keep her warm. Or to hide the newly-budded evidence that she was cold.

Paige bit off the chunk of apple, finally lowering it from her mouth and setting it on the counter. As she chewed, she watched Miles. Was he suddenly tired too? Again? Neither he nor Zoe had looked all that tired a moment ago. Whatever conversation they'd been in the middle of must've really been a private one. A sudden spike of jealousy shot through her at the thought of Zoe and Miles sharing private moments together.

Until his gaze fell on her. Then her jealousy vanished along with the air in the room.

Miles took in her outfit, or, well, lack of outfit while she chewed. And swallowed. And choked. Some people couldn't walk and chew bubble gum at the same time. Apparently Paige couldn't sit and eat an apple safely.

Tears pricked her eyes as she struggled to dislodge the tiny pieces of apple from the back of her throat.

Miles sauntered up to the counter calmly and reached beside her until he found her water bottle. He popped the top and held it out to her. She took a deep gulp or two and finally felt like she could breathe normally again.

"Thanks," she managed, finding her voice for the first time since he'd walked into the little room.

"Better?"

"Yes. I must have swallowed funny."

"Apples can be very dangerous." His eyes crinkled a little as he smiled, teasing her. He crossed over to the sink and wet a paper towel before returning to stand in front of her again. "And messy."

Miles wiped the damp towel across her lower lip, then down her chin and neck, stopping just below her collarbone. Good thing the apple hadn't dripped more. Much farther and he would have been wiping off her cleavage.

Her body responded to the thought, her nipples growing harder than they already were from the cool night air.

His gaze left her and traveled down the path his hand had just made then carried on to the hardened peaks clearly visible through the thin camisole. Damn it. Why hadn't she thought to at least grab a sweater before leaving her room? And now that she glanced down to where his eyes had gone, she realized just how teeny tiny her shorts were, riding up her thighs with only an inch of inseam fabric separating her from sporting a mini-skirt. A commando mini-skirt since she didn't wear panties underneath her pajamas.

Not to mention Miles currently took up residence between

her knees, his hands resting on either side of her on the counter. Damn, he was even hotter close up.

"Thanks," she mumbled, unable to think of anything better to say.

"My pleasure," he said, talking to her nipples.

If only she could find a way to make her body listen to her, she could cross her arms and cover herself. But her arms ignored her inner embarrassment.

"Everything okay between you and Zoe? Sounded like a serious conversation you were having when you guys came in here. I didn't mean to interrupt."

That did it. His gaze met hers. Holy hell. Those eyes… that hint of lust lingering in them.

"It was nothing. Just a disagreement about… something."

It sounded like a lame excuse and Paige didn't buy it. But she didn't have any good reason to press him further either. "If you say so."

"I do. And what exactly were you doing wandering around the hotel so late at night in barely more than tissue paper?"

"I ran out of snacks and water. I thought everyone was in bed already."

He raised an eyebrow questioningly. "You thought I was in bed too, didn't you?"

"Maybe," she said, not breaking his gaze.

"I haven't seen you much these last few nights. Not since the night we chatted by the fireplace. Everything okay? Or being antisocial?"

"Everything's fine. Just needed some space from the game." Sounded like a good excuse.

"I'm glad to hear that. But I have missed seeing you around in the evenings."

She hadn't thought he would.

"Maybe tomorrow night I'll see you around."

She couldn't help but notice his gaze flicker down her body again as he stepped toward the door. Then he disappeared through it without another word, leaving her alone with her thoughts.

Thoughts that threatened to take a walk in the gutter where images of Miles between her thighs took center stage. Only this time neither one of them were standing.

*

Miles closed the bathroom door and turned on the sink faucet. Leaning on the counter, he glared into the mirror at his reflection.

Way to go.

Two big errors in judgment tonight and they were only finishing up the first week of the show. He would have to be a lot more careful from now on. No more late night *talks* with Zoe. And definitely no more close calls by putting himself in intimate positions with Paige. Getting involved with Paige was a distraction he couldn't afford if he wanted to win the game with Ben. Yet every time he was around her, he found himself drawn to her, lusting for her, needing to be closer to her.

It had to stop.

He needed to stay as far away from that entire team as he possibly could. Maybe Paige had been doing him a favor these last few nights when she'd disappeared right after dinner, not surfacing again until the start time the next morning. And yet he'd just been stupid and admitted that he'd missed seeing her around.

Why couldn't he keep his big trap shut?

But he had missed seeing her sitting by the fire, sipping her hot chocolate, whether he wanted to admit it or not. Hell, he even missed seeing her slide the tiny tube of lip balm across her lips. Yes, that he definitely missed.

Damn it.

He had to put distance between himself and that team of girls. Zoe and Paige could be his kryptonite and he couldn't let that happen. Not when he had so much at stake.

Chapter Eight

Paige wandered into her room, closing the door softly behind her so as not to wake Zoe if she'd happened to fall asleep already. She couldn't stop her shoulders from drooping a little at the disappointment coursing through her.

"He didn't show again tonight, did he?" Zoe said from her bed where she was propped up reading. Reading a book. Not even a trashy magazine or anything, but a book without pictures and everything.

Paige stuffed down her disappointment like it didn't exist. She wasn't about to show weakness in front of Zoe. They may be partners and, God help her, roommates, but that didn't mean Paige was ready to share all her deepest and darkest feelings with the enemy all of a sudden.

"I don't know what you're talking about," she said simply.

Lie. She knew perfectly well. She'd been checking out the common room since her close encounter of the kissing kind with Miles in the kitchen a few nights ago. She'd gone from trying to avoid him to being the one who was now avoided. Every night since the kitchen incident, she'd gone to the common room to hang out with everyone. Only Miles was always missing. She didn't understand. He'd said he missed her, now he was MIA. It didn't make sense.

Zoe set her book beside her, trapping Paige in her lie. "What, you think I'm too thick skulled to notice you glancing around the common room looking for Miles to come in every time someone so much as sniffles?"

"No, I just…"

"If you want a guy like Miles, you're going to need better moves than that. Look at Eve. Every time that girl sees Miles, she's first in line to talk to him, flirt with him, touch him."

Zoe was right. Damn it. Miles would never notice her sitting in the room like a lump waiting when the room had girls like Zoe and Eve in it. But how would he ever see past those beautiful women to find her? It was useless.

"It doesn't matter anyway. I only wanted to say hi to him. He's kind of nice to talk to."

"Sure. Right. You're looking for good conversation and long walks on the beach." Zoe didn't even try to hide the mocking sarcasm in her voice.

"Fine, you caught me. I think Miles is hot, okay?" Paige said, walking into the bathroom to change into her pajamas. She might be roomies with Zoe but that didn't mean she felt comfortable enough to change in front of her. Not when it would give Zoe more ammunition to use against Paige when she wasn't expecting it.

No way. Her girly bits and pieces were staying hidden.

"And he's also funny, and nice to talk to, and he's super considerate, especially about his friend Ben. I heard from one of the other teams that Miles gave Ben the entire ten thousand dollars he won to help with his medical bills."

"That's sweet," Zoe said, sounding surprised.

"Did you know he teaches kids to rock climb? How could I not like him? He's everything a girl would ever want in a guy." Paige dropped the dreamy look she knew had to be on her face. She didn't have the patience to put up with Zoe making fun of her crush on Miles, even though this felt like a lot more than a simple crush. A lot more. Miles was amazing in every sense of the word. "Never mind."

"So do something about it," Zoe said when Paige walked back into the room.

Paige climbed into bed. "If it were only that easy."

"It is. What's so hard about going after what you want?"

"That's easy for you to say when you look like, well, when you look like *you*. But I don't look like you. Miles is way out of my league. And therefore a non-issue."

Zoe sat up and turned toward Paige. "I'm not interested—at all—in Jack Miles. And I can guarantee he's not interested in me either. So if you want him, then you go and get him but don't use me as an excuse not to go after him."

"It's not that easy."

"It is. You're making excuses for yourself so you don't have to risk getting rejected."

"Like you know what rejection feels like." Paige laughed at the absurdity of it.

Zoe was quiet for a moment while she examined the polish on her nails. "If you don't want my opinion, then stop whining at me about it." She got up from the bed and walked into the bathroom, slamming the door closed.

Did she want Zoe's opinion? Not really. But did she have any other choice? If they were allowed to make calls, she'd be on the phone with Cassidy in a second. But their cell phones had been confiscated before the start of the race and the hotel room phones had been disconnected except for room-to-room calls or emergencies.

Paige cursed her lack of confidence. If only she were more like Zoe, this wouldn't be an issue because she wouldn't feel like she wasn't good enough for a hot guy like Miles. But she didn't have Zoe's confidence. Or her looks. Or her style…

What if?

The bathroom door opened and Zoe climbed back into bed, turning off the bedside table lamp and plunging the room into darkness. But not before Paige noticed her eyes had been red rimmed as if she'd been crying in the bathroom. That couldn't be. Girls like Zoe didn't cry. It ruined their make up.

What if?

No. It was stupid. And bound to get her laughed at if she asked. And absolutely would be more hassle and nuisance then it was worth. She sighed and rolled over, trying her best to get comfortable.

If only she could be more like Zoe, minus the bitchy part, of course. Then Miles wouldn't have a choice but to notice her. Then she'd be closer to his league. And maybe…

No. I will not.

She sighed again and rolled onto her other side, toward Zoe's side of the room.

"Oh, would you just spit it out already?" came Zoe's voice in the darkness. She didn't need to see Zoe's face to know she was completely annoyed. "I'll never fall asleep with all that tossing and sighing so say what you need to say and get it over with."

Oh, yes. I'm a complete glutton for punishment.

"I. Well. Maybe you could…"

"I haven't got all night."

"Maybe you could teach me to be more like you. You know, have more confidence, be more irresistible to the opposite sex. That kind of thing."

"That really was hard for you, wasn't it?" Zoe giggled. Actually giggled. It sounded… bizarre.

"I've seen the way guys look at you and also the way you don't care unless you're interested in them too. In which case, you stake your claim and go for it, like you did on the show with Brad."

She harrumphed. "Immature surfer boy," she said quietly.

"So I was thinking…"

"Don't hurt yourself."

"If you could make me be a little more you," Paige continued, ignoring Zoe's comment, "then maybe I'll feel confident enough to go after Miles the way I want to."

"And what's in this deal for me?" Zoe said after a moment.

Paige rolled her eyes to the ceiling. Zoe would never do anything out of the goodness of her heart. She should have known asking her for something would come with consequences.

"What do you want?" Paige asked cautiously.

"I want to team up with Miles and Ben to work together. Form an alliance."

Paige breathed a sigh of relief. Was that really all? That was awesome, actually. Teaming up with the boys would give her more chances to get to know Miles. More chances for him to see her as his equal instead of the girl who was sitting on the counter in the kitchen in her tiny pajamas with apple juice running down her chin. Maybe he'd even look at her with more than a fleeting moment of lust in his eyes.

"Okay," Paige agreed quickly before Zoe could change her mind.

"And I want them to win," Zoe said with the confidence in her voice that Paige so desperately wanted to have too.

Paige stared at Zoe, stunned into silence for a moment. Had aliens come down from the sky and taken over her body because this girl who wanted another team to win didn't sound at all like the bitchy girl Paige knew and loved… liked… tolerated.

"But I thought you wanted to win. I thought you said you wanted the money and the prizes." Paige couldn't keep the shocked confusion out of her voice. "You really want to give away your chance at half a million dollars? Why?"

"My reasons are my own. Either you take my deal on my terms, or you don't."

Paige thought about it for a minute. Could she really give up her portion of the prize to Ben and Miles because Zoe said so? Because she wanted Zoe's help? Was the chance at winning Miles's affection worth the sacrifice?

She had come on the show as a way to spend time with Cassidy while she figured out what she wanted to do with her pathetic dating situation back home. Sure, it sounded great to have men come out in droves to court her with flowers and promises after she'd gotten kicked off *The One*. But the reality of it was more along the lines of annoying and confusing. She'd just wanted time away with Cassidy to figure out if it was time to jump back into dating or not.

And now here she was with a very good, very hot dating prospect in front of her. All she had to do was give up some money she hadn't really expected to win anyway.

That didn't sound so terrible.

Honestly, the chance of either of their teams winning was pretty slim anyway. Team Firefighters were basically kicking everyone's asses at this point with over a hundred caches found already and a pocket full of prizes like the pair of motorcycles they'd recently won. So what did she have to lose by saying yes? Nothing.

"Deal," she said before she could think about it any more. She needed this. Not only to try to win Miles's attention, but also for herself. She needed to learn to be more confident in every aspect of her life, not only dating. She was tired of people overlooking her and not taking her seriously—like Chip had, signing her up for the show based on a half-hearted "yes" she hadn't had time to think through, like her friends and parents back home had overlooked her opinion by forcing endless prospective suitors on her.

But no more.

Zoe's help was exactly what she needed to start the changes she wanted to make to her life. And once she was more confident in herself, she'd finally stop waiting for things to come to her and instead she would go after the things she really wanted. Like Miles.

"And you agree to listen to me and actually take my advice, no questions asked?" Zoe asked.

Oh jeez. She could practically hear Zoe's head getting bigger by the second.

"Yes."

"We start tomorrow. Now you better pipe down over there. You're going to need all the beauty rest you can get."

As Paige pulled the blankets tighter under her chin, a spike of excitement shot through her. Followed quickly by a spike of dread.

Had she really just made a deal with the she-devil Zoe?

*

Paige and Zoe parallel parked around the corner and a few streets down from Macy's in Herald Square. Yesterday had taken them all over hell's half acre along the Hudson Valley and nowhere near a shop where they could pop in and get started on Paige's new Zoe-ish style. But they'd had plenty of hours while driving around to work on her confidence level and her flirting techniques.

According to Zoe, it was all in the delivery and less in what you actually said. Half-lidded eyes, a subtle tilt of her head, a sultry smile, and a bedroom voice could make a man crumble to his knees—or so Zoe said in her lessons. But it was the practice that was even worse. It was hard to flirt while following an arrow on a GPS and even harder when it was Zoe she had to flirt with.

Paige tried to flirt with Evan a few times because at least she found him attractive. But every time she'd tried, all she could imagine was Cassidy watching it on TV and commenting on what she was doing wrong. Not that any of her flirting scenes with Evan would ever make it on air. Not when he laughed so hard he nearly dropped the camera on more than one occasion. He'd made it perfectly clear that he thought their plan was a bad idea, but he didn't seem to mind the comic relief she provided while practicing on him.

If Evan's reaction to her flirting was any indication, she still had plenty of work left to do.

That could wait, though, because today, finally, they'd ended up in the city. And according to their GPS arrow, they were heading right into Macy's. They walked into the building and were instantly greeted by the bright lights of the cosmetic counters.

"We should have a little look around for you," Zoe said, eyeing the nearest counter.

"No, we need to find the cache first, then see if we have any money to spare. I may have to borrow your makeup for a bit."

"I don't think so."

"Well, we can't spend all of our money on needless things, like new eye shadow, when we still have to buy gas and pay parking fees among other things for the next few weeks. You know as well as I do that Chip will never give us more money if we run out. And parking the first day put us way over budget right off the start."

Zoe shrugged. "There's always a price to pay for beauty, so either you pay it or you don't. It's your call."

Paige thought about it as they wove their way through the large department store trying to find the cache. After riding what had to be the world's oldest wooden escalators, the arrow finally narrowed down their target area to the shoe department. They searched as inconspicuously as they could but it was tricky in the busy department. With every shoe they peeked into and every table they looked under, the shoppers around them grew more and more interested in what they were doing.

Of course Evan following them around with his giant camera probably played a part in the spectacle too.

Finally, tucked back into the corner of the department, they found a shoebox marked with the purple logo of the show. They opened it to find the cache card as well as an envelope. They quickly snapped a picture of Zoe with the cache number, then she opened the envelope, smiling as she read the contents.

"I think our money problems have been solved." Zoe held two plastic cards and a note out to Paige to read. "We've each won a five hundred dollar shopping spree."

"After the show is over we can come back and get everything for my new me," Paige said, tucking the card into her pocket.

Zoe reached into her pocket and pulled the card right back out. "We're going to start your transformation right now."

"While we're racing? We're already way behind a few of the other teams with our count, we don't really have time for this right now. Maybe we can come back in a few days after we have more?"

"Nope. You agreed to listen to me and I say we start now. You're only putting off the inevitable if you want to snag Miles's attention."

Paige thought about it. True, she did want Miles to see her in a different way. But was she ready for that now? It didn't seem to make much sense to put it off for much longer. The competition only ran for so long and then the show would be done filming. If she wanted her best chance to catch Miles's attention, then she may as well do it now. Besides, that way they had many more chances to see each other and to practice her new flirting skills once they started their alliance with the boys.

"Where do we start first?" she conceded.

"Right here." Zoe walked off in the direction of the women's shoes.

"But I need my boots for hiking."

"Oh, silly girl. You have so much to learn." She stopped at a large display of shoes, picking up one that had a three-inch heel with thin black crisscrossing straps. "It's time to introduce you to some of my best friends."

Chapter Nine

Paige blanched at the sight of the tall stiletto heels in Zoe's hands. No way would she ever be able to walk in those let alone hike on some of the trails they'd already been on. Simply impossible if she wanted to complete the show without a broken ankle.

"Is there a training size for girls like me who like flats?" Paige asked.

"Sure, we could get you a kitten heel if you'd like, but then I'm pretty sure Miles would be more interested in making sure you were cuddled up nicely on the couch with your blankie and mug of warm milk. Is that what you want from Miles, to be tucked in and treated like a child in your little kitten heels?" Zoe put her hands on her hips.

"No, I guess not."

"Do you want him to look at you as if he can't get you out of your clothes fast enough so he may just put you back up on the kitchen counter again and have his way with you?" She held one kitten heel and one stiletto heel in her each of her hands. "Do you want to be tucked in at bedtime or have Miles rip your clothes off for sexy time in the kitchen? Your call."

Zoe made a pretty convincing argument.

Paige grabbed the arm of a passing salesman, stopping him. "I'd like to try a size six please."

"In which style, miss?"

She motioned toward the table of stilettos in a variety of colors. "All of them."

*

Twelve near death experiences later, Paige swiped her gift card to pay for her new silver sparkling five-inch heels. They were nothing short of spectacular—*if* she could learn to wear them without breaking her ankle.

Even just standing at the check out counter proved to be more than her weak ankles could handle. Her ankle kept rolling to the side every time she shifted her weight even slightly.

After she paid, she gripped the shopping bag with her hiking boots tucked away inside and wobbled after Zoe as she took off toward another department.

"Wait up, Zoe," she called, trying to catch up.

"We have lots of work to do before we get back to the race so hurry it up back there."

Paige tried her best to jog on her spindly heels and caught up to Zoe as she walked into the lingerie section, then stopped dead in her tracks. "Um, are we here to spend your gift card now?"

Please say these are for Zoe.

Paige held up a bra with so much padding in it a man could put it on and have perfectly shaped breasts. Not that most men would want them, but the point was, in this bra they could have them. No. No way could she ever see herself wearing one of these… contraptions. Besides, there was nothing wrong with her usual unpadded bras or the supportive sports bras she wore for the competition.

Zoe ignored her question and moved around the racks of bras, sorting through them with the efficiency of someone who worked in the store. Paige wandered quietly behind her, thankful that it was Zoe's turn to shop so maybe Paige could sit in the waiting area and rest her already sore feet.

When Zoe had an armful of bras of various colors, silhouettes, and materials, they made their way toward the changing rooms. Paige flopped into the black leather chair, which was even more comfortable than it looked. Instantly the needles in her feet eased a bit.

But before she could get really comfortable and slip her shoes off, Zoe pulled her from the chair and shoved her into a changing stall, thrusting the handful of bras after her.

"I don't need a new bra," Paige protested, sticking her head back out through the door. "You didn't even ask my size."

"Yes, you do need a new bra, Miss Uniboob." Zoe pointed at Paige's chest, drawing circles in the air, eyeing her breasts. "That is not going to get you a man. And don't worry about size, it wasn't hard to figure out."

"Uniboob?" Paige looked down at her own chest, offended at the comment. There was nothing wrong with wanting a little support for the girls while hiking and trekking doing God only knows what at each cache.

Zoe picked up one bra, black lacey with a strong underwire and a squishy balloon feeling thingy in each cup. "Start with this one."

Reluctantly, Paige closed the door, but not without noticing the laughter in Evan's eyes. When Paige got home, Cassidy was going to get an earful about her soon-to-be-husband's sense of humor at Paige's expense.

She disrobed and slipped on the first bra. It fit perfectly, thrusting her boobs up and out with exactly the right amount of separation between them. Huh. Maybe Zoe did know what she was talking about after all.

Pulling her shirt back on, she turned sideways in the mirror taking in her new silhouette. Not bad. Not bad at all. With her breasts lifted and supported, she actually looked slimmer. And her curves… wow.

"Any day. We still have a race to run you know."

Paige opened the changing room door and stepped out where Zoe and Evan could see her. She did a little spin for them. "Well, what do you think?"

Evan smiled and gave her a thumbs up. Encouraging. *I wonder how Cassy will feel about Evan filming this.*

Zoe tilted her head one way then the other, as if examining a piece of art. Maybe this was art to her. Then she cupped Paige's breasts in her hands and gave them a little lift, shake, and squeeze.

"Hey!" Paige squeaked. "I'm trying to pick up boys, not girls."

"Oh relax. I'm not hitting on you." Zoe winked at her. "If I was, you'd already have been picked up, played with, and thoroughly satisfied."

Paige's cheeks broke into flames.

"This one is good," Zoe said stepping back, "but try on the red one next. I think it will give you even better cleavage. And I really think what you're looking for is the full ka-pow effect."

"The what now?" Paige called from inside the stall where she wrestled out of one bra and into the next.

"When you walk into the room do you want guys to ignore you or do you want to knock them out cold with how hot you are? That glazed-over look of lust is the ka-pow effect. That's what we're going for here."

Paige reappeared in front of them, waiting to be groped. Zoe felt her up briefly then stepped back again, still evaluating her. Paige didn't know how to stand under such a scrutinizing stare so she put her hands on her hips like a superhero. Ka-pow did sound sort of superpower-ish—knocking guys out with a single chest-thrust.

"That one is perfect. The lift, the separation, the trajectory, it's all perfect."

"I want to look good, not become a torpedo storage device."

"And look at that cleavage. Stunning, right, Evan?"

He nodded, looking a little pink-cheeked himself at having to speak about his fiancée's best friend's cleavage.

Paige blushed and walked back into the stall again. After a few more breast exams, they made her purchases, spending the last of her gift card. As she swiped her gift card through the machine, she banged her arm into her boob, not used to the twins' new location on her chest.

Not to mention they were approximately two sizes bigger now, thanks to the power of a good push-up bra. She'd always been happy with her mostly perky full B cup breasts, but even she had to admit, looking at herself in the mirror with her larger "ka-pow" breasts paired with her new stilettos, she felt like a new woman. A more desirable and sexy woman.

"Before we get back to the car, let's input the new coordinates for the next cache in case it's close enough to walk to." Paige stumbled as they stepped onto the escalator to the lower floor.

Zoe rolled her eyes. "Really, it's not that hard. One foot in front of the other."

"It's because my new boobs stick out so much," she said looking down into her massive cleavage. "They've thrown my whole center of gravity off balance."

"There wasn't that much to push out. How could they throw you off so much? Want me to stuff a cookie or two into the straps near your shoulder blades to balance you out?"

Zoe's voice might sound sweet and innocent but Paige heard the sarcasm in it.

"Very funny."

Behind her, Evan snorted out a laugh.

Oh, yes. Cassidy would hear about this.

*

Miles tried not to let his frustration show while resting on a park bench facing out to the Hudson River. This should have been one of the easier caches to reach, but the length they'd had to walk from the car was grueling. Not only was it long, it was hot as hell today too.

Ben had been doing his best during the entire first week of the competition, but even still, they were far behind most of the other teams in their cache count with a mere thirty. No matter how well they thought they'd done each day, when they'd returned to camp, there would inevitably be some other team who had gotten at least double the number of caches they had. Usually it was Team Firefighters, although a couple of other teams were doing really well too.

Then there were teams like Zoe and Paige who also seemed to be struggling a bit with the caches, coming in at only about forty for the first week. But they were most likely still figuring out how to work together since they'd been thrown into this thing so suddenly. Once they got their groove going, they'd pick up the pace too and then it would only be Ben and Miles left at the back of the pack.

"I'm doing the best I can, I swear," Ben said quietly. He splashed his face with bottled water and looked up to the sky.

"I know you are. This is way harder than it sounded."

"Not for the other teams."

"Depends on the team."

"The good ones are getting a ton of caches. I really think there's no way for us to catch up. We may as well give up now."

Miles head shot up from where he'd had it resting in his hands. "No way. We're not giving up. We have as much chance of winning as anyone else."

Ben shook his head. "We don't. This is a waste of our time. We're never going to win."

Miles felt sick. This was not the same Ben he knew. This was some other guy who was beat down and broken. "Was it a waste of our time when we hit the peak of K2 just because there was no one there to give us a million dollars?"

"That's different and you know it."

"Except it isn't different." Miles shook his head. He had to find a way to get through to Ben. He had to find a way to prove there was something worthwhile about completing what they set out to do, regardless of whether or not they won. "Damn it, Ben. This doesn't even have to be about winning. Proving we can do it is enough. Together. Like we used to."

Ben stared out at the river, saying nothing for few minutes. He stood and started down the path again. "Well, get up. We're not going to prove anything with you lazing around all day without a care in the world."

Miles smiled, knowing he'd gotten through, at least a little.

*

"Pull over," Zoe demanded from the backseat.

"What's wrong? You're not going to throw up or something are you?" Paige swerved to the side of the road and into a free parking spot.

"Get out. We're making a pit stop."

Paige climbed out of the SUV, wobbling as her spindly heels hit the pavement. Some how she'd managed to forget she had them on while driving, but walking was a whole other story. As she closed the driver's side door, the weather-stripping rubbed against her newly expanded chest. Thankfully it didn't leave a mark on her shirt. She didn't need anything else drawing attention to her boobs.

"This way," Zoe said, trotting down the sidewalk.

"Okay, but to where exactly?" Paige caught up just as Zoe pulled open the front door to a store. "We don't have time for more shopping. We've basically wasted the whole day as it is."

"Oh, this isn't really shopping. It's more like research."

"Research?"

They stepped through the front door and it took a moment for Paige's eyes to adjust to the indoor lighting. When it did, she almost wished she couldn't see. Everywhere she looked, men stood around looking at various outdoor related paraphernalia. Fishing poles, tents, and an entire row of rifles lining one wall.

Paige grabbed Zoe by the arms, turning her until they were face to face. "This isn't any kind of research we need to do for the game, we already have everything we need provided for us. We're not even allowed to get any other kinds of equipment, or we'll be kicked out of the competition."

"We're not here to buy new equipment," Zoe said with a smile. She popped open the top button on Paige's shirt, showing off another inch of cleavage. "We're here to test the equipment we already have. And what better way to do that then with a few guinea pigs?"

Paige moved to do up the button on her blouse, but Zoe batted her hand away. "You want to get his attention, don't you?"

"Yes, but only one specific man's attention, not a bunch of random guys'."

"Trust me. I know Miles—guys like him." Zoe looked away. "And all of the guys in here are the same. If these guys respond, he will too. Just walk down the aisles and see what happens. I guarantee you'll turn heads."

"I don't know about this," Paige protested as Zoe forced her down the first aisle. As predicted, the couple of men immersed in their shopping were now interested in more than bait and lures. And they weren't too worried about hiding their drool either.

In the next row over, a man looking at camping tools dropped a small hammer on his foot as they passed. He didn't even flinch.

Okay, so maybe Zoe had a point.

"I think we can go now," Paige whispered.

"One more test, just to be sure." Zoe winked then walked over to counter in front of the rifles. She ignored the gawking men and sidled up to the counter like she belonged there. Paige followed, attempting to mirror Zoe's attitude and control of the situation. Zoe's attitude right now was exactly what Paige needed to learn. No time like the present.

"Can I help you, ladies?" the man behind the counter asked.

"Sure you can," Zoe said with a sticky sweet voice. "My friend here is in the market for a new toy. Maybe you can show her a couple to see what she likes the feel of in her hand."

What toy? And why did it sound so dirty?

"How about this one right here?" Zoe clicked her nail against the glass counter top. "Oh, or maybe that one over there. Paige, honey, can you point out the one I mean to the nice gentleman?"

Paige looked from Zoe to the glass counter. Underneath, handguns of all sizes and colors lay on display. Toys? Hardly. But she would play along if it meant they could get the hell out of here faster.

"This one?" she asked Zoe, pointing to the tiniest handgun she'd ever seen. It didn't even look real.

Zoe shook her head. "No, no. The one over there, way in the corner."

Paige slid her hand along the counter, stretching to point at the gun furthest away from her. "This one?"

"That's the one. Hold right there while this nice man gets it for you."

Paige glanced up to see the man behind the counter frozen in place, his gaze not anywhere near the gun she pointed at. She turned the other way. The men further down the counter stared, watching her too, only their eyes weren't focused anywhere near her face. Funny, she'd forgotten just how tight these jeans were until right now when she could feel the back seam riding up between her cheeks.

She stood straight and resisted the urge to pick her wedgie while waiting for the man to retrieve the gun she had no desire to hold. A low rumbling of conversation began around her again as the other shoppers apparently had decided to remember they had brains rattling around in their heads and not just life-sized googlie eyes.

"Here you go, honey. Now this is a gun you can be proud to carry." He put the firearm in her hands, the metal colder and heavier than she'd expected.

Paige fingered the gun cautiously for a minute. It really did feel strange to hold one. She'd never done that before. She'd never had reason to. "It's not loaded or anything, right?"

He chuckled. "That's right."

She took a step back from the counter and gripped the gun like she saw in the movies, standing with her feet slightly apart and her arms outstretched in front of her. "Freeze asshole." She laughed.

The sound of something crashing to the floor startled her and she shrieked, almost dropping the gun. One of the men further down the counter crouched on the ground, picking up the pieces of a tackle box that had spilled its contents all over the floor.

Zoe whispered in Paige's ear. "You can give the gun back now. I think our research here is conclusive."

Chapter Ten

Miles stretched out in the armchair, his head resting against the back and his feet propped up on the coffee table. It probably wasn't the most socially acceptable way to sit in a shared space with basically strangers, but he was past the point of caring. After the day he'd had, he needed to relax and not think about anything for a while.

The day hadn't been fun or even comfortable with Ben. There'd been no easy camaraderie like he was used to. No inside jokes or laughs of any kind actually. Only hours and hours of walking, driving, and logbook consulting. He'd had dentist visits that had been more fun than today.

And tonight wasn't proving to be much better.

Even though Ben had said he'd keep trying until they reached the end of the competition, he didn't seem to have much fire in him. It was as if the spark was gone. Fizzled out and replaced with lackluster nothingness. It was probably the worst condition he'd seen him in since right after the accident.

He raised his head from the back of the chair so he could drink his beer, finding Zoe and Paige chatting quietly with Ben off in the corner of the room at one of the tables.

What were they up to?

By the way their heads were all shoved together he had to assume it was something sneaky. Or at least something they didn't want everyone else to hear. But what?

Time to find out.

He pulled himself from the couch and grabbed another cold beer from the kitchen fridge. As he was heading over to join the conspiracy at the table, Eve stepped in front of him, blocking his path.

"Hey, Miles. You look tired tonight. Want me to give you a massage?" she asked, her eyelashes fluttering.

Nope.

"Thanks. That's really nice of you to offer." He paused, glancing over to the table where Ben and the girls sat, heads still bowed as if they were conspiring together. Maybe they were. Except for Paige. She might be listening to the others, but her eyes were locked on Eve. If eyes really could shoot daggers, Eve would be painted with a giant bull's-eye target.

Jealous? The thought made him smile.

"Great. Let's go back to my room so you can get out of that shirt. I have some delicious black raspberry massage oils. They're edible." She licked her lips.

"Eve, you're a beautiful woman and you make a tempting offer, but I'm not really on the market right now. I hope you understand." He started to move away from her, trying to ignore the hurt in her eyes.

Paige had gotten pulled into the conversation with Ben and Zoe again. Whatever they discussed, she found it more interesting than seeing him with Eve. Although you'd never know that by the look she'd shot at him a few seconds ago. Or maybe he'd misread her expression.

Regardless, he wanted to be a part of their conversation if it involved his partner. When he got to the table, he turned a chair around, straddling it and folding his arms along the back.

"What are you all whispering about over here?" he asked.

"Oh good, sleeping beauty finally woke up to grace us with his presence," Zoe snapped.

"I see someone's been hitting the bitch juice pretty hard tonight," he shot back with a smile. Damn, Zoe pissed him off.

"Zoe, stop. That's not going to help us convince him." Paige looked down at her hands, obviously embarrassed by their little outburst.

When she looked up again, he noticed she appeared about as tired as he felt. She had dark circles forming under her eyes and her hair pulled back into a messy ponytail, a few stray hairs framing her face. It took all the control he had not to reach out and tuck them behind her ear for her.

Damn. Even tired and in need of a shower, she was smokin' hot.

A vision of Paige standing in a steaming shower, rubbing a soap-filled sponge across her chest flickered to life in his brain. A shot of heat spiked through him, hardening him to half-mast instantly. Good thing his jeans were of the baggier variety tonight or his fantasy-induced semi would be on display for the neighboring tables to see.

Not something he wanted wandering eyes to find. Unless those eyes were deep brown and belonging to the fantasy-inducer herself—she could look all she wanted.

"Convince me of what?" he asked, addressing everyone at the table and not focusing solely on Paige. She could probably convince him of anything she wanted and all it would take was another moment between her thighs like the other night in the kitchen.

And there's full mast.

"Well," Paige started, turning her attention on him, "we have a little proposition for you."

Yes, sign me up.

He cleared his throat. "I'm intrigued."

Ben gave him the look that said he knew exactly what kind of proposition Miles was hoping for. "They want our help."

"It would be a mutual agreement actually. One in which both teams would benefit." The bitchy tone in Zoe's voice had disappeared. Good. He was sick of hearing that voice.

"We thought since both of our teams seem to be falling a little behind the other teams, maybe we'd all benefit from… an alliance." Paige whispered the last part, leaning in even closer as she did.

Miles found himself leaning forward too. Intrigued at the thought of an alliance or intrigued because of the beautiful woman?

"We're not that bad off," he said quietly, hoping Ben would back him up. "We checked off another six locations in our logbook today alone."

"That'll help you catch up to the firefighters who are well over a hundred at this point." Zoe rolled her eyes, like he'd seen her do so many times before. "Well, if you want to keep losing, don't let us stop you."

"You're not winning either, if my count is correct. You have what, five or ten more than we do."

"That's enough not to come in last."

"Possibly. But they said it would come down to point value in the end." Miles took a swig of his beer and shrugged. Zoe really knew how to get under his skin. "So let's say I'm entertaining this idea. How would this alliance work?"

Paige perked up. "We'd work together to find the caches neither of us have done and along the way, if we drive near any caches either of our teams have done, then we'll stop so that the other team can collect it too. And we'd have four sets of eyes looking for each cache instead of only two. That's bound to make them easier to find."

Miles nodded. Hearing Paige talk strategy was surprisingly hot. He enjoyed watching her take on the challenge of figuring out how their teams could work together and so far, it sounded like a pretty decent plan. Working with another team the way she'd specified could help a lot. And he and Ben had talked once before, earlier in the game, about the possibility of allying with another team. But were the girls really their best hope?

"We were just discussing how the prizes would work for caches we find together first and it seems like alternating the team who opens the cache would solve that little problem just fine. Then it's fair."

Seemed they'd come to an agreement before he'd even gotten to the table. Nice of Ben to consult his teammate. Although, he couldn't really be mad at Ben. The alliance did sound pretty good. The girls would tip them off to the caches they already knew about, they'd find the rest of them together, hopefully faster, and they'd still get a chance to find some prizes.

He glanced toward Paige where she sat quietly, waiting while he weighed the possibilities. An alliance with the girls would mean more time spent putting up with Zoe, who was already sufficiently annoying at base camp each night.

But it also meant spending more time with Paige. And that couldn't be a bad thing.

Well, it could be a bad thing if she distracted him so much he couldn't concentrate on finding the caches. But distraction by Paige certainly felt worth it at the moment.

And then there was Ben. This could be exactly what Ben needed to get him excited about being in the competition again. This could be the thing that gave him a little push to keep going and not give up all hope of winning. Sure, Miles had wanted to be the one to do that for him, but if he couldn't, then he still wanted someone else to. Maybe that was Zoe and Paige.

"Okay, I'm in if Ben is." If the smiles beaming back at him from around the table were any indication, everyone was happy with their new arrangement. "So what should we do first, allies?"

"First, we compare logbooks," Zoe said, flipping theirs open to the first page and sliding it to the middle of the table. The wall-mounted cameras might see what they were doing, but the other teams couldn't and that was all that mattered. "Then we decide where to begin our search tomorrow."

*

Miles kicked a tiny patch of dirt with the toe of his shoe while he waited for the start time to finally roll around. He hated this morning send off ritual they were forced to participate in for the show. But that was part of being on a reality show whether he liked it or not.

Now if only the rest of the teams would show up so they could get started… of course, it was his new alliance that was missing. Figures.

The girls came around the corner of the lodge and out to the front lawn where they started each day. Zoe looked her usual high-maintenance self, but Paige…

Well, Paige looked like a brunette version of Zoe.

Instead of her usual hiking boots, she came strolling—teetering, actually—toward them on the spindliest heels he'd seen on anyone other than Zoe. The sun reflected off the surface, causing a million sparkles to shoot from her feet.

Interesting choice for the day's activities, which included a fair amount of hiking if every other day they'd been on the show was any indication.

Along with her shining high heels, she wore another pair of tight jeans and her usual yoga top. Although there was something decidedly different about her shirt today. He couldn't quite pinpoint what was unusual about it. He was sure he'd seen her wear it at least once before, and yet it looked… even sexier than before somehow.

As they strolled up to the start line to join everyone else, Miles realized exactly what was different about Paige.

Boobs.

And cleavage. Where the hell had those been hiding? Maybe she'd been wearing one of those workout bras before today. Those things always made even the most voluptuous women look flat-chested. That had to be it.

And why the hell had she been keeping them under wraps? Breasts like those deserved to be served up front and center for the world to admire. Or at least every straight man in the area… and possibly some gay ones too. They really were great breasts.

Paige folded her arms across her chest and it was as if a fog lifted from his brain. As his gaze traveled up to her face, he noticed she was staring back at him, but he couldn't tell if her expression was one of amusement or annoyance.

"Welcome to day ten of *Treasure Trekkers,*" Spencer started. "Before you head out for the day, let's tell everyone at home how our teams are doing so far. The team who has stayed at the top of the leader board for the entire week is Team Firefighters with an outstanding one hundred and twenty-five caches logged so far."

The firefighters patted each other on the back. The other teams smiled and cheered a little, but no one was really thrilled with having a team so far in the lead.

"The next in line is Team Father Daughter who has a very impressive eighty-eight caches logged."

Miles tuned out while Spencer went through the ten teams, listing off their cache totals so far. By the time he got to Miles and Ben, the pit in his stomach had grown into a giant lump of embarrassment. He'd known the show would be a challenge, but somehow, he never thought they'd get this brutally beaten.

An alliance, even one with the stiletto girls, was looking better and better all the time.

"Now," Spencer spoke again, drawing Miles's attention back. "Before you head out for the day, we have a little surprise for you."

Great.

"Today we're mixing things up a little. Instead of racing with your normal partner, you'll each join forces with another team. One member of each team will pair up together for the day."

Well, that wasn't so terrible, Miles thought. At least they'd made their alliance last night so the choice was an easy one. Surely other teams had alliances formed in secret already too. Seeing who paired up together might even give them a little insight into the teams working in alliances.

"One more thing. All of the caches you find today will apply to both teams. That means if you find any prizes, they are to be shared. And any points for the cache are awarded to each team. So choose your partner wisely. This could help you or it could help another team. I'll let you have a moment to discuss your choice with your partner before we begin the day."

Miles and Ben moved to stand beside Paige and Zoe. Obviously as a new alliance, it wasn't a question of which team to work with, only how to split up.

"So how are we going to split the teams?" Ben asked as if reading his mind.

"I'll go with Ben and Paige can go with Miles," Zoe said as if it was already discussed and decided. Annoying, but definitely not worth the effort of complaining.

"Sounds good," he said, trying to come off as indifferent.

"Has everyone picked their new team and their new partner?" Spencer asked. The new teams all nodded and voiced their agreement. "Great. Then, treasure hunters, start searching."

The other teams raced into the parking lot while their two teams sort of moseyed. Miles sighed. This wasn't a better start then usual. Maybe teaming up with the girls wasn't going to be as beneficial as some of the other pairings.

"Paige and I'll go in our SUV and Ben can ride with Zoe." They nodded as they came up to the vehicles. The other teams were pulling out of the parking lot already so they were able to talk candidly.

"We'll take cameraman Evan with us," Zoe said, pulling Evan toward their SUV.

"No way," Paige shrieked, pulling on Evan's other arm. "He's coming with me and Miles, no exceptions. I know how you are, Zoe, and I don't trust you with him."

"Why, you two hooking up or something?" Ben asked motioning between Paige and Evan.

Better not be.

"No, he's engaged to my best friend. And I know how much Zoe loved flirting with him on *The One*. Cassidy would never forgive me if I left Evan in her care for the day."

Friend's fiancé.

Miles couldn't stop the smile of relief from coming to his lips. For some reason, it made him so happy to know she wasn't hanging on Evan because she liked him.

Ben sagged against the girls' SUV, already looking tired when the day had barely started. Maybe following each other around wasn't the most effective use of their time. Paige scooted past Ben, opening the back door and leaned in to grab her things, then transferred them quickly to the boys' SUV. Maybe going their separate ways would be a better idea just for today. That way, Zoe and Ben could travel a little slower while Miles and Paige tried to cover as much ground as possible.

As Paige slammed the door, she wobbled on her heels, falling back against the vehicle. Or maybe they were screwed either way with both girls in those silly heels. Of all the days she decided to wear ridiculous shoes. Still, they'd probably be better off on their own. Besides, the thought of spending the day alone with Paige was pretty appealing. And not only because of her new boobs. It was nice to hang out with her in the evenings with everyone else, but a little alone time on the race wouldn't be bad either.

"I know we talked about following each other around in the cars today and doing the caches together, but today all the caches we find will count for both teams even if we're not together. If we split up, we may be able to get more done, quicker," Miles offered.

Everyone nodded in agreement.

"Good thing we compared logbooks last night," Ben said. "All those other teams are going to have to waste time figuring out which caches neither of them have found yet. That'll save us a bunch of time."

Miles nodded. "We'll start with the first half of the logbook and you guys focus on the second half. Tonight we'll compare them again at base camp."

He walked around the front of the SUV to climb into the driver's side, but as Paige walked past him, she rolled her ankle on a loose piece of gravel and fell toward him. Instead of opening the door, he turned to catch Paige in his arms.

She peered up at him through surprised eyes. "Thanks," she said, her hands gripping his shirt.

"Is there a reason you didn't wear your usual hiking boots today?" he asked.

"They didn't go with this outfit."

Not true. They'd gone with that outfit plenty of other days. He'd noticed. She looked cute in her hiking gear. Cute enough he could imagine her in rock climbing gear at his side. Not that he wasn't enjoying the heels too. They made her legs look long and lean. The kind of legs he'd like to feel wrapped around his waist. But they were impractical for hiking and he'd much prefer she save those for a time that made sense so they could be enjoyed, appreciated.

No. She had some other reason for suddenly dressing up for the show, but finding out why would have to wait. They were already behind and now they needed to get on the road or they'd never get anything done today.

"Well, I wish you'd consider going back and changing into your boots before we leave."

She shook her head and a few hairs fell down around her face, dangling into her also-new cleavage. Now that new development he couldn't think of a single complaint for. He set her gently back upright on her feet.

"I like these shoes and I'm going to wear them." She smoothed down her shirt then pulled open her door. "Today you're stuck with me and my shoes."

Miles cocked an eyebrow at Paige's confident reply. Maybe she wasn't as shy and unsure of herself as he'd originally thought.

As she got in, Zoe passed by the side of the truck, pausing at Paige's open door. "Note he didn't complain about the new bra," she whispered loudly enough for him to hear in the front seat.

A quick glance in the rearview mirror revealed a red-faced Paige as Zoe pushed the door closed. Paige didn't say anything in response. She was far too busy examining her new shoes for words.

Interesting. New shoes, new bra—push-up by the look of that lift—and new pink cheeks to match. What exactly was Paige playing at?

He suddenly had a new mission for the day. Find out why Paige felt the need for these new wardrobe additions. Or maybe the better question was who were these new additions for?

Chapter Eleven

Paige slumped back against the seat and stared at the ceiling while the hottest man on earth followed her navigation directions to the next cache. If curling into an invisible ball of nothingness in the backseat was an option, she would have. But no. She had to sit in the back with her breasts feeling distinctly like torpedoes, aimed and ready to fire, while her cheeks still burned with embarrassment.

Great start to a day that was supposed to be filled with getting Miles's attention.

Maybe attention was the same as press—even the negative form was still beneficial.

There was no denying that he'd noticed her transformation. She'd seen the look in his eyes when she'd walked up this morning. She'd seen the look in his eyes when his gaze had traveled down to her chest and gotten stuck there. And there'd been no mistaking the look in his eyes when she'd been in his arms and he'd been peering directly down her shirt.

Nope.

He'd noticed the twins, in all their pushed-up glory.

She'd noticed something too. Namely how his chest felt under her hand when she'd held on to him, all muscular and firm. If there'd been any doubt in her mind about his physique before, it was long gone. He was rock solid. Climbing did his body good.

And she'd also noticed how hard his heart pounded against her palm. Just about as fast as hers had. Interesting. Maybe the bra was a better purchase than she realized.

This was definitely the ka-pow effect Zoe had mentioned. Miles had been so glassy-eyed when he'd caught sight of her new boobs, it was as if he'd been clocked a good one right upside the head. Ka-pow!

She could get used to this superpower.

"Take the next left and then I think we're going to have to go on foot from there," she said, directing Miles as close as she could to the cache location.

He turned left onto a side road then pulled over onto a grassy shoulder. There didn't appear to be any kind of trail to follow, but the cache was definitely close by. And hidden in the cluster of trees if her guess at distance and direction was right.

"Can I see that?" Miles asked, motioning to the GPS unit in her hand as they stood beside the truck. She handed it over, curious if he would come to the same estimation.

"It's through those trees somewhere, I think," she said, pointing off into the distance.

"I think you're right. Are you sure you don't want to change your shoes before we off road it?" He grinned, obviously teasing her.

Yes, I do, but I'm not going to because that's not what Zoe would do.

"Nope, I'm good," she said, setting her jaw tight and straightening her shoulders. She'd prove to him—and herself— that she could look good and still get the job done. She took a few steps forward, sinking into the soft ground of the ditch. And hopefully she wouldn't break her ankle while she was out here.

He chuckled and fell into step at her side. "So what made you decide on the footwear change all of a sudden? Hiking boots not working out so well for all the hiking we've been doing?"

Paige glanced to the side but he was looking straight ahead. Now what would Zoe say if she was in this position with him?

She'd flirt her ass off, of course.

But how? Paige wasn't a natural flirt. She didn't understand how people could put themselves out there like that by saying flirty things. Probably a big reason why she'd never really made any connection with bachelor Brad on the last show.

Did she want to make the same mistake this time around? It was only a little harmless flirting. And probably better to jump in and get her feet wet out here where she'd only embarrass herself in front of Miles and Evan and not in a room full of other teams, which was exactly what would happen if she waited to start flirting until she was back at base camp.

"I think your fascination with my footwear is rather interesting. Most men wouldn't remember what color shirt a girl wore today let alone her choice of shoes on previous days." She swallowed. Oh boy. "Maybe you have a hidden shoe fetish thing going on."

Fetishes were sexy-talk, right?

He chuckled again. "No. But I can't help it if I pay attention to things I like."

Oh, well then… What was I just saying?

She tried to make her voice sound sexy like the women in movies always did when they were trying to seduce someone. "So you do like the stilettos."

"I do," he said quietly. "But they don't strike me as being your style."

"You don't really know me well enough to know my style," she challenged, suddenly feeling like she had to defend her shoe choices. "Maybe these are the shoes I wear everyday in my normal life outside of the show."

Just then a tree root popped up out of the ground and grabbed her ankle on purpose as if the universe had a point to prove, causing her to stumble. Before she could catch herself, Miles caught her, holding her against his chest for the second time. It was even better than the first.

"You were saying about your normal shoes?" He smirked.

She met his gaze, putting on her best poker face. "That could have happened in flats."

"Could have, but didn't." He set her back on her feet, letting his hand linger on her lower back for a few steps while she got her balance again. A difficult task when his hand on her back made her knees feel like they'd been replaced with silly putty.

"Maybe you should save these shoes for around base camp at night and use the hiking boots for hiking."

"If Zoe can hike in stilettos, I can too."

"Not everything Zoe does should be copied."

Since when did men have anything negative to say about Zoe?

For the next quarter mile, they walked in silence following the arrow of the GPS. A few more minutes and they should reach the cache. Paige leaned in closer to the unit, watching the distance on the screen decreasing. Ten more feet.

The ground fell away beneath her and she was suddenly on her back, sliding down a very bumpy surface. After a short slide, she came to a stop, staring up at the canopy of trees.

Ouch.

Footsteps pounded down the slope after her then Miles was down on his knees in the dirt beside her.

Well hello there, Mr. Muscles. Let's get dirty together.

The image of getting dirty in the forest with Miles was a little more sex kitten than her usual train of thought. *Did I hit my head on the way down?*

Or maybe it was the influence of the super hot, super built man hovering over her with concern in his eyes that caused the shift in her mental state.

"Are you okay?" Miles asked, touching the side of her face and turning her head first one direction and then the other. Her eyes never left his.

"I'm fine. Just dirty—muddy," she clarified. Not that he could read her mind, but still. "I'll get up now."

"Let me help you," he said, standing over her and wrapping his large hands around her upper arms, pulling her up to stand in front of him. His hands dropped to her waist and she found hers groping his chest again. Seemed she couldn't keep her hands off of him. Not that the rest of her complained in the least.

"Thanks," she whispered, looking up to meet his gaze. The mix of concern and… something else made her breath hitch in her throat. Damn.

"My pleasure."

Her feet went out from under her again, but this time she didn't slide down the slope. Possibly because she'd managed to drag Miles down to the ground with her. Perhaps his body weight pressing her into the soft dirt was enough to stop her from going anywhere.

Definitely every inch of his tall, muscular body against hers was enough to cause the lightheadedness she now felt.

Or possibly the lightheadedness could be from his leg pressing against the junction of her thighs. He'd managed to anchor them both to the ground as she straddled his leg. Yes, that could cause lightheadedness to hit full force.

As could the length of something else currently pressing into her.

Either he suddenly had less blood traveling to his brain or he'd managed to shove a tree branch in his pocket on the way down the hill. A very large tree branch.

She stared up at him from where he rested, propped up on one elbow, staring back at her, his breathing heavy. She should probably say something, if only she could form words. Or thoughts.

He brushed the hair out of her eyes with his free hand. "You really need to lose those shoes."

"No," she said quietly. Sure, they may be death traps, but look where they'd gotten her. Just this morning she'd been hoping for a little of his attention, and now Miles was lying on top of her. Liking it too, if his tree branch was any indication of what was going on inside his head.

"Why not?"

"Because I like them," she said. She liked the position they'd managed to put her in too.

"You're going to get hurt. Tomorrow you leave the shoes behind or we don't work together anymore."

"Don't tell me what to do," she said, trying to wiggle out from beneath him so that maybe she could have more dignity while she stood up to him. But a twitch of something hard against her made her fall still again. She could have dignity from right where she was. "I'll wear whatever shoes I want."

"Tell me why you really decided high heels were a good idea and maybe I'll understand."

"That's my business."

He laughed, letting his head fall forward as he did. Any further and it would rest on her shoulder. When he looked at her again, his expression was serious. "Given our current predicament, I think it's my business too."

Could she admit it? Could she tell him the truth that she'd bought and worn the shoes so he'd finally notice her? What would a flirty, confident girl do in this situation?

She wouldn't tell him, that's for damn sure.

"I, um," she stammered. Great confident start. She cleared her throat and solidified her resolve. If she didn't say something flirty now, she probably wasn't going to get a more intimate opportunity. "I just wanted a little more… sexiness… with my outfit."

That was flirty, wasn't it?

Or now I'll die of humiliation when you bolt off of me like I'm covered in fire ants.

He raised an eyebrow at her. "You think the tight yoga tops you wear aren't sexy enough?"

You do?

"Oh, well." She looked away. No, actually, she didn't think yoga tops were sexy at all, but they were tight. And possibly paired with the bra it might be considered sexy. Sexy-ish. Hell, if yoga tops got Miles looking at her like he was right now, he could call them whatever he wanted to.

Wait a second.

"So you think I'm sexy?" Shocked didn't even begin to describe how she felt about this new tidbit of information. Huh.

"Was there ever a doubt in your mind after the way you looked in the kitchen the other night?"

"Oh," she said weakly, unable to think of anything more intelligent.

"Now, if you'd paired these heels with those tiny shorts and thin little tank top you wore that night…" He paused, leaning in closer. "Well, then concentrating on driving without staring into the rearview mirror would have been a real trick."

His mouth hovered over hers, his breath tickling her lips.

I should say something…

"Good thing then, I guess. We wouldn't want to end up in a ditch somewhere."

Not something stupid…

He smiled. "As opposed to the ditch we're in right now? No, I think I quite like this one."

Miles lowered his mouth to hers, so softly she wondered if she'd dreamed it. She tilted her chin for a better angle and kissed him back. Her breath froze in her lungs as his tongue slipped into her mouth.

He wrapped his hand around the nape of her neck, positioning her head just how he wanted it, trailing a line of kisses along her jaw to her ear where his then nibbled. "This ditch is pretty awesome actually."

She wished he would shut up and kiss her again. And she wished they were somewhere more comfortable than the ground. Not that the hard ground was much of a concern given the fact that Miles was currently nibbling on her neck and making good progress toward her collarbone. Every kiss sent another wave of heat quivering through her belly.

Then he kissed her again and there was no mistaking that he wished they were somewhere more comfortable too.

The sound of a twig snapping from somewhere near them broke their kiss. Evan stood only a few feet away, camera aimed right at their tryst happening in the woods. How had she forgotten Evan was here and that meant every moment with Miles was now caught on film?

Paige glared up at Evan. "Got that all on film?"

He nodded.

Miles climbed to his feet then pulled her to standing too, his arms wrapped tightly around her waist this time. "You wanna do me a favor and delete that footage?"

Evan shook his head.

"I'm telling Cassidy." It was a silly threat since Cassidy would probably love to see this all play out on TV like everyone else, but it was the only threat she had.

"Let's worry about the footage later. We've lost a lot of time already," Miles said, turning Paige to face him. "I'm taking the shoes."

"No, you're not," she said, trying to step away.

"Fine then, have it your way." Miles picked her up, tossing her over his shoulder, then smacked her on the ass. "Keep the shoes. I'll do this the hard way."

*

"How was it working with different partners today?" Evan asked as Paige and Zoe settled into their daily wrap-up interview.

"It was great," Paige said, possibly too enthusiastically judging by the expression of amusement on Zoe's face. "I mean, it was fun in a different sort of way."

Evan smirked behind the camera. Of course, he knew exactly what kind of fun she'd had today. The question was whether or not he'd bring it up in the questions. She wasn't quite ready to share her thoughts about it yet, even if the viewing audience would get to see what actually happened.

"I really enjoyed hanging out with Ben," Zoe said. "He was funny and easy to talk to all day. A big contrast from my usual partner."

"Hey," Paige griped, swatting Zoe on the shoulder for her rude comment. "I'm funny and easy to talk to too."

"Sure you are, in a Paige sort of way. But let's face it. It was nice for both of us to get a little break from the other for a day, wasn't it?"

"True."

"Does that mean you would be up to racing with Team Everest again if that twist happened a second time?"

"Sure," both girls said together.

"What about forming an alliance with them since you all seemed to get along so well? Would you consider doing that with Ben and Miles or perhaps a different team?"

Paige and Zoe looked at each other. They'd talked about it, decided on it basically, but did they want to share that in the interview? Would anyone else get to see this footage before the show actually aired? What was the best way to answer this question without lying?

"I… we—" Paige started, still unsure of what to say.

"What Paige is trying to say is that we've decided to keep our strategy to ourselves, for right now. We can't be too careful when there are so many teams around to compete with. So for now, our strategy is off the table for discussion during these daily wrap-ups."

Evan glanced down at his questions. "Okay, then. I guess that's all I have for you since the rest of the questions Chip wanted me to ask are strategy based. I'm sure he'll be thrilled with your decision." He laughed, getting up and straightening out his papers. "And he thought Cassidy was the one who would give him trouble."

"Well, Chip should know better than to underestimate me. If he gives you any lip about it, you send him my way and I'll deal with him myself," Zoe said, a twinkle in her eye and a smile playing on her lips as if she'd started daydreaming. She walked out of the room and left Paige to stare after her without another word.

Zoe thinking about Chip in a daydreamy way? Odd. Very odd.

"Do you really think Chip will be upset with us? Because we probably could talk a bit about our strategy if we really had to." Paige didn't like the thought of the producer being mad at her.

"He'll be fine." Evan put down his camera. "Between you and me, you're making a good choice to keep things tight-lipped."

"Thanks for saying that, Evan." Paige relaxed.

"And by tight-lipped, I don't mean smooching with your alliance members." Evan laughed and walked away.

Paige's cheeks grew hot. Thank God Evan had said that last part off camera since she still hadn't had a chance to tell Zoe about the kiss with Miles yet. And she didn't need Zoe cracking comments on camera either.

Chapter Twelve

Miles stretched out on his bed, his hands folded behind his head as his muscles ached at the abuse they'd taken during the day. It had seemed like an easy enough cache to get—wander a few hundred feet into the woods, search around a bit, log it, and get back to the SUV and on to the next one.

Then Paige had taken her spill down the hill on those ridiculous heels and he'd been a goner ever since. He'd had to carry her the rest of the way to the cache, not that he'd minded all that much. Aside from the difficult terrain, having Paige over his shoulder had been rather awesome. And the little smack on the ass he'd given her hadn't been too shabby either.

But it had slowed them down. As had their kiss. Damn, that kiss…

And of course it all had to happen on a day he'd been hoping to make up for lost time. He'd really thought he'd be able to knock out a solid ten caches with Paige, instead of the five he and Ben usually logged.

Not matter how hard he tried, he couldn't seem to keep focused on the game. Either he was worrying about how Ben was holding up or he worried about what kind of trouble Zoe was getting herself into. And now he had to add Paige to his list of worries too. He had to worry about whether or not she was going to twist her ankle in those stupid shoes. And he had to worry about whether or not he'd have enough blood flowing to his brain at any given time while in Paige's presence to function at a normal human level.

None of which was conducive to running a fast race. Exactly the reason they were still pulling up damn close to last place.

At least with today's combined caches, both his team and the girls' team had been able to move up in the ranks two places. Finally they weren't dead last.

"I expected you and Paige to rack of up the points today. What happened?" Ben asked, walking out of the bathroom.

"Those shoes happened."

Ben laughed. "I think Zoe's finally corrupted her. And of all days when we really could have used the help."

"I hear you. You and Zoe did okay getting another seven caches too. How was it with her today? Was she unbearable?"

Ben sat on the edge of his bed and slipped off his prosthetic, massaging the reddened skin for a minute, then sliding under the covers. "Actually, she was great. I've never seen her be so nice before."

"Are you sure you took the right girl with you today? You didn't accidentally grab some Zoe lookalike?"

Zoe wasn't nice to anyone. Not even herself.

"I know. I thought it was all a big joke at first too, but if it was, she kept up the act all day."

What was Zoe playing at? There had to be some reason for her sudden attitude change toward Ben, but what? Was there some kind of twist in the game she'd figured out and they hadn't? Because no part of Zoe was nice to another human being without a good reason.

Or maybe it was because she could relate to Ben's injury… the way it had changed him…

Yes, that could definitely explain Zoe's sudden change of heart and attitude toward Ben.

"Well, regardless of the reason behind it, I'm glad to hear you didn't have to put up with Zoe being a bitch all day."

"And despite the shoes, how was it with Paige?"

"Fine."

"Just fine?"

Miles sighed. How could he describe his day with Paige? Distracting, tempting, sexually frustrating. "Yep. Fine."

"Huh," Ben said between yawns, "because I could have sworn I overheard Evan and another cameraman talking about some kind of kiss in the mud. Sounded like there's a budding showmance in the mix."

Damn.

"There may have been a kiss."

A really fan-fucking-tastic kiss.

After an amazing kiss like that, maybe it was finally time to tell Paige about his past with Zoe. It seemed like Paige and Zoe were getting along better now than they had been at the start of the show. Maybe his previous connection to Zoe wouldn't affect Paige's opinion of him anymore. Maybe he could have a fair shot with her even if she found out the truth.

Possibly, he could tell Zoe they didn't need to keep things a secret anymore. After all, the groundwork had been laid already, in more ways than one.

"Never could resist a pretty brunette in heels, could you?" Ben laughed and rolled over. "Just don't let it screw up our partnership with them. On second thought, maybe we shouldn't make an alliance with them if you're starting to fool around with Paige. It could complicate things more than it's worth."

"It was one kiss, not a complication."

"Still. Maybe we're better off on our own."

Miles glanced over to Ben. What was the right decision for their team? Working with the girls could lead to complications, especially if he had to watch Paige in those heels and yoga tops everyday. But the girls were also pretty stubborn and that might be just what they needed to get enough caches to win.

Not to mention, the thought of Paige falling down another hill without anyone to rescue her but Zoe made him break out in a cold sweat. What if something worse happened and he wasn't there to help?

That settled it.

"An alliance with the girls is our best option right now if we really want a chance to win. Even if we only pair up with them long enough to collect most of the caches they've already gotten, it will be worth it for the points alone. After that point, we can reevaluate the situation."

"I'll give it another day, but if working with the girls holds us back in any way, we're on our own again."

"Deal," he agreed reluctantly.

It really was the only option. That way he could get Ben closer to winning. Miles could already see the spark of excitement coming back to Ben. If they won, it would be all it took to make Ben realize how much he'd missed having a little more adventure in his life.

And if he got to flirt with Paige a little more along the way, that was pretty okay too.

*

"How did it go with Miles yesterday? You didn't really get into specifics in the interview last night, and then you scurried off to bed before I got another chance to ask you. But I could tell you were leaving out some good stuff," Zoe said while brushing her already perfect looking hair.

Every morning, Zoe managed to beat Paige out of bed and into the shower. And every morning by the time Paige woke up, Zoe was already shampooed, blow-dried and had her makeup fully applied. It made Paige feel very lazy. Not exactly what she wanted to feel when the alarm went off at six each morning.

"Aside from acting like an idiot, not bad."

"What do you mean?"

Paige sighed and stretched out her still half asleep body. She couldn't believe yesterday had actually happened. It felt more like a dream than reality. A great dream she didn't want to wake up from. "I don't know how you do it."

"I'm awesome. That's how."

Paige rolled her eyes. "I didn't even finish my thought yet."

"Well, I'm awesome at basically everything. You'll have to be more specific."

Paige rolled out of bed and walked into the bathroom, turning on the shower. "Hiking in heels wasn't easy," she called through the open door as she stepped into the hot water. "I'm not sure I can keep wearing them. I may have to go back to my boots."

"Not if I burn them first."

"I'm serious. I fell. Down a hill. Miles had to come and rescue me."

"What's the problem then?" Zoe asked. "You wanted his attention, so mission accomplished."

"I kind of hoped for a less embarrassing type of attention." Paige finished her shower, toweled off and pulled on her clothes before walking back into the bedroom. As she combed her hair, Zoe touched up her makeup for what had to be the third or forth time that morning already.

"What did Miles do when you fell?"

"He rushed down the hill after me to make sure I was okay." Paige's lips tingled at the memory. Or possibly because of the minty lip balm she'd applied. The warmth settling deep in her belly, however, was definitely from the memory of Miles lying on top of her.

"And were you okay?"

"I'm here and not the hospital, aren't I? Of course, I could have been a little more seductive and a little less feminist."

"Have you learned nothing from me yet?" Zoe asked, sounding exasperated.

"He told me to lose the shoes and I told him not to tell me what to do. Somehow I don't think that was the flirty response I should have made."

Zoe sighed. "Amateur."

"So teach me, oh wise one. Teach me how to be like you," Paige teased.

"You can't teach this," Zoe said, waving a hand down her body. "I guess you can dress a girl up, but you can't make her sexy."

"Gee, thanks."

"It's what I'm here for." Zoe slipped into her heels then eyed Paige.

Paige couldn't help but feel pathetic in comparison to the blonde bombshell of a teammate she'd been stuck with. "Why should I even bother attempting to flirt with anyone when you're around?"

"Gee, thanks," Zoe said, mimicking Paige's earlier sentiment.

Paige almost felt bad for saying that. Almost.

"Oh, come on. I know that didn't hurt your feelings. Seriously, how is Miles ever going to fall for plain old me when perfect you is around to remind him how much better he could have it with another girl?"

Zoe shrugged. "True. But I happen to know for a fact Miles isn't interested in me. He's interested in you. You need to be more confident."

"Whatever." Paige pulled her hair into a knot at the nape of her neck, approximately where Miles's hand had been the day before… when he'd kissed her. Maybe Zoe was right. Maybe Miles was at least interested enough to kiss her. But then if he was really interested, why hadn't he tried to kiss her again yesterday? After that first cache, he'd been focused on "making up for lost time" with the others. That didn't sound like a guy who was interested in scoring with the girl who tried to flirt with him.

"Are you really going to make me say this?" Zoe huffed.

"Say what?" Paige was too annoyed with herself to try and figure out what the hell Zoe was talking about.

She sighed and rubbed her temples as if whatever she had to say was torturous. "You have no reason to feel pathetic. Miles or any other guy would be lucky to have you. You're smart, and pretty, and sort of sexy in your own hiking boots and tank top kind of way."

Paige's mouth dropped open. Had hell actually frozen over? She peeked out the window and into the sky. Nope. No flying pigs. Wow. Zoe Oliver had just paid someone a compliment. And only the hiking boots part had been the tiniest bit backhanded.

Whoa.

"Um, thanks?" Paige shook her head then pinched her arm. It hurt. "Are you dying or something?"

Zoe wasn't nice to anyone. Certainly she'd never been nice to Paige. Therefore, she had to be suffering from some terminal illness.

"No. I'm not dying. I'm sick of hearing you be pathetic. It's throwing off my mojo." Zoe walked to the door and paused with her hand on the doorknob. "I'll be waiting out front whenever you've gotten ready for the day."

"I am ready," Paige said, looking down at her outfit; shorts, a fitted shirt with a hint of sparkle and—sigh—her high-heeled torture devices as soon as she strapped them on her feet.

Zoe eyed her. "Oh. In that case, make sure to smile and bat your eyes a lot. And touch his arms if you can. Even better, make sure to tell him how big his arms are. No guy can resist a girl who comments on the size of his… biceps." With a giggle, she disappeared out the door.

Paige slipped into her heels then stood in front of the full-length mirror in the corner eyeing her outfit. "Maybe Zoe's right."

Oh God. Had she really said that out loud?

Her denim cut-offs were cute and—she turned to evaluate her rearview in the mirror—short. So those could stay. But maybe her top wasn't quite eye-catching enough. She grabbed a different one from the closet and slipped into it. It wasn't her usual yoga top style, but it was still fitted in all the right places, especially with the help of the push-up bra and a low scoop neck that offered a glimpse at the twins. She didn't want to put the girls totally out there, but showing them off a little to Miles couldn't hurt her chances.

Or her self-confidence, which, according to new, nicer Zoe, she didn't need to be so worried about.

Maybe today she could get attention from Miles without falling down a hill.

Chapter Thirteen

Paige stood at the edge of the lake but couldn't make out anything other than the small waves breaking the surface. The other side of the lake looked completely uninhabited and according to their GPS units, it was also too far away to be the next cache location. That only left one possibility. The cache was somewhere on the lake.

"It's out there," Ben said from beside her.

"Only one way to get it then," Miles added. "But the boats are only big enough for two so we'll have to split up."

"Ben, can you help me with this boat?" Zoe called, attempting to push the canoe away from the shore enough that they could get into it without getting stuck on the sand.

"I guess that means you're riding with me." Miles pushed the other canoe into the water then held it still while Paige climbed into it.

If she wasn't mistaken, she heard a low whistle from his direction when she held the sides and crept into the front position. Perhaps her shorts were a touch shorter than she thought. Good. At least she knew Miles was paying attention.

He handed her an oar and took another for himself. Together they paddled out toward the middle of the lake, pausing every so often to check the coordinates were still ahead of them. Neither spoke much other than to comment on the beautiful, picturesque surroundings. Zoe and Ben in the other canoe floated a few feet away, their chatty conversation drifting over the water. Both of them laughing and sounding as if they were having a great time. The cameramen filmed from their own canoe, capturing the footage from where they could see all of the contestants at the same time.

"Have you noticed how well they've been getting along since their day alone together?" Paige asked quietly, turning slightly in her seat so she could see Miles better.

He nodded. "Everyone likes Ben. I think they bonded or something."

"Bonded horizontally in the backseat of the SUV maybe. I can't imagine Zoe bonding on any other level."

"No way," Miles said shaking his head. "Ben is married and one hundred percent committed to Tammy. Him and Zoe just seem to get along. That's all. I wouldn't read too much into it. She's simply decided to be nice to Ben for whatever reason."

"I wish she acted that nicely to me. I'm her partner and all I get is sarcasm and arrogance."

"Those are Zoe's specialties."

"True. I guess I shouldn't expect anything else from her. It's not like we're suddenly going to become best friends or anything."

"I think Zoe's one of those people who has more going on inside than she lets people see. She and Ben are actually a lot alike in that way. It's probably why they hit it off so well."

Paige scowled. "Maybe they should be teammates then. At least they seem to work well together which is more than I can say for Zoe and me as a team."

Miles smiled. "I like that idea. Then you and I could be a team. I promise I'd keep the arrogance and sarcasm to a minimum." He leaned forward, his breath tickling the back of her neck, raising little goose bumps along her skin. "And I promise I'd try my best not to kiss you again, but even my best might not be enough to resist you."

She sucked in a breath. So their kiss hadn't been a big mistake. He hadn't been caught up in the moment. He might even want to kiss her again.

Say something flirty now.

She turned and met his gaze. "And I promise I wouldn't stop you." She bit her bottom lip, holding her breath.

"This partnership is sounding better and better every second," he said, leaning in, his mouth inching closer to hers. She tilted her chin a tiny bit, bringing her mouth a fraction of a breath closer to his. Her eyelids grew heavier as his lips brushed against hers.

"We found it," Ben yelled.

Paige jumped backward, startled by the sudden sound. The boat wobbled back and forth with her sudden weight shift and she shrieked, gripping the sides with her hands. Her oar splashed into the water.

Her heart pounded in her chest, but not just from being startled. She put her hand to her mouth, rubbing where Miles's lips had touched hers. The heat from the brief kiss still radiated through her body.

Miles cursed under his breath. He leaned over the edge of the canoe and retrieved her oar before it could float away then paddled over to where Ben and Zoe were coming up on a small floating buoy. Right in the middle of the buoy was a plastic case, waiting to be opened.

"Whose turn is it to open this one first?" Paige asked.

"Yours," Miles replied. "Go for it."

"How?" she asked. The buoy was only a foot or so away, but it drifted with the water's current, as did their canoe.

"Just reach for it. I'll try to hold the canoe steady."

Paige scooted closer to the edge, cautious not to shift her body weight too quickly and risk throwing the canoe off balance again. Outstretching her arm, she leaned out of the canoe and into the buoy. She'd just reached the clasp on the container when she felt her hand slip off the edge of the canoe. Before she could pull her upper body back into the canoe, she tipped over the side.

Cold water surrounded her as Paige popped up through the surface, sputtering and coughing from the bit of lake water she'd swallowed on the way in. As she caught her breath, the sounds of laughter greeted her.

"Thanks for your concern," she muttered to no one and all of them.

"Now's not the best time for a swim, Paige." Zoe laughed.

Paige splashed water at her, but missed. "Want to join me in here? I'll tip your canoe if you're not nice."

The smile fell from Zoe's face. "Don't you dare."

"Oh, relax." Paige swam over to the buoy, trying her best to ignore the chuckling brats around her. She flipped open the clasp. "Nothing."

Great. Even a fall in the water couldn't earn her a kick-ass prize like some of the other teams had found. Team Father Daughter found keys to new cars, Team Sisters had found one thousand dollars each, and Team Firefighters had found tickets to the next Super Bowl. She and Zoe had found nothing but cache numbers and a measly five hundred dollar shopping spree at Macy's. Pathetic.

She grabbed the cache card and swam back, the cold water already making her teeth chatter too much to stay in even a moment longer. When she reached the side of the canoe again, Miles lifted her out of the water without any trouble. The canoe barely moved. His biceps, however, were another story entirely. They flexed and bulged and looked beyond delicious. She wanted to wrap her hands around them while they scooped her out of the water and settled her back into the canoe. But she didn't.

"Zoe," she called, starting to shiver, "snap the picture so we can get out of here."

She held up the cache number card and turned so Zoe could take her picture, not bothering to smile.

"Paige," Miles said.

She turned to look at him, holding the card out so she could then take his picture. He snapped a picture of her on his GPS unit.

"That's not going to count for you guys getting the cache," she said.

"I know." Miles smiled and handed her the GPS unit, taking the card from her and holding it up for his turn in front of the lens. "That one was for me to enjoy later."

Her cheeks were the only warm part of her body while she shivered. "Perv," she teased, not meaning it. She folded her arms across her chest, only then realizing how cold she really was. She could cut glass with the hardened peaks in her soaking wet, bordering on see-through shirt. Her cheeks burned hotter as she glanced up to find Miles still smirking.

Zoe and Ben had already started back to shore. "We should head back too," Paige said. "Are you going to put the cache card back for me or do I have to go for another swim?"

"I think you're cold enough without another swim." Miles paddled the boat right up beside the buoy then leaned over and slipped the card back into the box and fastened the clasp.

He made it look so easy.

"Thanks." Paige reached for the oar, her arm shaking from the cold.

Miles put his hand on her arm, the warmth of it instantly dancing along her skin. She wanted to wrap herself in his big arms and snuggle against his body heat.

"It's okay. I'll paddle us back."

She nodded and settled back onto her seat and attempted to look as if she wasn't completely freezing, but her uncontrollable shivers gave her away.

Miles stopped paddling and pulled in his oar. They were still a long way from shore and from the heater she already longed for in the SUV. "Why are... you stopping... here?" she asked between shivers.

"Because you're already freezing and you'll be an ice cube by the time I get you back to shore if this wind doesn't let up."

The wind had picked up since they'd left the shore and a large bank of clouds had hidden the sun. But she could manage until they got back to the truck and then she'd crank the heat. "I'm okay."

"No, you're not." Miles pulled off his T-shirt in one quick motion and held it up in front of him. "I won't peek and the others are too far away to see. Slip your wet shirt off, and put mine on instead."

Paige eyed the shirt in front of her and weighed her options. She could freeze in her wet clothes until they got back to the base camp, or she could take his shirt and at least one part of her would be warm and dry. She glanced over to where Evan filmed from another canoe. He nodded and turned his camera away, getting some long shots of the scenery.

Not liking her other options, she peeled her wet shirt over her head and pulled on Miles's instead. Then she unfastened her bra and slipped it off. No sense wearing a dry shirt with a wet bra.

She hugged the soft, dry cotton shirt against herself, Miles's scent drifting up around her. Closing her eyes, she breathed in deeply, forgetting where she was. All she could focus on was the distinctly manly scent infiltrating her mind, making her feel slightly lightheaded. Funny, she hadn't even needed his lips this time, just his smell.

The sound of a throat clearing popped her eyes back open.

"Okay, then," Miles said, looking uncharacteristically uncomfortable as he picked up his oar again.

Odd considering in all the time she'd known him so far, she hadn't seen him look anything but completely collected and put together at every moment. Even when Spencer surprised them with the twist in the game, he'd taken the news in stride. The only time she'd seen his demeanor change was when she'd fallen and he'd thought she'd been hurt.

Interesting.

Also interesting were Miles's muscles as they rippled and pulled beneath his taut skin. Oh, hell in a handbag, he was beyond hot.

Scorching. She should probably turn around in her seat and face forward, since it wasn't like they were in a rowboat. But she couldn't pull her eyes off the miles and miles of perfectly tanned skin in front of her.

Maybe that explains the nickname.

Every time he dipped the oar into the water and pulled it back, every inch of his upper body tightened. And every time he withdrew the oar from the water and reached forward for another stroke, she'd let out the breath she hadn't meant to hold.

Between the awkward breathing, the sway of the canoe shifting her back and forth in her seat while the inseam of her increasingly uncomfortable denim cut-offs rode up higher and higher between her thighs, and her budded nipples rubbing against the soft cotton of the Miles-scented shirt, she thought she might actually faint. Add in a half-naked Miles for eye-candy and it was all too much. All too good.

By the time Miles had rowed them back to shore, into the wind the whole time, they'd both worked up a sweat. It was all she could do not to jump across the two feet separating them in the canoe and tackle him right then and there.

Best. Canoe ride. Ever.

When she'd finally gathered up her discarded shirt and bra and climbed out of the canoe onto solid ground, Zoe and Ben had come back to the shore to greet them.

"Well, what do we have here?" Zoe smirked. "I never thought about doing it on a canoe before, but I guess you've proven it's possible.

"We didn't..." Paige trailed off, too embarrassed to speak a full sentence.

"I loaned her a dry shirt, that's all." Miles stood confidently as if he had no reason in the world to be embarrassed about his shirtless state. Of course, he didn't. No one that hot would be embarrassed. "So where are we off to next?"

Back to business as usual. Good. That was good. Wasn't it?

The thought of the canoe ride still caused her head to swirl, but that wouldn't do her any good now. Best to move on and forget that moment. Like Miles did so easily. Apparently a half-naked canoe ride was no big deal to him. Maybe she wasn't a big deal to him either.

"Can I have the keys?" she asked Miles, holding out her hand. "While you guys figure out where we're going next, I'm going to go defrost myself."

She jogged to the truck and cranked the heat on high, then laid out her shirt and bra across the dashboard over top of the vents near the windshield. Maybe if she blasted them with heat for a few minutes they would dry off enough to slip back into. She couldn't let Miles walk around shirtless for the rest of the day. And stopping back at base camp for more clothes would take up way too much time.

As her skin started returning to a normal temperature, the back hatch opened and Miles popped his head inside, rustling around in a backpack for something. A moment later, he pulled open the driver's side door and leaned in toward her.

"Feeling warmer?" he asked.

Her gaze roamed down his still naked chest. She nodded. Much warmer. "My stuff should be dry in a minute and then you can have your shirt back."

"Keep it," he said with a sexy smile. "It looks good on you."

"You're just…" She swallowed, her throat feeling parched. "You're going to be comfortable like… that… for the rest of the day?" She nodded toward his chest—his very naked, very muscular, close-enough-she-could-touch-it chest.

He cocked an eyebrow at her. "I might. How would you feel if I did?"

"I, um. That would be, um, fine." She closed her eyes and took a deep, steadying breath before opening them again. Yep. Hot, shirtless guy still inches from her cold, needy body. Damn.

Where the hell was the confident Paige she'd been trying so hard to channel?

That Paige had gone on vacation the second the shirtless hunk showed up and left behind super un-flirty Paige in her place. Well, that wasn't going to fly with a guy like Miles.

"You wouldn't hear a complaint from me," she said, dropping her tone to something that hopefully sounded seductive and not like she suffered from a throat infection.

He stood frozen for a few minutes as if thinking about what to do next. "Maybe another time."

For a second, she thought he might lean in and kiss her again. Oh God, if he did, she wouldn't be able to keep her hands off him. His chest had felt amazing with clothes on. With nothing separating her skin from his, she might not be able to control herself. If only he'd kiss her again so she could find out.

But he didn't.

"Today we have caches to find and the other halves of our teams are waiting for us to hurry up. So you scoot into the back and I'll drive. I can't risk your shivers veering us off the road." He paused leaning closer, running his fingers along her jaw and across her lips. "I can't risk being distracted by you either. And enjoying this look in your eye because I'm bare-chested will have to wait until another time, or I'm afraid we won't make it out of the parking lot."

He stepped back from the door and pulled on a new, clean shirt. She passed in front of him with barely an inch of space between them. Her knees had never been shakier and she couldn't blame a single quiver on her chill. Nope.

"Where did that come from?" she asked, referring to the new shirt as she settled into the backseat, thankful there was great second-row venting in the vehicle. And also thankful she didn't have to give back Miles's shirt yet. She wasn't ready to part with it.

"Years of mountain climbing and hiking taught me to always come prepared. Anything you need, I probably have either in my backpack or on my person."

Oh, I bet you do...

Chapter Fourteen

Miles braced himself in the backseat, cursing his poor lack of judgment for letting Zoe behind the wheel. He knew better than that. Her driving history was proof. She spooked easily behind the wheel and drove as if her life depended on getting where she was going as quickly as possible. If he ever made it back to base camp in one piece, he'd never let her drive him anywhere again. Ever.

Even without her driving, they were incompatible for a road trip of any length. Always had been, always would be. They'd been forced into a few road trips as children and the hours in the car, sharing a backseat had always been grueling. Torturous.

"I can't believe I let you have the keys," Miles griped as his seatbelt tightened. If she slammed on the breaks one more time, he was going to lose his mind. And possibly the granola bar he'd gulped down at lunch.

"Stop your backseat driving," Zoe snapped.

"I'm not sure what you're doing is called driving so how could I possibly be commenting on it?"

"Just because you're a pansy behind the wheel, doesn't mean I am. Besides, if you want to get to the finish line before the check-in time cut off, then we need to hurry the hell up."

"True, but I'd still prefer to get there alive."

Zoe didn't respond. Probably just as well. Her snotty comments would only succeed in getting them into yet another argument. And distracting Zoe while she drove like a complete maniac would only make the entire situation more dangerous.

Nope. He'd sit back and pray.

Then after they were safely checked in at base camp, he'd pull Zoe aside and give her a piece of his mind. Not that it would make any difference. She never listened to a thing he said anyway. But it would make him feel better to get his aggravation with her off his chest.

He leaned back and closed his eyes. Maybe if he didn't look, they would magically transport themselves to base camp and he could stop staring down the freeway of death from the backseat. Yes, eyes closed were better.

Miles let his mind wander out of the game and over to Paige in the other SUV with Ben. He'd had an awesome day with her, driving in comfortable silence or chatting about the game while hunting caches all day. He would have much preferred being in her SUV for the return trip too if they hadn't been in such a rush after the last cache and jumped into the wrong trucks. He'd thought for sure he'd slipped into the backseat of the one Paige had revved the engine of, but sadly no.

"I think it might be time to tell Paige the truth about us," he said, trying to take his mind off the car ride from hell.

"About time. It's really not that big a deal."

"Not to you, but you're not the one who gets picked on by the tall bitchy blonde girl all the time. Paige might care if she knows she has to spend more time with you if she chooses to be with me."

"Hey, I've been nice lately. I've hardly teased her at all and you have to admit, I've had a lot of material to work with."

True, Zoe hadn't teased Paige as much as she could have lately. As far as he knew, she hadn't said anything to Paige about sliding down the hill and today she'd barely said anything about the fall into the lake. Maybe things were settling down enough between all of them that it wouldn't matter anymore if Paige found out the truth.

Paige… Damn, that girl looked hot in his shirt. And when she'd gotten too hot on the last walk and had rolled up the sleeves and twisted the bottom hem into a knot just above her hip… well, shit. He'd never felt so knotted up inside. He was the one who needed a dip in a cold lake after seeing that.

Didn't matter that the knot in his shirt would probably leave it stretched out, even after washing. Nope. What did matter was the strip of lightly tanned skin peeking out from between her denim cut-offs and the now knotted edged of his soft cotton shirt. Not to mention the lack of a bra beneath it.

Just the thought of her bare skin rubbing against the fabric of his shirt made him hard.

His shoulder slammed into the door as the car shifted violently. "Damn it, Zoe," he yelled, his eyes popping open and the image of Paige vanishing. "Are you trying to take out the competition? We're supposed to be allies now, remember?"

"While you were having a catnap back there, I got us to base camp," she said, pulling into a parking spot while the sound of gravel clinked against the undercarriage of the truck. "Now stop your bitching and run. We're almost late."

Miles threw open the back door and hopped out, thankful to see Paige and Ben pulling in behind them. Somehow Paige had managed to keep up with Zoe's crazy driving.

The four of them ran across the parking lot toward the line painted on the front lawn where they started and finished each day during the race. Of course, all of the closer spots were already taken by the other teams. Spencer waited beside the line, glancing down at his watch as he waved them on.

When they hit the grass Zoe swore and fell to the ground. She gripped her ankle in her hands.

"Are you okay?" Miles asked as they all crouched around her.

"Do I look okay?" she shot back.

"Well, at least your bad attitude isn't broken. Can you walk on it?" Miles wrapped his arm under her shoulders and lifted her to her feet.

She took a small step, attempting to put weight on it, but cried out in pain and went weak in his arms. "You guys go ahead. You're going to be late."

"No," all three of them said at the same time.

"We started together, we'll finish together too," Ben said.

Miles scooped Zoe into his arms and started toward the check in line together. Ben and Paige walked beside him. There was no sense in them running ahead since both members of the team had to be present before check in would count. Either they would all make it in time, or they'd all be late. Either way, it looked like their alliance was standing strong.

"You are the last teams to check in tonight and you're both late," Spencer said without much showmanship. "As such, both teams have incurred a two hour penalty for tomorrow's start time. That means you will be able to officially start your search in the morning at ten. I'll see you back here then."

Miles didn't wait around to talk to Spencer about it more. He needed to get Zoe's ankle looked at by the staff medic as soon as possible. With any luck, she wouldn't have to go for x-rays. But if she did, they had a few extra hours before they were allowed to start racing again, which would hopefully be more than enough time to get her feeling better.

Just off the lobby of the lodge's main entrance was a small room normally used for extra supplies. During filming, it had been turned into a makeshift first aid station. Miles set Zoe on the tiny cot inside the door.

"What happened?" the medic asked Zoe.

"I twisted it running for the check-in. It's just a sprain. Give me a couple Ibuprofen and a tensor bandage and I'll be good to go."

The medic ignored her while he twisted her ankle gently one way then the other. It was obvious she tried to keep her poker face on but it wasn't working. Every time he moved it, the color drained from her cheeks.

"You need to have this x-rayed to make sure it's not fractured. I don't think it is, but I can't let you race again without knowing for sure. Some of these caches are too dangerous if you have a bad ankle."

"It's fine," Zoe protested, moving to get off the bed.

The medic put his hands on her shoulders, stopping her. "Do you want me to kick you out of the race?"

"No, of course not."

"Then you'll do as I deem necessary and you'll get x-rayed. If the x-ray shows no fractures, I'll let you race tomorrow. No x-ray, no race."

Damn it. Why did Zoe have to wear those stupid heels all the time? She was asking for something like this to happen. And now she'd gotten Paige to start wearing them too. It was a miracle they both weren't in ankle casts by now.

"Fine," Zoe said quietly, looking distinctly pale and worried. Not at all like the tough girl she usually was. "Let's get this over with."

Miles could tell she was trying her best to be strong, but it wasn't fooling him. "Maybe we should go with you?"

"Only room for one more in the ambulance."

"I'll go," Ben said, stepping forward and putting his hand on Zoe's shoulder before anyone else had a chance to speak.

"No, it should be me. I'm her teammate," Paige said. Paige didn't appear to like the idea of going to the hospital any more than Zoe appeared to.

"You still stink like the lake. I don't want you in my ambulance, thanks."

Always the kind and appreciative Zoe.

While the three of them bickered about who should go with Zoe, Miles followed the medic around the corner to where the wheelchair was stored. "How bad is her ankle?" He couldn't help but worry even if she put on a strong face.

"Between you and me, I think she's fine. I'd be surprised if she needs more than ice and a pain reliever, but the show is very cautious. Chip can't risk a lawsuit over a sprained ankle."

Miles breathed out a sigh of relief. Good. Zoe would be fine.

They just needed an emergency room doctor to tell the show that. Now he could relax and not worry.

"Okay, you two. Let's go." The medic rolled a wheelchair over to the doorway while Paige moved out of the way. Ben took his place by Zoe's side. After she was comfortably seated, they walked toward to ambulance now waiting out front.

"Send an update from the hospital if you can," Paige called as they disappeared out the doors.

They stood unspeaking, watching as Zoe and Ben were loaded into the ambulance. Ben really was the perfect choice to go with her. He was calm and comfortable in the hospital after all his surgeries and treatment over the last couple of years, while Zoe was anything but calm in a hospital setting. Knowing Ben was by Zoe's side helped put Miles's mind at ease. And Ben would do a better job of comforting Zoe than he ever would.

And in case he needed any distraction tonight while he waited up for them to come back, he still had Paige in his shirt to deal with.

*

"Is it safe to assume your two teams are now part of an alliance?" Evan asked, eyeing Paige who still wore Miles's shirt over her petite frame. As soon as the ambulance pulled away, Evan had insisted they do their daily wrap-up segment. That way, when news came from the hospital, they would be free to deal with it. Miles couldn't help but have a little more respect for Evan since he had singlehandedly gotten everything taken care of for them to have the interview area first.

"Are we part of an alliance?" Paige asked him, her eyes and tone of voice clearly asking more than that. Was it safe to share the information with the cameras yet? Was there any way to hide it now?

Were Paige and he really "only" an alliance or were they something more?

"I'm afraid there's no point in hiding it anymore," Miles said with a shrug. "Everyone is sure to find out when they realize we were all running to the check-in line as a unit. Yes, our two teams are officially in an alliance together."

"How is it working out for you so far? Has the alliance been beneficial?" Evan asked.

Depends what you mean by beneficial. I've definitely seen a few perks to the arrangement. Like time with Paige.

"Sure. Our teams have been working really well together." Miles smiled at Paige, thinking about the ways the two of them had specifically worked well together. As if she knew what he was thinking about, she blushed. Her cheeks turned the pretty shade of pink he loved on her.

"Does your alliance put you at an advantage over the other teams?"

Paige shook her head. "No more than any of the other alliances who have already formed."

"Are you aware of other alliances between teams? Who are they?"

"Well, I don't know specifically, but we can't possibly be the only team who's figured out how to make an alliance work in the structure of this game. I couldn't give you names or anything, though." She looked down at her hands, twisting them.

Miles felt an ache grow in his chest for her. He didn't want her to feel bad about anything, certainly not about some silly interview questions. He reached across the armrests of the rocking chairs and took her hand in his, squeezing it gently. Her eyes met his, a connection of understanding sparking between them. His touch brought her comfort and seeing her comfort brought him a feeling of contentment. He liked being strong for Paige.

"We can't be one hundred percent sure of anyone else's business but our own, but Paige is right to believe there are some tight groups forming. Every night in the common room, more teams are talking in hushed voices or not even coming out of their rooms. The game is definitely on and we're trying to stay with the pack."

"One last question and I'll let you go," Evan said, reading his notes. "Tonight Zoe was injured and taken to the hospital. How do you think her injury is going to affect your teams in the race?"

"As long as the doctors say she can race, it won't change anything for us," Paige said. "Zoe wants to win money and prizes and she's not going to let any cache or injury stand in her way. She's way too feisty for that."

Evan signaled that they were done then packed up his camera and notes.

"You really think she's going to race as hard as she has been?" Miles asked.

"Maybe you don't know Zoe as well as I do, but she's not going to let anything stop her, especially not some silly sore ankle."

Miles sighed. He did know Zoe, better than Paige realized, and sadly he had to agree with her. Zoe was going to race hard and then he'd have three people to keep watch over.

*

Paige watched silently as Evan packed up his things and left. As they walked out of the filming area for the next team to go, Paige couldn't help but let her mind wander back to Zoe being carted away in the ambulance earlier. Sure, Zoe annoyed the crap out of her, but she still worried that her ankle might be broken. And not because it would put them out of the competition, but because being stuck with a cast and not allowed to wear her heels would probably make Zoe even harder to live with.

"I guess I should get cleaned up since I apparently stink," Paige said as they turned away from the doors.

"I can't smell you." Miles laughed.

"Only because you sat in the truck with me all day. You're used to my stink by now."

"Or maybe Zoe was just being Zoe and you don't actually smell like anything but yourself."

Myself with a hint of you from your shirt, she thought, resisting the urge to bury her nose in the fabric surrounding her.

"Maybe." Paige swiped her hair away from her face. She felt disgusting even if she didn't smell it. "Either way, I do need to wash the lake out of my hair and off my skin. I can only imagine how much goose poop is in that lake."

"Maybe a shower is a good idea after all," Miles said. "I'm starved. Why don't you go shower and I'll scrounge us up some food and bring it to your room while we wait for Zoe to call."

Miles. Alone. In my room?

"Yes," she said too quickly. "I mean, that sounds okay."

"Good. See you in a few." Miles wandered off in the direction of the kitchen while Paige bolted for her room.

If she was going to get an evening alone with Miles, away from the game, she'd better clean up. She couldn't have him in her room when she looked like this. It wouldn't take long for him to find food so she had to hurry.

She cranked the shower to hot and steamy. It would take heat and lots of soap to make her feel clean again. Quickly, she scrubbed and rinsed her hair. While she waited for the conditioner to soak in, she soaped up the rest of herself with body wash. When she was sure she was clean, she rinsed off and stepped out of the shower.

Toweling off, she reached for her clothes only to realize that she'd forgotten to grab something clean to put on. The thought of getting back into her denim shorts was most unappealing. But maybe it wasn't so terrible to slip back into Miles's shirt for a few minutes while she found something clean to wear. It was either that, or her towel.

At least her towel was clean, which was more than she could say for Miles's shirt. Even from a few feet away she could make out the distinct layer of grime on it. She would definitely have to wash it before giving it back.

Was Miles out there waiting already or would he wait in the hall? Maybe he was still finding some food for them.

She pressed her ear against the door and held her breath, listening for any kind of movement in her room. Hearing nothing, she pulled her towel tight around her chest and made a beeline for the closet on her side of the room. Halfway across the room, she heard a cough and froze mid-step. A cough that came from inside her room.

A cough that came from the incredibly hunky mountain climber currently sprawled across her bed and propped back onto her pillows. Oh, how she wanted to climb that mountain.

Shit. Maybe the shirt would have been better than the towel.

"I didn't realize you would be in my bed—in my room… Um, hi." She smiled, trying to look casual.

Miles took a swig of his beer then set it on her bedside table and sat forward. "Sorry. I thought you realized I planned to wait in here, not in the hall."

"I forgot my clothes."

Brilliant response.

He raised an eyebrow. "I see that. Would you like help finding them?"

She bit her bottom lip, suddenly wondering if she could convincingly pretend to drop her towel by accident. No. She'd never be confident enough to pull a move like that successfully. Best bet was getting into clothes quickly.

"I should be able to manage." She stood unmoving. Or maybe she couldn't manage.

What should she put on? It seemed a little late to put on a whole new outfit. But staying in her towel really wasn't the best idea either. At some point the towel would unwrap and her bits or pieces would end up exposed. He'd already seen her in her pajamas so those might work.

She took a moment to actually look at what he wore—a pair of beat up gym shorts and a clean T-shirt. By the look of him, he'd stopped into his room to clean up too. How had he managed all that and the dinner waiting on plates on Zoe's bed while she'd barely accomplished the quickest shower of her life?

That settled it. If he could be in comfortable clothes, she could be too. The only problem was that her pajamas were currently lying on the bed beside Miles. Meaning, she'd have to get close enough to Miles for him to hand them to her.

And she had to try not to get too close or she might risk doing something stupid—like try to climb his mountain.

She took a tentative step toward him. He leaned forward a little more on the bed, a questioning expression playing on his face. Another couple of steps and she was only a foot from the bed, and from him—altogether too close for her current state of nakedness. Especially with such a hunky guy looking up at her from her bed… his eyebrows arched.

"I thought you said you didn't need my help, but now here you are." Miles's voice sounded huskier than usual. Maybe he was tired. "Do you need my help?" he asked, reaching out his hand to stroke the little indent beside her very naked kneecap.

Maybe he was horny.

She gasped. *Oh God, yes I need help. But no… Or maybe.*

Squeezing the looped edge at the top of her towel tighter so there was no risk of it coming undone, she pointed with her free hand to the pajamas beside him. "I. Pajamas. You."

Paige tried to calm her breathing, which was difficult because she suddenly felt as if she'd run a marathon since showering. Maybe if she could stop hyperventilating, she'd actually be able to form a coherent sentence.

Or maybe she'd be able to think straight if Miles wasn't still massaging a circle on her knee while he waited for a response.

Or possibly it was the tingles dancing along her nerve endings that caused her brain synapses to short circuit.

Miles grabbed the tiny pile of clothing beside him then stood. Hot damn, he was tall. And she was still very naked. He held out her clothes, gripped tighter in his fist than seemed necessary given the lightweight material.

"Your pajamas." He smirked.

She opened her mouth to respond, but no words came out. Seemed every thought she could've possibly had was washed down the drain during her shower. All thoughts except for the ones that involved tackling him onto her bed. She touched his hand as she reached for her shorts and camisole and tried again, unsuccessfully, to speak.

"I think you do need some help getting dressed since even forming a sentence seems too challenging for you right now." He held out her camisole and shrugged. "No different than on the canoe earlier really. Only this time I'll hold up your towel while you slip into your pajamas. I promise I'll even try my best not to peek."

She nodded.

Yes. Okay. At least then she wouldn't be in a towel or naked. And since her body no longer seemed to function in its current state, she saw very few other choices. The thought of walking to her bathroom to change felt like an unachievable option. She took the top he offered her and met his gaze.

Miles removed her other hand from the top edge of the towel, pulling the secured end free. As the towel loosened from around her chest, his fingers brushed against her skin. She worried she might actually burst into flames.

Or jump him.

Either was a plausible option.

He slipped the towel from her body, holding it out in front of her a couple of inches. His gaze flickered down momentarily before meeting her eyes again.

"I promised I'd try not to peek." He cleared his throat. "I tried."

She blushed, unsure of how much he could even see with the towel up at her chest height. Of course, he was a good amount taller than her. He probably had a pretty clear peek at all the goods. The cool air of the room drifted across her rear, sending a chill up her back, beading her nipples instantly. She shivered.

His gaze faltered, falling to her chest again.

Her suspicions about his view were immediately confirmed as his eyes glazed over and his breath came out in a ragged sigh. "Please, Paige. For the love of all things holy. Put your pajamas on quicker."

Paige glanced down to the towel he still held, his knuckles almost as white as the bathroom linen. Screw it. He obviously wanted her as much as she wanted him.

"No," she said, dropping her pajamas to the floor.

"No what?" he asked, his voice very deep and forced.

"Neither one of us wants me to put those on, so I'm not going to." She pressed her now pajama-free hands to his chest, smiling as he took in a shaking breath. Maybe she did have what it took to turn a guy like Miles on. "Drop the towel, Miles."

Chapter Fifteen

Miles did as he was told and dropped her towel. A second later she was in his arms, her naked body pressing to his clothed one. She went up on her toes and wrapped her arms around his neck, kissing him. His hands traveled down her back as he did, coming to rest on her ass. Goddamn, it felt even better than it had looked in those little jean shorts she'd worn all day.

Miles groaned into her mouth and pulled back from her, propping his forehead against hers as he tried to catch his breath, which was coming fast and hard. "I've been trying not to do this all day. You looked so damn hot wearing my shirt."

He slid one hand up her ribs until he cupped her bare breast in his palm. "Knowing you weren't wearing a bra underneath it…" He flickered his thumb across her tight bud, enjoying the response he got from her body. "Knowing my shirt was brushing against your bare breasts…" He kissed her deeply then pulled back again so he could finish his thought. "It almost drove me mad. I've never been jealous of a shirt before, but I was today."

Scooping her into his arms, she wrapped her legs around his waist. She was so petite. Had she always been this tiny? She always seemed so big and full of life when they were searching for a cache or dealing with Zoe. How was it that such a big personality fit into such a tiny package?

He laid her back on the bed, forcing her to unwind her legs from around him. Staring down at her, he took off his shirt. Paige looked self-conscious as she crawled backward on the bed toward a throw blanket. He grabbed her ankles, sliding her back down to where he'd put her. She didn't have a single good reason to be self-conscious and he wasn't about to let her hide. No way.

He'd been dreaming about seeing her—all of her—for so long, he wasn't about to let her ruin the view by hiding.

"You don't need that," he said, motioning toward the blanket. "I want to see you."

She lay still, waiting for him while he stepped out of his shorts. Propping himself up on one elbow, he sank down beside her, taking in every aspect of her body. The gentle curve of her hip, the concave dip of her abdomen, the valley between her breasts—all of it the most gorgeous thing he'd seen. And he'd seen a lot.

But none like her.

Miles closed his eyes as she ran her hand down his chest, pausing only briefly around his belly button before plunging south to the hardened length aching for her. She stroked him slowly, sending waves of heat through him and he rocked his hips slightly.

He bent forward, dipping his head to suck one taut nipple into his mouth, enjoying the gasp she made as he did. After a few minutes of her arching against his mouth while she stroked him, he pushed her hand away and took his mouth south. She moved her hips in time to his tongue, climaxing hard and fast.

As her breathing calmed, he searched his shorts for his wallet and cursed himself for not bringing it with him. Standing beside the bed, looking down at Paige, waiting for him, reaching for him, he cursed himself again.

"You don't happen to have protection, do you?" he asked, rubbing a hand across the back of his neck.

Paige sat up on her elbows. "You're joking, right?"

He shook his head. "I'm afraid not." He was so ready for her he thought he might die from blood loss to his brain if this situation didn't rectify itself soon. "You brought some with you, right?"

"No. I didn't plan on needing any. Didn't you bring some? You're a boy. Don't boys always have some handy?"

"Yeah. In my wallet. In my pants pocket. The pants crumpled up in a ball at the foot of my bed in my room."

Paige smiled and fluttered her eyelashes at him. "So run on down the hall and get them. I'll wait here."

"Oh, sure, no problem. I'll just run down the hall with this," he pointed to his erection, "flapping in the breeze. That won't be obvious to any of the teams I'm bound to run into along the way. And when they inquire where I'm off to in my current situation, I'll be sure to tell them I'm heading back here to you. Sound good?"

"Point taken," she said, biting her lip. Now he wanted to bite her lip.

He looked around. "Where are Zoe's things?"

"I know you want to fool around, and believe me, I want to too, but I can't let you violate Zoe's privacy by going through her things." Paige sat up and pulled the blanket around her. "You think Zoe's okay, right? I feel a little bad that I'm not, you know, pining away with worry while she's at the hospital."

"She's fine, trust me. I asked the medic before they left. He thinks it's a sprain or less." He opened the bedside table and took a quick peek. Nothing that looked anything like a condom. "It's the show's policy to be extra cautious since we're not on set all the time."

He closed the bedside table drawer harder than he meant to and it banged loudly in the quiet room. "Damn it. Where the hell is a condom when you need one? I know Zoe will have one around here somewhere."

"I really don't think you should be doing this. I don't care how bitchy she is, you can't go through her things like she doesn't matter." Paige's voice held a distinct hint of annoyance.

If she knew what he knew about Zoe, she wouldn't be riding him about it. She'd be helping him find what he was looking for *then* she'd be riding him because of it. And he'd be happily buried balls-deep inside her right now.

He stopped and stared at Paige. "Listen, I'm not going to violate Zoe's privacy. I just need her makeup bag and I'm sure there will be a condom in it. That's all. I swear I won't touch anything. I know Zoe." He sighed, cursing his slip of the tongue. He couldn't think straight without proper blood flow. He did want to tell Paige about his past with Zoe, but right when he was about to get busy with Paige probably wasn't the right moment. "I know girls like her. They always come packing protection."

Paige thought about that for a moment. "It's on the bathroom counter. But I swear to God, if you snoop in her things for longer than just a peek for a condom, I'm going to tell on you. And Zoe will totally kick you." Her eyes glanced down quickly then back up.

He had no doubt that Zoe would, or where she'd kick him. But luckily, he also knew Zoe would get over it. One quick peek inside Zoe's normal polka dot makeup bag was all it took to find a row of wrappers. Tearing one from the line, he closed the bag. Then opened it again, taking another.

Who was he kidding?

Miles trotted back to the bed, crawling his way up her legs with kisses as he went. Paige giggled when he got to her inner thighs and pushed him away.

"Miles," she practically murmured. "Enough already."

He hadn't ever heard anything more wonderful. Sheathing himself, he settled between her legs as she wrapped them around his waist. When her heat surrounded him, he thought he might actually pass out. He'd been thinking about this moment for so long—finally getting to live it was better than amazing.

He curled over her as they moved together, kissing her lips and neck and anywhere else he could reach. When she scratched her nails down his back, he picked up the pace.

She responded with little gasps. When her breathing finally gave way to one last moan as she arched into him, he let himself give in too. Collapsing onto the bed beside her, he pulled her into his arms while he tried to catch his breath.

If he gained nothing else from this entire TV show experience, just one kiss from Paige had made it all worthwhile. This other stuff with her, beside him, satiated because of him, was icing on the cake.

*

Paige rested her head on the pillow next to Miles, running her hand up and down his stomach in lazy sweeps. She wasn't trying to entice him into round two, although she could already see the stirrings of interest. For now she was content to be here with him, in his arms—his amazing, strong arms.

"I'm a terrible teammate," she said, realizing she hadn't thought much about Zoe—other than during the whole condom incident—and she'd been at the hospital for a couple of hours already.

"Why do you say that?" Miles asked then yawned.

"Because my teammate is at the hospital with a possible broken ankle and I'm here in bed, getting sexed up with a hunk on another team."

Miles laughed. "You have met Zoe, right? I'm pretty sure she'd do the same thing in your position. In fact, I think she'd applaud your timing. And I'm also sure she's fine. She would have been in a lot more pain if her ankle was actually broken. The medic wouldn't lie to me if he thought there was a real chance she was injured. Nor would Ben leave me here in the dark if they discovered something major was wrong at the hospital. I trust Ben, especially in a hospital. He'll call if there's anything to worry about."

"So it's the whole 'no news is good news' thing?"

"Exactly." He kissed her forehead. The gesture of comfort hit the spot she needed soothed.

"You don't think they're still waiting to be seen and don't even know yet if it's serious or not?"

He shook his head. "No way. Chip Cormack is way too pushy to let one of his contestants sit in the waiting room all night. I'm sure he's pulled whatever strings necessary to get them in to a doctor right away."

She sighed. "I hope you're right. And I really hope they call soon to tell us."

"I don't. In another forty-five minutes, I'll be happy for an update, but right now, I have other, more important matters to attend to." Miles rolled her over so she lay on his chest. If his body was any indication of his mindset, it was obvious he was already way beyond thinking about Zoe.

Paige wasn't as sure of Zoe's situation as he was. But maybe he was right about one thing; they could wait a little longer to hear back about her status.

And in the meantime, he made a pretty convincing argument about how they should spend their time—starting with the rock hard desire pressing against her thigh. And hopefully ending with a bite of that dinner he'd brought for them, which they still hadn't so much as glanced at. Hunger could wait.

*

Paige scrunched her eyes against the blinding light. A bang that sounded like the door closing startled her. "Miles?" she mumbled trying to figure out where she was and what time it was. Had he come back for more?

"What?" Zoe asked as she shuffled to her bed.

"You're finally back. I can't believe it took so long to wrap a sprained ankle." Paige sat up and rubbed the sleep from her eyes. She stretched. Her body ached in the most amazing ways after her few fun-filled hours with Miles.

"Seriously. Then Chip showed up with a bunch of legal waivers and forms. God, is this what Cassidy went through every time she fell on *The One*?"

Paige laughed. "I think she finally signed a stack of forms and told the medic to fill in the dates as needed. So you're really okay?"

"I'm fine. A little sore. I have a splitting headache and a serious case of exhaustion." She flopped onto the bed, pulling the blanket over her then clicking off the light.

"Thank goodness. I'm so glad you're okay." Paige closed her eyes again, getting ready to settle back into another amazing dream featuring Miles.

Now that she had real life details of his body to draw on, it seemed her mind couldn't stop putting him in all kinds of interesting scenarios and positions that would never happen in real life. Her current favorite was one very detailed dream involving a canoe, a couple of strategically placed life jackets, and some Cirque du Soleil inspired balance.

"Thanks." Zoe yawned. "Now if you don't mind, I'm too tired to talk."

Paige yawned back. "Me too. You can tell me all about your hospital visit in the morning."

"Deal. And you can tell me all about why our room smells like sex."

Paige cringed and pulled the blankets over her head. Damn it. She couldn't get anything past Zoe.

*

Paige picked at her breakfast and tried not to look directly at either Miles or Zoe—or even Ben, for that matter. All of them seemed to have big grins on their faces every time they looked at her this morning. It was as if all of them were in on some kind of joke and she was the only one who didn't know what was going on.

"What?" she finally asked, unable to take it anymore. "Why do you guys keep looking at me like that?"

"I'm just admiring the nice color in your cheeks this morning," Zoe said with one of her sticky-sweet smiles. "Some might even use the word glowing to describe you."

Paige glanced to Miles. He couldn't seem to hide his good mood this morning. Just seeing his smile and the twinkle of deviousness in his eyes was enough to make her cheeks burn.

"I guess I got a really good sleep last night." Paige went back to attempting to eat her fruit salad.

"I'm so glad to hear my hospital visit didn't keep you awake with gut wrenching worry." There was no mistaking the sarcasm in Zoe's voice.

Paige blushed deeper but for a completely different reason. "I was worried. Ask Miles."

Zoe raised an eyebrow questioningly. "Really? Now why would Miles know about your emotional state last night?"

Oh, no. Why did she say anything to defend herself? She would have been much better off with Zoe thinking she was an uncaring bitch. Now she'd have to put up with Zoe's relentless teasing and questions.

"I…" She paused, trying to think of a feasible excuse. She couldn't think of anything except Miles's sculpted body hovering over hers.

"Paige and I had dinner together last night while you two were at the hospital. She was very worried about you."

"But you weren't? Sweet."

Miles nudged her with his elbow. "I knew you were too tough to let some silly ankle bother you. Unless of course there was some very hot doctor on staff in the emergency room last night, in which case you'd suddenly feel as if you were dying and need chest compressions or mouth-to-mouth."

She laughed. Actually laughed. It wasn't often Paige heard that particular sound coming from Zoe. "You know me too well."

True. Why was that exactly?

"Too bad for Zoe the doctor was female," Ben added. "Beautiful enough to be on one of those medical drama shows on TV, but female nonetheless. Poor, poor Zoe. Not a Dr. Hunky to be seen last night."

"Just as well. I'm only here for the game, not for hooking up with random doctors."

They continued eating their breakfast in silence for a few minutes. The only sound in the common room today came from the large flat screen TV in the corner of the room playing the local news. All the other teams had already left for the day over an hour ago.

"Speaking of hooking up," Zoe said, breaking the silence. "Anyone care to tell me how condoms went missing from my makeup bag?"

Paige inhaled a piece of melon.

She coughed, tears springing to her eyes. When the piece of food dislodged, she took a shaking breath then coughed a few more times. She wiped the tears out of her eyes only to find Zoe looking at her with fake innocence on her face.

Zoe already knew the truth. She'd probably figured it out the second she'd walked in the room last night. Paige suddenly remembered Zoe's comment about the room smelling of sex. Did sex have a smell? Maybe lust mingling with pheromones.

"About that," Miles started.

Paige shot him a look. Was he really going to tell her what they'd done? How had she been so stupid to let him take condoms from Zoe? Of course Zoe would notice. She noticed everything.

Damn it. Paige should have insisted Miles go back to his room and get his own condoms, erection flapping in the wind, as he'd so eloquently put it, and all. Anything another team would have said or assumed would be better than having to look at the expression of amusement currently gracing Zoe's beautiful face. Paige could already hear the jokes and teasing she'd have to put up with for the rest of the day.

"I may have—" Miles started, but was interrupted by a breaking news bulletin on the television.

They all turned to see what had happened. The view of the scene was from a circling helicopter. Below them, in the center of the screen, an emergency rescue boat was pulling something—or someone—into the boat on a bright orange backboard.

The words on the ticket tape running along the bottom of the screen sent a chill down Paige's spine: Has reality TV finally gone too far?

"Oh my God. That's one of our teams."

Chapter Sixteen

Miles stood from the table, drawn to the television. One of the teams from the show apparently had been rappelling down the side of a cliff and had fallen into some body of water. Where they were and what had happened was still unclear.

One thing was very clear—whatever cache it was they'd been trying to reach, was now off limits. He couldn't risk Ben or either of the girls getting hurt the way the team on television seemed to be. No cache points or prizes would ever be worth it if one of them got hurt.

Not after the accident that had happened on the mountain with Ben. Miles would never let something like that happen on his watch again.

"Which team is it? I can't tell," Ben said to no one specifically.

Miles just shook his head. He had no words. It didn't matter what team it was, only that one of them had gotten hurt. Hopefully not hurt too badly. Not like Ben had.

"I can't tell either. I wish the helicopter would get closer." Zoe stood right in front of the TV. "They're way too far away to even see if it's a team of girls or guys."

"I'm sure we'll hear news later tonight when we get back to base camp. And if no one says anything, then we'll find Chip and make him tell us." Paige looked determined.

"Why don't we find one of the production assistants right now and ask them?" Ben questioned.

"We don't have time," Miles said, finally pulling his gaze from the news long enough to check his watch. "We're supposed to check out in a few minutes. There's probably another penalty for checking out late too. I'm sure Spencer is already waiting for us on the line with his speech about how we all suck for coming in late yesterday."

The others nodded and followed him out to the front lawn. Sure enough, Spencer was there with a huge primetime-worthy smile on his face. Chip, however, was missing. Normally he was on the sidelines watching every start and finish of the day, but not today.

Miles's stomach sank. Shit. It really was one of their teams that had been injured. No way would Chip miss something like their late start if he didn't have somewhere more important to be. And what was more important than the drama of a penalty other than the drama of a tragic accident during filming?

That accident on the news was more serious than he thought. They would have to be extra cautious on their hunt today. He couldn't let the same kind of accident affect either of their teams.

An uneasiness washed over Miles as the four of them stood shoulder to shoulder on the start line. Maybe they shouldn't tempt the weird vibe of the day and skip one day of the show. Go have coffee somewhere and wait out the time they were supposed to be finding caches.

"Welcome to the start of day fourteen. You're officially halfway, so congratulations. All of you have done very well up to this point."

A unanimous grumble rippled through them, confirming he wasn't alone in his belief that his team sort of sucked. A stark contrast from the success they'd always had climbing. His chosen alliance team didn't seem much better.

"Now, we need to take care of some business," Spencer started with his serious tone. "Last night you had some trouble reaching the check in on time when Zoe took a nasty spill. How are you feeling now, Zoe? Are you able to continue in the competition?"

Zoe smiled but Miles could see her discomfort as she shifted her weight off of her bandaged ankle. She was remarkably shorter in sneakers.

"I'm fine," she said. "I'd be one hundred percent again if that annoying medic had allowed me to wear my heels."

"How long are you off your heels?" Spencer asked.

"Hopefully only a few days, but it could be as much as a couple of weeks."

Spencer smiled and nodded as if he really cared. Miles doubted he was even listening to what Zoe said. "Great. Okay. I won't keep you any longer. Your day starts now."

Spencer looked surprised when none of them took off in a sprint to the vehicles. But with Zoe's ankle and the breaking news about one of the other teams, it seemed as if no one was really in a hurry to get the day started.

"So how are we working today?" Ben asked, breaking the silence. "Are we going together again?"

"That was the plan, wasn't it?" Paige asked, looking to Miles for confirmation.

He nodded. "Yep. But with Zoe's hurt foot, I think Paige and I should be the drivers." It sucked not getting Paige all to himself in his truck, especially after the mind-blowing night they'd had, but it couldn't be helped. His memories of the night would have to be enough to get him through the day. Then hopefully he could spend tonight making a whole new set of memories with Paige. He just had to figure out where those memories would be created since Ben and Zoe would both be at the lodge tonight.

Good thing he had all day to figure it out.

"So what cache number are we headed for today?" Zoe asked, flipping through the logbook. "We may as well get going since we'll be lucky to find more than one or two today."

Miles flipped open his logbook too and scanned the pages. "Looks like we're on number 218."

Zoe and Ben walked off to the vehicles to get settled while Paige and Miles made sure they entered in the same coordinates. Looked like it was a bit of a drive away, but definitely doable and the may even be able to hit another one before the day was over.

Miles slipped his hand around Paige's lower back and pulled her close. "Be careful today, okay?"

"I always am."

"I don't believe you in those silly heels." Miles couldn't help but worry after Zoe's fall last night and the news this morning. Teams were getting tired. They were getting sloppy. And now they were getting hurt. He couldn't let that happen to his teams. "Zoe wore sneakers, can't you wear some too?"

"No. Why would I do that when these heels are so damn sexy?"

She peered up at him with a twinkle in her eyes that made him want to throw her over his shoulder and cart her back up to her room. But not for new shoes. She was right. Those heels were damn sexy. They made her legs look long even though she was petite. And the way her calves curved practically made him drool.

But sneakers would be safer.

"Just put on your sneakers, would you? Otherwise I'll have to stay right beside you all day to catch you when you fall."

"And that's supposed to persuade me to take them off?" She ran her hand up his chest and he wondered if she could feel how hard her touch made his heart pound. Wrapping her hand around the back of his neck, she pulled herself up until her mouth was almost on his, which wasn't as far as usual with those heels of hers. "I think you just persuaded me to never take them off again. Not when wearing them makes you look at me like this. Not when the only reason I put them on to begin with, was to see this very look in your eyes when you look at me."

"Trying to manipulate my emotions, huh? Nice."

She smirked. "Not manipulate. Gently persuade. A nudge, if you will."

"You know, it's more than just the shoes that do it for me." It was everything. Her shoes, her hair, her tiny frame that seemed to fit so perfectly with his. Her personality that was shy and unsure one minute and confident and witty the next.

He closed the gap between them, pressing his lips to hers, accepting her invitation when her mouth opened letting him in to explore. And it was certainly her kisses that did it to him the most. He could kiss her all day. And then all night.

"We have to go. Tomorrow I'm going to hide those shoes so you have no choice but to wear your hiking boots again." He leaned forward to whisper in her ear. "I've had dreams about you in those hiking boots too, you know."

He smiled when he heard her suck in a shaky breath, her body trembling. Then he kissed the spot below her ear and enjoyed hearing a tiny moan escape her in response.

"You guys need more of my condoms?" Zoe yelled, sticking her head out the back window of the SUV. "We might need to make a pit stop at the gas station on the corner if you guys are going to bang like bunnies for the last two weeks of the show."

Miles laughed. He ran his hands down her back and gave her bottom a quick squeeze before putting some distance between them. "Leave it to Zoe to ruin a perfectly good moment."

Shaking his head, he pulled Paige back toward the waiting vehicles and the impatient teammates inside. He smacked her on the ass before disappearing around the side of the truck. "See you at the next cache."

"Don't leave me alone with her to explain," Paige whisper yelled after him.

"Explain what?" Zoe called, the teasing obvious in her voice even if he couldn't see her face. "I already know you guys banged while Ben and I sat bored at the hospital last night."

Miles heard Paige start to protest as she climbed in and closed the door. He'd wish her good luck, but knowing Zoe, luck played no role in how long he and Paige would get teased today. Probably all day. And possibly all day tomorrow too.

"You finally done sucking face with Paige?" Ben asked as Miles handed him the GPS unit and started out of the parking lot.

"We weren't sucking face." Miles grinned like a teenage boy sneaking back from behind the bleachers with the cheerleading captain. Hell, he had been that teenager, but that didn't even come close to comparing with kissing Paige. She was in her own league.

"Well, whatever you call it, I call it wasting time we don't have today. So knock it off."

"What the hell's your problem?"

"The girls are my problem. I'm not so sure this alliance is beneficial to us anymore. Now instead of one lame player, we have two. It doesn't look like Zoe's going to be better anytime soon and we already know I'm not going to either."

"You're not a lame player. And neither is Zoe. So what if we're not the fastest? We still have two weeks to find the rest of the caches. I'm sure we won't get all of them before the end of the show, but no one will. We have as much chance of winning as anyone else does. Better now that we're working with another team."

"I'm sure she'll still get into bed with you even if we're not in an alliance with them anymore."

Miles gripped the steering wheel harder than necessary. It wasn't about that at all. And who the hell was Ben to say shit like that? "Listen, what happened with me and Paige last night has nothing to do with our alliance and you know it. If you're in a bad mood today, then that's your problem, but leave the rest of us out of it. Now which way am I supposed to turn?"

*

Paige slowed and pulled up beside the boy's truck along the side of the road. Up ahead, a sea of lights and emergency vehicles crisscrossed the roadway, making it impossible to go any further. She rolled down the passenger side window. "Doesn't look like we can get any closer."

Miles nodded. "I think we found out where the accident happened earlier."

"Think they'll open it back up soon?" Zoe asked from the backseat.

"No. And even if they did, we're not doing it." Miles clenched his jaw.

"You're right," Paige said. "They'll probably need some time to get everything cleaned up and ready again. We'll come back in a couple of days."

"No, we're not doing this one. Not today, not another day. It's obviously too dangerous." Miles called out the window.

Paige didn't really care for Miles's tone or male posturing. She could do what she pleased when she pleased, but getting into it with him right now didn't seem like the best use of their already screwed time. She'd talk to Zoe about it later and together they would decide what was best for their team.

"Maybe we should start heading back toward base camp," Paige offered instead. Better to get at least a few caches done today versus no caches. "I think there's a couple others with similar coordinates that might be along the way."

"Sounds good."

Zoe and Ben each entered in the new coordinates into their respective GPS units while Miles and Paige turned the vehicles around in the road. As they drove back the way they'd just come, Paige glanced into the review mirror, shocked at how many emergency vehicles had been called in.

The other team was going to be okay, weren't they? It wasn't like these caches were supposed to be life threatening or anything. Chip was a sucker for creating great television but he wouldn't put his contestants in real danger.

Even Chip wasn't that scummy.

Before they made the first turn toward the next cache, another team drove past them heading into the chaos they'd just left.

Apparently they weren't the only team on cache 218. Hopefully Paige and Zoe and the boys would be way ahead if this other team kept following in their footsteps today.

Fifteen minutes later, they pulled up as close as they could get to a new cache. Paige all but jumped out of the car the second she twisted the key from the ignition. The entire drive Zoe had made little comments and hints about Paige and Miles together. It was unnerving. And awkward. And Paige really didn't feel like getting teased anymore. Surely Zoe would pipe down now that they were with the boys again.

"Hey, Ben, want to share my GPS unit with me?" Zoe asked, looping her arm through his. "I think lover boy probably wants an excuse to get cozy and grope Paige again."

"Hey," Paige scoffed. She pulled out her lip balm to give her lips a coat before heading out on whatever trail the cache location forced them down. *Cherry or mint flavor?* "I'm right here. I can hear you."

"So can I," Miles said, coming up and looping his arm across her shoulders. "I don't mind getting cozy if you don't."

Definitely cherry. Cherry is way better for cozy situations.

"And here I thought I'd signed up for an adventure show, not a dating show," Ben said with annoyance.

"No one said they had to be dating to fool around, as was evident last night. I'm so glad to know my hospital visit didn't affect either of your libidos. I'd hate to think my poor, possibly broken ankle had put a damper on your evening activities."

"I offered to go with you," Paige said. It wasn't fair. She had offered and Zoe had shot her down. And she'd worried about her while she'd been there too. She'd just happened to distract herself from her worries by spending the night with Miles. "You told me I'd stink up your ambulance."

"Don't let her make you feel bad. Zoe's just annoyed that someone is getting more attention than she is for a change." Miles glared at Zoe as she walked away ahead of them, focusing only on her GPS instead of Miles's words.

"Miles, be nice," Paige said quietly. "Maybe Zoe really did want me there and I was too busy with…" Her gaze flickered between him and the floor.

"With me." Miles held her gaze. "But do you regret it now?"

She shook her head. No way did she regret anything about last night. Well, maybe she regretted not having her own condoms with her. That was pretty stupid. A grown adult, *single*, woman should always be prepared for anything. Or anyone.

"Good. Then let's not let her ruin what was an unbelievably awesome night."

He thought last night was unbelievably awesome? Awesome!

"Okay."

"Come on, lover boy," Ben called from further up the trail. "We really are wasting time again."

Miles staring at her almost like he had last night in her bed made everything else around her disappear. Ben and Zoe ceased existing.

Miles brushed his fingers across her lips then cupped her jaw in his hand. "I can't wait to get you alone again."

When he kissed her, she was thankful for his height and strength because she didn't know if she could hold herself up without having his strong arms to cling to. Strong arms that attached to an even stronger torso. One she couldn't stop imagining hovering over her, sweat glistening across his tanned skin.

"Tonight," she heard herself whisper, although she hadn't planned on saying anything at all, much less inviting him into her bed again.

"If you insist." He stepped away from her, his eyes appearing as lust-filled as she felt. He took her hand in his and led her down the path toward where Zoe and Ben had already disappeared. She wobbled once or twice on her feet before her knees finally felt strong enough to hold her.

How much longer until check in?

The sound of gravel under tires cut into her thoughts. She turned just in time to see another SUV from the show pulling in to the parking lot. Paige couldn't tell if it was the same team that had turned up at the other cache earlier or not, but either way, they would have to hurry if they wanted any shot of getting the cache first.

Paige and Miles sprinted to catch up with Ben and Zoe who were already disappearing around a bend in the trail. Annoyance bubbled up inside of her. Maybe if she and Miles hadn't gotten distracted in the parking lot, they'd be further along and almost at the cache already. Now they were going to have to rush if they wanted to find the cache first.

"We have to hurry," she called as they joined Ben and Zoe. Together the four of them set out jogging toward the cache, following the little arrow on the GPS. Paige thought they might actually beat the other team, but moments later, Team Frat Boys shot past them, leaving behind a wake of laughter and jeering.

Paige slowed her pace along with the others and groaned in frustration. They just weren't fast enough to beat the other teams in a foot race. And now Team Frat Boys would never let them live it down.

Chapter Seventeen

Miles paced the length of the common room while they waited for Chip to address the group. Spencer was already here getting his makeup touched up, which meant whatever was going on, was also going to be filmed. This was out of the show's normal context so it couldn't be good.

And that worried him.

"What's all this about?" Sam asked, his daughter by his side. "I heard someone say something about an accident today, but no one seems to know what's going on."

Miles glanced around the room, the uneasiness settling into him making his stomach feel heavy. Why hadn't anyone told them anything yet?

"We saw the local news this morning after everyone else left," Ben said. "There was a breaking story. Something about a reality show and an accident. We think one of the teams got hurt."

"Oh no," Kristin said from beside her father, holding her hand to her mouth. "That's awful. Who's missing tonight? I didn't realize a team hadn't checked in."

Miles scanned the various teams huddled together. Paige and Zoe sat at the table where they'd had breakfast together earlier. Eve and Rayne—Team Sisters—stood by the fireplace. He shifted, shoving his hands in his pockets to keep from fidgeting. Damn it. Who was missing?

A shot of pain in his shoulder forced his attention away from figuring out who wasn't accounted for in the room. And annoyance shot through the rest of him at the sight of the grin on Team Frat Boy's faces. If either one of them punched him in the shoulder again, he was going to have a really hard time not returning the gesture.

"Sorry about stealing that cache out from under you guys today," Dean said without a hint of actual remorse.

"It was just one of those situations where we needed to get in and get out as fast as we could. I'm sure you understand how it is," Chuck said.

Miles ground his teeth together. If there was anything he hated more than a pretentious frat boy, it was two pretentious frat boys. "It's fine. No worries."

"Oh good. I didn't want you to think we were being inconsiderate to your partner's special needs. We just had our own needs to meet." Dean smiled and patted Chuck on the shoulder. "Like that trip today, right?"

"Hells yah!" Chuck cheered. "Cancun here we come."

Great. Just what spring break needed—a couple extra jerks drinking on the beach.

"Can I have your attention, please?" Chip asked, walking into the room and saving Miles from any more unwanted conversation with Tweedledee and Tweedledum. "Gather around."

Spencer joined Chip at the front of the room as the cameramen all took their places where they could see both the contestants and the host.

"Thank you all for joining us tonight. It's unlike our usual format to film on your off-hours, but this is a very abnormal circumstance." Spencer's brow creased. "Chip Cormack, the show's producer, has asked us all here this evening. Chip, why don't you tell us what's going on?"

Chip turned to face the teams. "I'm sure some of you have already noticed that one of our teams is missing tonight." There was a rumble around the room as teams either confirmed that they did know or realized now that they hadn't. Chip raised his hands to quiet everyone down again.

"This morning, shortly after the start of the day, Team Firefighters attempted our hardest cache and they were involved in an accident. They are in stable condition at the local hospital and will both make a full recovery, but the doctors have decided they are unable to continue in the race."

A couple of gasps and a sob caused Chip to stop talking. Eve from Team Sisters held Rayne as tears flowed freely down her cheeks. Rayne must have been closer to the firefighters than Miles had realized. Sure, he'd seen them together a few times around the common room, but he hadn't suspected they were so tight. Obviously they were if she was crying.

As he watched, Eve glanced over at him, catching his eye. She appeared even more concerned while watching him than she did to be holding her upset sister. He got the distinct impression she was worried about him too. But why would she worry about him? Maybe she didn't want to see any of the teams hurt.

A shiver ran down his spine. How would he feel if it were Paige and Zoe lying in the hospital? His chest constricted at the thought. Well, he'd never let that happen, would he?

"What's happened to them?" Rayne asked, her voice shaking as she tried to hold back her tears.

"They were rappelling and we think they didn't hook in properly. They fell to the water below and were rescued by the emergency boats. But they both suffered from water inhalation along with a few cuts and bruises they endured during the fall against the rocks. The good news is, they have the best doctors at the hospital and are being very well taken care of. The doctors have assured us they will not suffer any long term physical effects from this ordeal, but they are not allowed to return to the game."

"Can we see them?" Rayne asked. "I'd like to see them tonight."

"I'm sorry. I can't allow that. But if you would like us to pass along a message to them, please speak to one of the production team members and they'll make sure it's done."

Chip looked around as if waiting to see if there were more questions. The room was silent except for the occasional sniffle.

"What cache did the accident happen at?" another team asked. "Should we take it off our logbook?"

"I can't tell you what cache it is and there's no need to remove it from your logbooks. We've had safety crews out all day working to make sure the cache is completely safe and in perfect working order. Tomorrow morning the cache will be officially reopened."

"Thank you for filling us in, Chip," Spencer started. He turned to face the contestants again while Chip left the room. "I know this is all a bit shocking for you. But at least this tragedy has a silver lining for you remaining contestants."

Miles waited impatiently for Spencer to continue. Sometimes the drama of the show really got on his nerves.

"As I'm sure you're all aware, Team Firefighters had been leading the pack with the most cache finds for the entire show so far. As it was, they had seventy-five percent of the caches already found and were well on target to finding all of them before the end of day twenty-eight. The rest of you were much closer in your number of cache finds."

Spencer's smile was huge. "Good news. Now that their team is out of the race, the leader board is very close. The difference between our new team in first place—Team Frat Boys—and last place—Team Models—is now only fifteen caches. That means this is still anyone's game to win—or lose."

The frat boys let out another obnoxious cheer while the other teams congratulated themselves on not sucking as badly as they had this morning. Even Miles couldn't stop the smile from spreading across his lips at the thought that they might actually still have a chance to win. Now, instead of being in the back of the pack, they were solidly in the middle. And the middle could win if they started finding caches faster.

"Okay, everyone," Spencer said. "I'll let you get back to whatever you were doing. Make sure you get some rest tonight because I think for many of you, the game is officially back on."

*

Ben motioned for Miles to follow him and together they joined Paige and Zoe sitting in the rocking chairs on the porch where they filmed their daily wrap-up each night. They both looked pretty darn excited.

"What's going on? Are we interrupting your filming time?" Miles asked. The girls had been scheduled first thing after Chip's big announcement and he had no idea why Ben had dragged him along.

"No, we're all doing the interview together," Ben said.

"This is allowed?"

"Yep, because we're an alliance we can film these together," Paige said, tapping the chair next to hers for Miles to sit.

Evan and their cameraman checked interview notes for a moment then signaled that filming had started. "Let's start with this big announcement. How do you feel now that Team Firefighters is out of the running and off the leader board?"

"Well, we feel sad, of course," Paige said. "Everyone was shocked when they got hurt enough to be forced out of the game."

"And we're excited because now we can totally still win," Zoe said, excitement ringing through her voice.

"That's right. Spencer informed everyone in the common room of the same thing," Ben said shrugging. "But I'm not going to cheer about it at another team's expense."

"Do you think you stand a better chance at winning now?" Evan asked.

"I do. Not all of the other teams were as far behind as we were. Now we really have a chance." Paige practically bounced up and down in her seat.

"I hate to seem happy that the firefighters are off the show, because we're not," Miles said. "But it definitely evens up the playing field a lot for our alliance. Although we've still got our work cut out for us if we want to make it to first place. We're a good number of caches behind."

Miles leaned forward, resting his elbows on his knees. He needed a massage in the worst way. Too bad the show didn't provide those to contestants at base camp. Of course, Eve had offered to fill that position for him on multiple occasions, but he couldn't take her up on it. Now, if Paige offered a massage that would be a different story entirely.

"Unless," Zoe said, dropping her voice low as if there were others around eavesdropping instead of the cameramen, "we get a really good cache that's worth a lot of points and one that the other teams probably won't attempt."

Miles didn't like the sound of where this was heading. "What cache are you thinking of?" he asked cautiously, fearing he already knew the answer.

"The one we tried to get today." Paige smiled.

"What cache was that?" Evan asked.

"The one we couldn't get because the cache was currently closed while rescue teams saved the firefighters. But now it's open and if we head there tomorrow morning, we could be the first ones to find it."

"And there's bound to be a great prize in it since Chip said it's the hardest cache they hid." Zoe smiled. "I've already heard a couple of other teams saying they're going to leave that one since they're too afraid to follow in the firefighter's footsteps."

Miles shook his head. "No way."

Ben sat forward on the edge of his chair. "If we go fast, we could beat all of the other teams. We've already found the general location so we'd be able to drive there quicker than the teams who have to rely completely on their GPS."

"You're all kidding, right?" Miles asked.

Paige pulled her usual lip balm from her front pocket and applied a coat before talking again, and Miles's thoughts drifted momentarily to later tonight when he'd hopefully get Paige alone again so he could taste that lip balm for himself and find out which flavor she'd picked—cherry or mint. Either was fine with him.

"There was another team who showed up as we were driving away yesterday," Paige said, "but there's no way to know if they're going for the cache or not since I didn't get a good look at who was in the vehicle."

"And there's a good possibility it was one of the teams that now says they're not going to try that cache." Ben nodded along with the others. "It's settled then."

Wait, what's settled?

"The only thing that's settled here is that we're not doing it." Miles's pulse raced, thumping in his head like a marching band. No. He wasn't going to let it happen again. "We're not doing it and that's final."

Zoe and Paige stared at him as if he'd grown a third head. Well, they could look at him however they wanted, he didn't care. He wasn't letting either of them—and certainly not Ben—anywhere near that cache.

"You're kidding, right?" Zoe mimicked his earlier words. "You don't really think you can boss us around, do you?"

Miles clenched his jaw. Ben leaned back in his seat and folded his arms across his chest. Everyone was silent.

Evan cleared his throat. "So this alliance is still going well then?"

Miles ignored his question. "I'm not trying to tell you what to do."

"Really? 'Cause I'm pretty sure you just did," Paige said. Her eyes told him everything he needed to know. She was offended that he'd spoken to her that way. And he knew he shouldn't have.

But damn it, it was hard to listen to them talk about doing something so stupid. And dangerous. And stupid.

He locked eyes with her. "I didn't mean to tell you what to do. I know you can make your own decisions. But I can't sit here and listen to you guys discuss something that is obviously dangerous. I can't…" His voiced dropped off as he fought to stay in control of his emotions as the memories of his last climbing excursion with Ben flashed through his mind.

If only he'd made better decisions that day. Maybe then Ben wouldn't have been hurt.

He turned to Ben. Surely he didn't have to spell it out for his friend. He cleared his throat, hoping his voice would be stronger than he felt. "Ben, you know it's too dangerous. You know it's too—challenging."

"Do the rest of you think that cache is too dangerous to get?" Evan asked.

Paige's voice was soft, as if she was talking to a temperamental child. "It's not dangerous. Chip said safety crews worked all day to make sure it was safe."

"Chip's an asshole whose only concern is for himself and the show." She flinched at his words, shifting away from him. Miles instantly regretted snapping at Paige.

"You will edit that out," Miles said to Evan through clenched teeth.

Evan shrugged. "I'll do what I can, dude, but I can't make any promises."

If they'd all get it through their thick skulls already, then he could focus on apologizing to Paige for coming off so gruff and overbearing. But he couldn't even think of what to say to her to make the flicker of hurt in her eyes go away. And he wouldn't be able to think of what to say until they stopped all this nonsense about going to that cache.

"That may be true," Zoe said calmly, "but Chip wouldn't put us in danger. He wants a good show, but he also cares about the contestants' wellbeing."

"I can do the cache," Ben said. "I'm a lot stronger now than I was before."

Miles shook his head again. He wasn't going to give in. He wasn't going to risk it. "No. It's too dangerous. All the other teams are smart for turning their backs on that stupid cache."

Zoe kept her tone low and controlled. "But there could be a prize in the cache. It would make sense. There haven't been that many big prizes and it's obviously one of the hardest caches to reach."

"That's not a convincing argument," Miles said dryly.

"If it's hard to reach, the show is going to reward whoever finds it," Zoe insisted.

"She's right. We're doing the cache." Ben shrugged as if his mind was made up.

"No, we're not," Miles said, his mind equally as made up.

"While you guys sort this out between yourselves, Paige and I will go get it tomorrow and then we'll let you know how hard it is." Zoe smiled sweetly at him.

"The hell you will." He was so angry they were putting him in this position he could barely see straight. Why wouldn't they listen to reason?

"The hell I won't," Zoe shot back.

"It's too dangerous," he said through a tight jaw. "We're not risking it. None of us are. Your ankle is a warning to all of us just how dangerous this game can be."

"My ankle is a warning that running in heels on wet grass is a stupid idea. That's all."

He wasn't going to cave in. Not on this. Any other cache they wanted to try was fine. But this one—this one that had already taken out one team—wasn't happening. "No."

"Stop being such a coward," Zoe said, her eyes narrowed at him in a way he hadn't seen for a long time. "This is about you, not the cache."

"Wanting to keep the people I care about safe doesn't make me a coward." And how dare she insinuate it did. She didn't know anything about him anymore. Hell, she never really knew anything about him before either. She'd never bothered to know him.

Miles looked around at his teammate and alliance. They were wrong about the cache. But judging by their ignorant arguments, he could only assume that talking to them was useless right now. He needed to figure out how to get through to them, but to do that, he needed some distance so maybe he could start thinking clearly again. All he could think of right now was what could happen if he conceded.

Zoe could hurt her ankle more and be forced out of the game.

Ben could be physically unable to do the cache with his prosthetic. And knowing Ben, he'd pick that cache to be the one he finally got his confidence back on and would do it just to prove he could and would end up even more hurt.

Paige... Shit. He couldn't even imagine what he'd do if something happened to her because of him.

"I said we're not doing that cache. It's off the table and I'm not discussing it again." Miles turned to Evan, finally remembering they were supposed to be filming the daily wrap-up. "Is our time up? Did you get all that?"

"We've got more than enough for the day," Evan said, shutting off his camera.

"Good." Miles stood from his seat and walked out of the room without waiting for more complaints. His decision was made and he was doing it for their own good, even if they couldn't see that.

Chapter Eighteen

Paige took a deep breath and stared at the closed door. Did she really want to do this? Did she really want to get into it with Miles? What if he hadn't calmed down yet?

Had she calmed down?

She'd been furious at the way he'd decided their course of action for the show. It wasn't his job to make decisions for everyone. Especially not for Zoe and Paige. Ben maybe. But even Ben hadn't been thrilled with Miles.

So less than thrilled, actually, that Ben had found Chip and arranged to spend the night in another room stating that it was either a night away from Miles to give them both a little breathing room, or he would walk away from the show tonight.

Needless to say Chip found him a suitable room to sleep in for the night.

And Paige needed to talk to Miles and find out exactly what was going on with him because obviously something was wrong. Even in the few weeks she'd known Miles, she'd never once seen him speak to anyone in the demeaning way he'd spoken to them an hour ago.

This wasn't just about a silly cache.

Forcing her shoulders back, she tried to mentally center herself for whatever state Miles was in. If he was still angry and upset, she needed to remain calm. And if he'd finally calmed down, then she needed to say the right things to keep him that way. Regardless, she needed to stay strong and let him know that whatever this hissy fit of his had been about, she wasn't just some little girl he could boss around.

Maybe she had been at the start of this show, feeling timid and unconfident. But something had changed recently. Something inside told her she didn't have to be that timid, pushover girl anymore. Maybe it was the heels. Maybe it was the push-up bra. Or maybe it was learning she was so much stronger than she'd realized, able to do even the toughest caches they'd found.

And she was certainly going to prove that to herself once and for all by doing the cache Miles had so arrogantly forbidden.

Feeling her resolve firmly in her stance and her emotions safely in check, she knocked on the door. Moments passed with no sound of movement from inside the room. She knocked again. Harder this time. He had to be in there. They hadn't seen him anywhere else around the lodge and it wasn't like the place was very big.

Still nothing.

She knocked one last time. If he didn't answer then she'd take another loop around the lodge and grounds then come back and try again. She just couldn't go to bed with this hanging over her head. She'd never sleep with the fight unresolved.

The door opened to reveal Miles, hair rumpled, eyes tired, chest... bare.

"What can I do for you tonight, Paige?" he asked, leaning against the doorframe.

Um...

"Did you come to tell me how awful I am? Because there's no need. I'm fully aware."

She'd been prepared to find Miles in a lot of different conditions, but half naked wasn't one of them. All that strength and resolve she'd felt a moment ago vanished like a puff of smoke at the sight of the gorgeous man in front of her. The man who looked like he could use a good friend to lean on. He could lean on her.

"Did I wake you?" she managed to ask, finally forming thoughts now that she'd pulled her gaze up from chest level. "I thought maybe you weren't in there after all the knocking."

"No. I was just hoping whoever it was at my door would go away."

Oh.

Now would be a good time to find that resolve again.

"Well, I'm not going anywhere until we've had a chance to talk about what happened earlier. So you may as well let me in. Unless of course you'd rather the rest of the teams hear our business."

She folded her arms across her chest, hoping it made her appear more determined than she felt. Seeing Miles without his shirt made it infinitely harder to concentrate on why she'd come to see him to begin with. She had to stay focused.

He eyed her for a moment, finally stepping aside to allow her into the room.

Once in, she didn't know where to go. Her choices were one of two beds or the floor. Ben's bed was still made up, the zip-up sweater he always had with him lay on the bed where he must have dropped it after returning from the day.

The other bed was clearly Miles's and clearly unmade. Had he been lying in bed when she'd gotten here? The thought of his lean body lying there half naked made a flurry of butterflies spring to life in her belly.

Focus.

She didn't feel right sitting on Ben's bed since even though he was a part of her alliance, she really didn't know him that well. It felt a little bit like a violation of his privacy. That only left Miles's bed. Miles's rumpled, ready to be used bed. The mess of sheets was almost an invitation to mess them up even more. Perhaps by rolling around in them getting sweaty with the shirtless hunk currently watching her with a mix of annoyance and amusement on his face.

"Sit. It's not going to bite." Miles walked to his bed and threw the covers back roughly into place so the bed appeared slightly more made. Then he propped the pillows against the headboard and leaned back, his stomach muscles tightening as he did. Her stomach tightened too watching him, but for an entirely different reason.

Paige perched on the edge of the bed. Now that she was here she had to figure out what to say. "I had this whole big speech planned out for you and now that I'm here, I don't remember any of it."

"Well, you better think of something soon. Ben's bound to get tired at some point and want to go to bed. Unless of course you don't mind saying whatever it is you're here to say in front of him."

Still in a bit of a mood. Well, she had news for him that ought to set him straight on how he should be speaking to people versus how he had spoken to them tonight.

"Ben's not coming back tonight." Except she didn't like the concern in his eyes. So she added quickly, "He's fine. He asked to sleep in another room tonight to give you both some space."

The concern left his eyes replaced by sadness. "I'm sorry to hear he felt he had to do that." Miles watched her. "So what, he sent you here to check up on me?"

"No. I came here because I want to talk to you."

"So talk."

"So be rude."

He sighed and she noticed the tension in his shoulders for the first time. He was not his usual self. "I'm sorry," he said simply.

"Thank you." She shifted on the bed so she could face him straight on, sitting cross-legged. "I want to know what's going on with you and this whole 'I forbid you to do the cache' thing, because I know that's not who you usually are."

"You don't really know anything about me. How can you know that's not how I am?"

She thought back to the night before when they'd been together. He'd been gentle and giving and not the least bit overbearing or demanding. Not to mention how he'd taken care of her after she'd fallen in the lake, literally giving her the shirt off his back. And how he'd carried her after she'd slid down the hill in her heels so she couldn't slip again.

Those weren't the actions of a man who didn't care about the people around him and how they felt. So what had happened tonight to spark this change in him?

"I know you're a good man who's had a shitty night. The only thing I don't know is why? But you can tell me. I want to know. I want to understand why you spoke to us the way you did. And I want to help you sort out whatever it is that's going on with you tonight."

Miles stared at her for a moment and she thought she might crawl across the bed and right into his lap and comfort him. The way he looked at her with pain in his eyes instead of the lust she'd grown accustomed to was surprising.

He sighed. "I'm sorry for the way I acted. But I'm not going to change my mind. I can't let either of our teams attempt that cache."

She felt her annoyance level start to rise. "But it's not your choice what Zoe and I do. We are our own team. Don't you get that?"

He pushed away from the wall, leaning toward her, anger flashing in his eyes. "Don't you get how dangerous it is? Do you really think I'm going to let any of you get hurt just to try and win some stupid prize in some stupid game?"

"Why is it suddenly your responsibility to keep us all safe?"

"It's always been my job to keep my team safe, and now that I'm involved with you and…" He paused, sighing. "Zoe's on your team. Your team is my responsibility too. I'm not going to fail again." The anger creasing his features faded with his words and he rested his head into his hands, his shoulder slumping.

"What are you talking about? You haven't failed anything." She inched closer, placing her hand on his knee.

When he looked up at her, she gasped. The pain, the deep-rooted sorrow etched in his very being, was laid out for her to see.

"Ben's accident. The accident that nearly cost him everything…"

Miles's voice wavered. He cleared his throat. "It was my fault."

"No. I'm sure it wasn't. And I'm sure Ben doesn't think it was either. If he did think that, he'd never have agreed to do this show with you."

Miles shook his head. "It doesn't matter what he thinks, I know the truth. That day, I knew there was a good chance the weather could change, but I ignored the reports."

Paige didn't say anything. His eyes glazed over as if he was reliving the memory. She took one of his hands in both of hers, holding it tightly while she waited for him to continue.

"We were so close to the top. I knew we'd make it to the summit that day. And if we didn't go then, the storm blowing in would prevent us from continuing and we couldn't wait it out on the side of the mountain for days. I thought we'd make it up and back with plenty of time to spare. Then we'd make it to the lower base camp to ride out the storm before heading home."

Miles met her gaze and she wanted to take his pain away. Her breathing quickened with his story, unable to imagine living through the scenario he described.

"I was right about us being able to make the summit at least. We were on our way down when the winds picked up without warning. The storm came hours earlier than it was supposed to. We tried to get down the mountain faster, but the terrain was really rough. Ben slipped. He slid down the side of the mountain, loosening rocks along the way. And when he stopped against an outcropping, a large boulder tumbled after him, narrowly missing his body, but catching his foot."

Paige sucked in a breath, fighting back the tears pooling in her eyes. She couldn't even imagine what that must have been like for Ben. Or for Miles. Any anger or annoyance she'd felt coming to talk to Miles was long gone.

"The boulder crushed his foot and ankle bones so badly that by the time we finally got him to a hospital, they had no choice but to amputate. He is the way he is now… because of me." He sat up straighter. "I can't let something like that happen again. To any of you. I won't make another mistake like I made with Ben."

Paige didn't say anything as she climbed into his lap and wrapped her arms around his neck, pulling him close. No wonder he was always so worried about everyone. He'd been carrying around his guilt about Ben for a couple of years now. But it wasn't his fault. Accidents are called accidents for a reason.

He wove his hands around her waist and buried his head in her neck. She stroked her hands up and down his back, comforting him and fighting back her own tears.

"You didn't do anything wrong," she whispered in his ear. "The accident wasn't your fault. Ben is a grown man who makes his own choices. He chose to go up to the summit with you that day."

Miles didn't reply so she took his face in her hands, forcing him to look at her. "You are one of the kindest and most caring men I've ever met. I may not have known you for very long, but I'm certain you would never do anything on purpose knowing it would hurt someone else."

She didn't wait for him to respond. She pressed her lips to his, kissing him tenderly as if doing so might somehow ease away his pain. The tension in his arms around her waist disappeared.

She pulled back to look him in the eyes again. "You've carried this around too long already. It's time to let your guilt over an *accident* go. I'm sure Ben would want that too if he knew."

Miles brushed his fingers along her cheek. "I'll try. But only if you agree not to put me in the position of having to get over another accident. Agree not to attempt that cache."

Paige thought about his request. Could she convince Zoe not to go for the cache?

If Zoe knew why, then maybe she'd agree. "I'll talk to Zoe about it and see what she says, but we'll still have to consider what's best for our team. If your mind is set, then you're going to have to tell

Ben the reason your team can't do it. And 'because I said so' isn't going to cut it. You need to tell him how you feel."

Miles smiled for the first time since Paige walked into his room. "You want me to talk to another guy about my feelings?"

She nodded, smiling back. "It would do you both some good."

"I can think of something else that would do me some good right about now." He shifted her in his lap, the evidence of his intensions pressing into her. "You're an amazing woman, Paige. I'm lucky to have you here tonight."

Paige wiggled in his lap, teasing him while he gripped her hips in his hands. "I think a little stress relief is just what the doctor ordered."

*

Sun streamed in the through the window, casting the room into a bright yellow glow. Paige squinted against the offending light and peered at the bedside table clock. Time to get up and ready if she wanted to eat before the race day started at eight.

Under her cheek, Miles shifted. "Time to get up already?"

"Looks that way," she said with a yawn, carefully turning away so she wouldn't accidentally blow her dragon breath on him. Morning breath was so not sexy. But it also wasn't correctable at the moment considering she wasn't in her own room and didn't have her own toothbrush handy.

After spending another few hours with Miles last night, making sure all of him felt better, they'd passed out from exhaustion. She couldn't remember a better night. Ever.

"I should go," she said, crawling over Miles to get out of bed. "I need to get back to my room before anyone sees me do the walk of shame."

"Nothing shameful about what we did last night." Miles stretched and walked Paige to the door. He bent, giving her a quick kiss on the lips. "I'll see you at breakfast and we'll talk to Zoe and Ben together about the cache, okay?"

Paige groaned. "Great. Just what I need to go with my breakfast—a splash of bitchy Zoe. She's never going to listen to us if her mind's already made up."

"Don't worry. Zoe will listen to me. She never wants to, but she always does."

Odd comment to make when they'd only known each other a few weeks.

"Why do you always make it sound like you've known Zoe for years when you only met when the show started?" Paige asked. A sinking in her stomach warned her that she didn't really want to know the answer.

"I've been waiting for the right moment to tell you—to explain about my past with Zoe." He sighed and wrung his hands together as if he was suddenly nervous about something. "I didn't tell you at first because I was worried you'd look at me differently once you knew, but I didn't mean to keep it a secret this long."

Nervousness made Paige's voice shake. "Tell me what exactly?"

"Zoe's my sister."

Chapter Nineteen

Paige closed her door and leaned her head against it, letting her eyes flutter shut. She'd walked down the hall in a daze, not caring if any of the other teams saw her leave Miles's room in the same clothes she'd been wearing yesterday.

Zoe and Miles were siblings.

Holy shitballs.

Well that explained how they were both so damned good-looking. And why they spoke to each other and about each other as if they'd known the other for years. Because they had.

How? How was that even possible? He was Jack Miles. She was Zoe Oliver. They didn't even share a last name. Maybe he'd been joking.

"Look what the cat dragged in," Zoe said, walking out of the bathroom with her hair and body wrapped in a towel as if she'd just gotten out of the shower—her makeup perfectly applied already as always. She flopped down on her bed and started massaging moisturizer onto her legs. "Someone had a good night."

"I, just…"

"Don't bother. I noticed you weren't here when I got up to shower." Zoe walked to the closet and pulled out her outfit for the day. "No sense in trying to deny your walk of shame."

Paige didn't bother. She had no idea what to say to Zoe.

"Your brother just rocked my world," didn't seem entirely appropriate. "I can't believe you're from the same family" seemed rude. Her initial reaction of "Holy fuck!" seemed really hard to explain in other, more eloquent words.

"Miles is your brother."

"Oh good. He finally manned up and told you."

"We're partners and you knew but you didn't tell me."

"Of course I knew. Brother. Sister. That's not something I could un-know."

Paige felt her annoyance with Zoe rising exponentially with this conversation. Perfect timing for the shower she needed to have anyways. As she ducked into the bathroom, she heard Zoe chuckle from behind her. She shivered as she stepped into the shower.

Zoe and Miles—family.

And she really liked Miles.

And she really didn't care for Zoe so much. Not that she was as terrible as Paige had originally believed. If being forced to be together for the last few weeks did anything, it was show that maybe there was a teeny tiny real person inside of Zoe buried under the giant, sarcastic bitchy outer shell.

Hoping for a relationship with Miles outside of the show also meant accepting a relationship with Zoe as his sibling. Could she sign up for that? Was Miles worth it?

An image of him from the night before flashed through her mind.

Maybe he was worth the annoyance of Zoe.

Paige stepped out of the shower and toweled off, sad that she couldn't smell Miles's cologne lingering on her skin anymore. Maybe she'd have to stop by his room to check on him later for another quick dose of his cologne to take with her for the day. She could already imagine his lips trailing along her neck as he kissed her in the spot behind her ear that tickled.

Tonight couldn't come soon enough.

But then Ben would most likely be back in the room with Miles. That could make fooling around awfully tricky. Maybe she could plead with Chip for a spare room of her own… claim Zoe was driving her crazy. That would be believable. Then she could spend another amazing night in his arms.

Of course that would also mean she would fall a little harder for him and risk getting closer to Zoe by proxy. The question popped into her mind again as she dug through her closet for something cute to wear. Was Miles worth it, knowing he was forever attached to Zoe?

Yes.

Maybe.

Zoe couldn't possibly be that bad once they got to know each other better. Already they were getting along better on this show than they had on *The One*. Surely, if they were connected because of Miles, they could figure out a way to be around each other without fighting or constant sarcasm, couldn't they?

"Apparently screwing my brother leads to an inability to hold conversations," Zoe said, sarcasm at full throttle. "If I'd known how quiet it would be, I would have gotten you two to hook up sooner. I wonder if there's a way to accomplish this level of speechlessness without having to make you squeal with ecstasy? I'm not sure I like you that much."

Paige's mouth dropped open. She needed to say something back but what could she say to that? The longer she sat there thinking, the more Zoe's comment rang true. "I. He."

"Bumped uglies last night? Yep, old news."

"I'm not quiet because of sleeping with Miles, which is none of your business by the way. I'm quiet because I can't believe that you and he share the same genetic beginning. You're so completely different from each other."

"We're really not that different actually."

She bit the inside of her cheek thinking about Zoe's comment. If they weren't so different, then how exactly were they the same? And could she live with Miles's similarities to Zoe?

Damn it. How the hell out of all the people in the whole world, had she ended up in bed with Zoe's brother? Fate was a cruel, cruel bitch.

"How exactly are you like him?"

Zoe shrugged. "We're both determined and driven. We're both independent. We're both hot."

"At least he doesn't share your amazing modesty," Paige mumbled. "How are you guys siblings when you don't even share the same last name? That doesn't make sense."

"Not all of us grew up with the perfect mother and father who loved each other with a white picket fence, two point five children, and a dog. Our parents split when we were little. He stayed with dad, and I went with mom. We changed our last names after my mom remarried. It just made things easier. People asked fewer questions."

Paige hadn't thought Zoe had grown up in anything less than perfection. To hear her life hadn't been all luxury and extravagance like she'd made it sound made Zoe somehow more real. Almost as if she could have been someone Paige might be friends with if they hadn't met under such difficult circumstances during filming of *The One*. Almost.

"Why didn't you tell me Miles was your brother right away? Why did you two keep it hidden, especially after Miles and I started getting more interested in each other?"

Zoe smiled. "And miss the chance to see this moment of horror when you realize you've slept with my brother? Not a chance. If he wasn't going to tell you, there was no reason for me to ruin the surprise. Besides, I knew sooner or later you'd figure out our connection."

And that was why they'd never be real friends—Paige didn't take pleasure in other people's embarrassment or discomfort.

Realization about Miles's motives for not telling her about Zoe sank in fully. Of course he wouldn't tell her they were related when Zoe behaved the way she did. Who would want to be related to her when she acted so awful to other people?

And he was right. As much as she hated to admit it, Miles had been right. Paige probably would have judged him unfairly based on Zoe's actions.

She slipped into her heels, cringing a little as the familiar pain stung her feet again. Damn. How long did it take to break in stilettos? Hopefully not much longer or her feet might stop working altogether.

"You don't need to bother with those if they're hurting you. You've already succeeded in snagging Miles. I doubt he'll even notice if you wear your boots again." Zoe tied her sneakers, after a long jealous glance toward Paige's heels.

Paige shook her head. "No. I like them." *They make me feel confident.* Not that she'd ever say that to Zoe, the girl who would surely ooze confidence even while wearing a garbage bag. Whether or not Miles liked her shoes was beside the point now. Every time she put them on, she felt not only taller, but physically, mentally, and emotionally stronger too.

And she really liked feeling this way.

What if she wore her stupid hiking boots or sneakers again and the feeling disappeared? Best not to risk it now while she really needed to keep feeling this way. After the show would be soon enough.

So stilettos it was. She'd enjoy when Miles looked at her with that twinkle in his eyes that told her he couldn't wait to be alone with her again.

"We should go," Paige said, standing from the bed. Her toes complained about being shoved into the tight shoes again, but otherwise she was getting more and more used to the heels every day. She walked to the door without wobbling once. Definitely getting better at the whole balance thing too. "The boys are probably already waiting for us in the common room. You and I need to decide if we want to go for that other cache or not."

Zoe shrugged. "I think we do. It will guarantee us some great points and maybe even a prize. How can we not go for the cache? If we don't even try to get it, we may as well just concede to losing. I don't know about you, but I'm not a loser."

Paige nodded. Funny how a few weeks together could make them start agreeing. "We should have just enough time to try and convince Miles to go for the cache while we eat breakfast."

Zoe smirked. "We can try, but I hate to break it to you… Miles can be pretty stubborn when he wants to be."

Paige felt confidence surge through her. "Nothing I can't handle. Besides, we're our own team and we can make our own decisions, regardless of our alliance with the boys." She took out her lip balm but Zoe stopped her before she could even pull off the cap.

"On behalf of every makeup person in the world, please use a lip gloss instead of that crappy wax." She shoved the dark crimson tube of gloss toward Paige. "Real women wear gloss."

Paige eyed the tube, contemplating whether or not she should give in and take it. Zoe hadn't steered her wrong yet, but she hated lip-gloss every time she'd worn it for a special occasion. She couldn't imagine putting up with the feel of it on her lips for an entire day outside.

But Paige did want to be confident like Zoe was, so didn't that mean she should start standing up for herself even if it meant standing up to Zoe?

"No thanks," Paige said easily, feeling stronger and more confident. "I hate the sticky feel of it on my lips. And honestly, I can't imagine Miles liking it either."

Zoe rolled her eyes. "Seriously, if you start telling me what he likes in the bedroom next, I'm going to hurl. It's one thing to know you're hooking up, but it's another to find out what he likes and how he likes it."

"Don't worry, I don't plan on sharing any details about anything with you." Paige had no desire to discuss her love life with Zoe… ugh, his sister. Besides, the more distance she could put between the fact that Zoe and Miles were siblings, the better. Not to mention, she didn't need another reminder that she was totally falling for Miles and that meant being stuck with Zoe in her life forever.

*

Miles watched as the girls sat down at the table with Ben and began eating breakfast. This wasn't going to be easy. He knew a fight waited for him at the table and all three of them would gang up on him. But it didn't matter. He would do whatever he had to so they would all stay safe.

And after being in the common room all morning, drinking way more coffee than any one human needed to consume, he was pretty sure he'd come up with the perfect argument. Now he had to convince them of it.

He grabbed a bottle of water, unable to even consider drinking another sip of coffee, and headed for the table. He sat and tried to produce a confident yet understanding expression. It would be best if they decided this wasn't a good idea for themselves versus him putting his foot down again like he'd tried, and failed, to do last night. Zoe never responded to that attitude and if Paige's annoyance at him when she'd shown up at his room last night was any indication, she wouldn't put up with an attitude like that from him again either.

Apparently more of Zoe was rubbing off on her than she realized.

Not that he minded a strong woman. As long as Paige didn't also adopt the bitchy side of Zoe, they'd be fine. Bitchy and strong were totally different things and Zoe often didn't seem to understand the difference between the two. Hopefully Paige would.

"What's our plan for today?" he said with an easy smile. He'd play it cautiously and see what happened.

They glanced at each other, no one meeting his gaze.

Not a great start.

Paige looked at him. Her shoulders were high and full of tension even though her facial expression was laidback and casual. She probably thought she was fooling him. But years of teaching people how to climb had giving him an uncanny ability to read body language, even if they didn't want to say what was really on their minds.

"We've decided we're going for the cache," she said simply, not needing to explain what cache she meant. There was only one in question. "It's the best thing to do for our teams despite the minor risk involved."

"You have? I see. And all of you are in agreement?" he asked.

Ben and Zoe nodded.

"And I'm only now finding out about this group decision that affects me as much as it affects you?" he asked.

"Yep. Sort of like how I just found out that you and Zoe are siblings." Paige crossed her arms, looking at him with a mix of annoyance and teasing.

Oh yes, she definitely could be happier with him right now, but at least she didn't seem angry. Annoyed, yes. Annoyed she could get over quickly and maybe she already had if the teasing tone was any indication. Sure, he'd kept the truth from her for a few weeks, but he'd done it for a good reason.

"Would it have made a difference with how you feel about me?"

"Maybe." Paige sighed and rolled her eyes. "Probably not."

And there was his answer. He would never know for sure if things would have escalated to the point of being intimately involved Paige if he'd told her about Zoe earlier. But now they were together and he could talk to her about it. They could work it out because now Paige knew the real Miles and not simply the guy who happened to be related to Zoe Oliver by blood.

"And I guess I'm out numbered with this decision about the cache," he said, changing the subject. He needed to figure out a way to stop them from going for that stupid dangerous cache.

"You are." Ben smiled. "But don't let it bruise your ego too much."

Miles was quiet for a moment. "So when are we going for that cache?"

"Today," Zoe said. "First thing. Let's get in and get out before any of the other teams have a chance."

He nodded along with them. They all looked so pleased with themselves. With their plan. Under different circumstances he might have felt that way too. But not this time.

"Well, we should be able to take our time today," he started. He worked hard to keep his voice as casual and nonchalant as possibly. It was crucial they didn't think he was bullying them into this decision, even if he wanted to. If it kept them from getting hurt, it was worth it.

"What do you mean?" Paige asked. "Everyone will be headed there right away."

"That's not what I heard around here this morning."

"No? What did you hear?" Ben asked.

"Sounded to me like every team had taken it off their list."

"Why would they do that? It doesn't make sense when they know there's a good possibility there's a prize available."

He shrugged. "Seems half of them think it's disrespectful to the firefighters to go after the cache they got hurt on and the other half think it's bad luck. Like the cache is cursed or something." He forced himself to chuckle even though he didn't feel like laughing. He had to agree with the sentiment of the other teams. If only his teams would get on board too.

Miles took a sip of water while he let that settle. "I was thinking, since no one else is going for that cache, it will be safe sitting there a while. Maybe we would be better off trying to do some of the other caches that are hopefully closer, faster, and easier. And since we know where that other one is, we can run over to it anytime we find ourselves close by. Saves going out of our way for one cache and possibly losing a whole day completing it."

By the expression on their faces and the change in their body language, he felt pretty confident they would agree with his plan. It was a good plan, no doubt. But since he wanted them to figure it out for themselves, he needed to give them a few more minutes to decide.

"I'm going to grab another pastry. Anyone want anything?" he asked, rising from the table.

"I'll take one," Paige said. "Thank you."

He smiled at her and she blushed slightly. He wandered off to the buffet table, taking much longer than necessary to gather two little pastries on plates. Glancing over to the table while he reached for a couple of extra napkins, he saw the three of them huddled with their heads together. After lingering near the food as long as he could without feeling awkward, he wandered back to his teammates and set Paige's pastry in front of her then took his seat again.

"We've decided to leave that cache until later and risk that the prize will still be there when we get around to it," Paige said.

Good.

"And we will get to it before the end." Zoe's voice was determined.

Well, at least it wouldn't be today. The longer he could delay them, the more chance there was that they'd forget about it, another team would go for it and get it, or they'd decide it wasn't worth the risk. Any way he looked at it, delaying even another day was a success.

Finishing the last bite of his pastry, he leaned back and laced his fingers behind his head. His tension and stress vanished. "Sounds like you guys have it all figured out."

Chapter Twenty

Paige shifted in bed and snuggled closer against Miles's side. Funny how she felt like she'd always belonged there even though they'd only been together a few weeks. Felt like a lifetime already.

She yawned, trying to shake off the tiredness before another grueling day of caches and driving and searching hit her. Didn't matter how much sleep she got each night, she still felt tired each morning. Of course, lying in bed with a naked Miles probably wasn't equivalent to sleeping soundly. She'd barely been able to choke down dinner each night before exhaustion settled in. Last night, she'd even been too tired to fool around, which was saying something considering Miles had brought her to his bed again, wrapped his arms around her, and wore only his boxer briefs. Just thinking about it now made her girly bits tingle. If only she could wake up enough to do something about it.

But the last week had been too much. Together, they'd managed to find an outstanding seventy-five caches, putting both teams only one place back from Team Frat Boys who still had a five-cache lead. Team Retired Grandparents and Team Husband and Wife were close on their heels. Every day they started out knowing they had to find as many caches as possible to keep their tie together for second and third place.

Of course, in the end, it would all come down to point value per cache not the number of caches alone. But logic told them that the more caches they had, the more points they would collect.

And after each of the long days this last week, they'd come back to the common room to strategize. The noise of the room during the first two weeks had tapered off considerably as everyone made the final push to the end leading into this last week. Some teams didn't even bother hanging out in the common room every night anymore, preferring instead to hole up in their rooms where they could plan their next day in private.

Paige, Zoe, and the boys didn't feel the need to hide out. They liked to be out in the open, enjoying their time in the evenings for more than just strategizing. Sure they'd done a lot of that too, but they'd also played a few rounds of chess, goofed off, and eaten way too much for dinner. Seemed their stomachs had become bottomless pits from all the exercise during the day.

After they'd finally given up planning for the next day, their teams split up for the remainder of the evening. Paige and Miles would grab hot chocolate and cuddle on the couch in front of the huge stone fireplace, chatting about their lives outside of the game, and Zoe and Ben would usually go stretch out in the girls' room where he could rest his leg and they could talk. About what, Paige had no idea, since talking to Zoe usually meant lots of sarcasm. But Ben didn't seem to mind at all.

In fact, Ben seemed happier now than he had at the beginning of the show. If Paige had to wager a guess, she'd say Zoe was too. Odd how the two of them suddenly got along so well. After their hospital excursion, they seemed to have bonded in a way Paige and Zoe hadn't. Come to think of it, Zoe was calmer, more polite, and hadn't said one sarcastic thing to Ben in all the times Paige had seen them together.

Ben and Zoe's newfound—whatever it was—also left lots of time for Miles and Paige to be alone together. Most nights it was *all* night since Ben ended up falling asleep while talking to Zoe in the girls' room.

And yet Miles insisted Ben was faithful to his wife Tammy without question. Paige couldn't help but wonder why someone like Ben would want to spend so much time alone with Zoe. He must see something in her that the rest of the world was blind to.

Paige didn't mind giving up her bed at all. Miles's bed was way more comfortable for sleeping anyways… well, after he finally let her sleep each night. The other teams didn't even bat an eyelash in her direction during her walk of shame each morning anymore either. Their blooming romance—"showmance" if you asked the Frat Boys—was old news with the end of the show nearing and everyone so focused on winning.

Miles's fingers trailed down her ribs and back up again, her bare skin tingling with the sensation. She hadn't bothered to bring pajamas with her to Miles's room each night since she wouldn't have stayed in them for long anyway. The appreciative smile on his face each night when she climbed into bed in only her panties was worth the lack of clothing. And she was never cold wrapped in his arms.

His hand slid down her side and slipped under the material of her panties, coming to rest on her rear. He squeezed and she tried to wiggle away from his wandering hand. She needed to get up and get to her own room, not fool around with Miles. Fooling around would lead to a late start and none of them could afford that.

"Miles, stop. We have to get up." She turned her head and yawned away from him. "We don't have time for any of that this morning."

"Still too tired? I let you sleep all night to recoup." He kissed her head while his free hand found her breast, caressing it until her nipple peaked into a tight bud. "You seem awake enough."

She rolled onto him, kissing his neck then his collarbone and chest. Oh, yes. She'd love to stay and play this morning, and judging by the tenting in his boxer briefs, he'd love it too.

Paige stopped kissing his body and stared into his eyes, hovering over him. Every morning she woke up in his bed, she felt herself fall a little harder, a little deeper. It wouldn't take much longer before she was a total goner. Seeing his beautiful eyes stare back at her with lust and something that looked an awful lot like love in them, she didn't mind falling further. As long as he fell with her.

Was he falling for her too? Or was she the only one losing her head in this arrangement?

"You are so beautiful," he whispered, his voice raspy as if there was more than the early morning making his voice sound that way. "I think this might be the best alliance ever."

"So it's all about the game, huh?" she teased, but her insides twisted with fear that she might be right. "I'm just an ally, nothing more."

He flipped her over and was suddenly hovering over her, his eyes serious and full of heat. "You've never been part of the game to me."

Miles kissed her hard on the mouth, the intensity full of passion and something more she couldn't pinpoint. With his lips on hers, his tongue in her mouth, his hand pressed between her thighs—her worries about the game vanished from her mind. He wanted her and damn it, she wanted him too. There was nowhere else she wanted to be right now than in his arms where she felt desirable, confident, and in control.

The show could go on without them if need be.

*

Miles hadn't been able to wipe the grin off his face all day. Going to bed with Paige each night and waking up with her each morning for the last ten days had been amazing. And every time they'd been together, his connection got deeper.

Deeper than he'd ever felt with anyone.

He wasn't a settle down and get married kind of guy. He liked variety and the freedom to come and go as he pleased. But there was something about Paige that made him believe he'd never get bored with her. Maybe it was the way she only had to glance his way and he got hard. Or maybe it was the fact that they could talk about anything together. He didn't feel like he had to hold back what he felt or thought with her. Like how he'd finally been able to confide in someone about the accident and how much it still bothered him. He hadn't been anywhere near ready to tell someone that before.

Because Paige wasn't just anyone.

She was completely amazing in every way. And feeling that way for her scared the shit out of him.

He hadn't expected to get involved with anyone while on the show. He'd been here for Ben only. Then he'd met Paige and all that changed. Every kiss seemed to throw him further over the edge and pretty soon there'd be no coming back.

Not that he really wanted to come back anyway.

He watched her hips sway as she walked in front of him down the path, feeling almost hypnotized by the movement. The grin on his face grew. If he could take her into the brush to steal a few more kisses right now, he totally would. He glanced to the side and surveyed the nearby foliage. Maybe he could take her behind that bush for a few minutes without being missed.

"We're here," Zoe said from beside Paige.

He pulled his mind back from where it had wandered off to do dirty things to Paige in the bushes and focused on the path ahead of him. Except there was no path anymore.

A wall of rock went straight up. Miles tracked a path from the bottom to the top, mentally noting all the notches to grip with his fingertips and the tiny cracks and crevasses to tuck his toes into the wall. Years of climbing made it easy to spot the best route up the cliff.

An easy climb. A couple of minutes up, a couple of minutes down. No sweat.

Small rocks fell from above, showering down the side of the cliff.

"Watch out below," Dean called from the top ledge, swinging his leg over and beginning his climb down. A few minutes later, he and Chuck stood in front of them.

"You guys going up?" Chuck asked.

"Yeah," Zoe said, squaring her shoulders. "We're all going up."

Chuck and Dean elbowed each other laughing. "Sure you are," Dean said. He turned to face Miles. "Too bad you've got so much dead weight on your team. This would be an easy climb for you. For the others, not so much."

"Watch it," Miles said, balling his hands into fists at his sides. He wasn't a fighter, but hearing some jackass call his friends dead weight could make even the most even-tempered person irate.

They ignored his comment and laughed again, jogging down the trail.

Miles clenched his jaw. It wasn't true. Neither his teammate nor the girls were dead weight. He took in the others who stood there watching him, not saying anything as if they waited for him to admit he felt that way about them.

"Those guys are jackasses. Don't listen to them." But even as he said it, he couldn't stop himself from evaluating them. Paige in her heels with the open toes. Zoe with her ankle still bandaged and weak in her sneakers. Ben with his prosthesis, still unsure of whether he could climb or not.

And his fear that something would go wrong if they tried to climb the cliff.

"So let's get going then," Paige said, moving to stand right in front of the cliff. She grabbed hold of the rocks with both hands then tentatively put the ball of her foot on a small ledge. As she pulled herself up to find a place for her other foot, Miles watched as her arms quivered a little at having to hold the majority of her body weight.

Damn it. He couldn't let her do this.

"Come on back down, Paige," he said, taking a step toward her.

She glanced over her shoulder, "No, I'm good. I can do it."

She reached up a little further then looked for the next place to put her feet. He could see where she should step, but instead of her choosing that spot, she placed her foot on a precarious looking outcropping.

"Not that one," he said, coming up behind her, raising his arms to catch her if she fell. "Put your right foot over one spot further."

"This one is fine, Miles."

Paige put her foot where she wanted instead of where he suggested. As soon as she shifted her weight to move her hands again, her foot slipped. Paige shrieked and stumbled to regain her footing while clinging to the wall. Her arms and legs shook as she looked back down to him, fear in her eyes already and she was only a few feet off the ground.

He reached up and grabbed her by the waist, guiding her as she climbed back down to solid ground. When her feet hit the trail, she turned and buried her head in his chest. Her entire body trembled in his arms.

"It's okay. You're on the ground now."

She pulled away and glanced back to the wall, freeing herself from his protective arms. What he wouldn't do to keep them safely wrapped around her for the rest of the show. "I'm okay. I just got freaked out. You tell me where to put my feet and I'll listen this time."

He smiled and kissed her. "Good. Leave them right where they are."

"What?" She took a step back. Not the reaction he wanted, but unfortunately the one he expected.

"Stay right here, both feet on the ground."

"No. The cache is up there and I'm going to get it."

He shook his head. "No you're not. None of us are."

"What?" This time it was Ben's voice with a touch of disbelief mixed with annoyance.

Miles prepared himself for the fight he was about to have on his hands. Ben wasn't going to like him very much in another minute or two. "I think we should skip this one. Go back to the trucks and find another cache to hit. We still have lots of time left today."

Ben threw his hands up. "I can't believe you. Why did you bring me on this show? Just so you could keep telling me what I can and can't do? Just to keep proving to yourself how much better you are than me?"

Ben's words stung like acid. "No. That's not it at all. I can't believe you think that."

"What else am I supposed to think? All you've done this whole time is tell me what I'm not strong enough to do. So thanks for bringing me on national television just to point out my shortcomings."

Miles shook his head. That wasn't what he'd meant to do at all. It was the exact opposite of that. "I didn't. I wanted you to remember how much fun we had climbing together so maybe you'd start doing it again. I wanted you to realize that you can still do all the things you used to so that when I ask you to join me for a climb, you'll actually say yes for a change."

Ben folded his arms across his chest. "Well, if that's your goal, you've been going about it ass backward."

Miles didn't know what to say. Had he screwed up that bad? One glance around at the unhappy faces greeting him and the answer was clear. Yep. He'd screwed up big time. But how could he fix it now?

"I'm sorry. It wasn't my intention to make you feel weak."

"Then let me do this. You know as well as I do that this is a baby climb compared to the mountains we've conquered."

He wanted to say yes, but what about Paige and Zoe? Paige obviously couldn't climb in those heels and seeing her try once was more than enough. And Zoe's ankle would never be strong enough to make the climb.

"Great. So it's settled then. Let's go." Paige moved toward the cliff again.

Miles grabbed her arm and pulled her back against his chest. "I can't let you do that again," he said softly. "You can't climb in those heels. You'll fall and get hurt."

"No I won't. I'll be fine."

"If you guys can do it, we can to," Zoe said.

No way. He couldn't watch all three of them on the rocks at once. Certainly he couldn't catch all three if they fell.

"No way. I'm sticking to my original plan. We all go back."

Ben swore and looked as if he wanted to punch something. Probably he wanted to punch Miles. And after everything, he probably deserved it.

"I'm going up that cliff and you're coming with me. We're a team and as an equal half of that team, I'm making a decision for us. Finally. We're climbing up to that cache and if the girls can't come too, then we're going without them."

Ben turned to face Zoe. "You know why I have to do this, right?"

She smiled and nodded, stepping away from the rocks and heading back down the trail. "Come on, Paige. Let's go find another cache to do."

"What? You're not going to put up a fight about being equally as strong or capable or anything?" Paige called after Zoe, looking disappointed. When Zoe didn't stop or answer her, Paige turned back to Miles. "You coming with us? Wasn't this an alliance where we do all the caches together or we don't do them?"

Miles looked back and forth between Paige and Ben. What was the right choice? He didn't want to walk away from Paige or break his alliance, but he had come on the show to prove to Ben he could still climb. Now they were in the position to climb and he couldn't very well say no. He knew Ben was strong enough to do this. Maybe it was the thing that would really convince him to start climbing again. If he didn't take this opportunity with him now, he may not get another one.

"You know climbing is all about trusting your partner," Ben started. "How can you expect me to trust you on a mountain again if you can't even trust me to climb this?"

Ben was right. Miles had to trust Ben to make good judgment calls if he wanted a climbing partner again. And he needed to start proving to Ben he did trust him. Starting today.

He faced Paige. "I'm going with Ben. You can wait at the trucks for us if you want or I'll catch up with you at base camp tonight."

Paige glanced back to where Ben stood, waiting. "I get why you need to do this climb with Ben after everything you told me about the accident the other night. But why can't you help us climb too? Aren't we important to you too?"

Of course she was important to him, but in this moment, he had to do this with Ben and only Ben. This was the entire reason he'd come on the show to begin with. He couldn't change his goals now. That wouldn't be fair to Ben or to himself. If Paige and Zoe would have been in better condition to climb, he absolutely would have helped them. But they weren't and he couldn't risk any of them, even on this simple climb.

"You are important, but I can't watch all of you at once. It's not safe for you to climb in those heels and Zoe's ankle would never be strong enough. But Ben and I can make it to the top."

"And Zoe and I can't so you're going to ditch us instead of sticking with us. Nice."

"I'm sorry, but I need to do this for him even if it means I have to do it without you."

She narrowed her eyes, hurt and anger flashing in them. "So that's it? You use us as long as it's convenient for you and the second you can't benefit from us you bail? Nice. I thought our— alliance—meant more to you."

Paige turned and walked away.

Shit.

Tonight he would explain his choice to Paige when they were

alone in his room. Until then, he had to focus on getting Ben up to the cache and back safely.

"Let's go," he said, motioning for Ben to start up the hill in front of him.

Chapter Twenty-One

Paige pushed the rocking chair back and forth, hoping the motion would calm the turmoil boiling inside. So far, it wasn't working.

"Can you knock that off, it's making me seasick." Zoe leaned back in her rocking chair, closing her eyes.

Paige stopped rocking and stared at Zoe instead.

"What?" Zoe said, her eyes still closed.

"Doesn't it bother you at all?"

"Yes, I'm completely sick of these stupid daily wrap-ups, interviews, whatever the hell Chip wants to call them. No matter what you call them, they suck."

"On that lovely note, let's get started," Evan said. He flipped the switch to turn his camera on. "Now that we're getting closer to the end of the game, how are you holding up? Is the pressure getting to you yet?"

"I'd be better if we could have a day off from these wrap-ups," Zoe said, looking completely bored.

"We're holding up just fine. Our team is doing great. We've collected a lot of caches lately, so we should be set up okay going into the end."

"And how is your alliance with Team Everest going? Still strong and united?"

Paige felt her blood pressure spike at the mention of Miles's team. "We have no alliance. I don't know what you're talking about."

Zoe turned to face her. "We don't have an alliance? Damn. That's news to me."

"Has the alliance been going well in your mind, Zoe?" Evan asked.

"Yeah. It's been great. We've been getting a ton of caches since we started working together and we've actually been having a lot of fun hanging out together too. This no alliance thing is definitely news to me."

Evan addressed his next question at Paige. "What changed with your alliance in your opinion?"

She wanted to ignore him, but couldn't. The camera would keep rolling until she answered. "It's only an alliance if the teams actually work together. When one team goes off on their own leaving the other team behind, I think that effectively ends the partnership."

"Did that happen with your teams today?"

"Yes. Miles and Ben chose to do a cache we weren't able to do and that, in my mind at least, ends the alliance."

"So you won't be working with them again tomorrow?" Evan asked.

"Yes, we will," Zoe said, rolling her eyes. "Paige needs a night to cool off about everything and we'll be back on track with our alliance."

"No, I'm done with your brother, Zoe. Done."

"Paige, calm down. You just need a little distance before you talk it out with Miles. Everything will be fine again after a little make-up… *talk*." Zoe winked at her.

"You really think I'm going to jump into bed with him again after he betrayed me this way?"

Zoe nodded her head toward the camera while staring at Paige. "You might want to ask Evan nicely to edit out that last part about sleeping with my brother. Viewing audience and all that stuff."

Paige clenched her jaw and rubbed her hand across her forehead. Great. Just what she needed, the whole world hearing about her relationship with Miles and her subsequent betrayal by him. Awesome. Let the good times roll. Well, she wasn't going to risk saying anything else stupid.

Paige stood from her rocking chair and pulled her hair back off her face into a messy ponytail. It felt so good to get it out of her face after a long day in the heat out on the trails. "I don't know if you had more questions or not, Evan, but I'm done for the night."

*

Paige filled her plate at the buffet then scanned the room for a place to sit and eat. Ben and Miles already sat at their usual table, laughing and joking while they ate. No way in hell was she about to join them. Not after Miles had turned his back on their alliance... and on her.

She sat on the sofa in front of the fireplace, balancing her plate in her lap. Hopefully the warmth of the fire would take away the chill she felt run down her spine every time she looked at Miles, her anger and hurt still pulsing through her.

He'd chosen Ben.

Not their alliance. Not her. Ben. His buddy. And only Ben.

Everything she'd done during this show to try and become more confident and stronger—more *desirable* to a guy like Miles—had all been for nothing. Didn't matter how much more confident she was, guys like Miles or Ben or any of the others from her past would never chose to be with her. No matter what she did, no one would ever see her as the kind of girl they wanted to stick with forever. She was always just someone they were stuck with temporarily until they could ditch her.

At least now she knew where Miles's loyalty lay, and it wasn't with her. The only thing lying with her was his hot body. Too bad. She'd miss cuddling up against his gorgeous sculpted body tonight. But more than that, she'd miss falling asleep while talking to him about everything in their lives. She'd miss listening to his stories about his adventures. She'd miss telling him about her life back home.

She glanced over when she heard Miles laugh at something Ben said. Well, he wouldn't miss her, would he?

Paige turned back to her food, not really tasting what she ate. It was just something to stop the annoying monster in her stomach, not something she took any pleasure in tonight. The sooner she ate, the sooner she could head to bed and put the day behind her. Tomorrow she'd feel better about everything. Hopefully.

Or at least she'd feel better about the show. Miles was a whole other problem that would probably bother her for a while longer.

Halfway through her plate of food, Zoe walked into the common room. Paige nodded at her but Zoe looked right past her then wandered over to Ben and Miles.

Nice. Traitor.

Not even Zoe cared that Miles had chosen Ben over Paige. Why would she? Obviously she cared more that her brother was happy than she cared about her own teammate. Now that Zoe had this new bond with Ben, she probably cared more about him than she did about Paige too.

Paige was a team of one again, just like she feared she would be that very first day when Cassidy had bailed on the show. Before she could dwell on it any longer, Zoe and Ben walked out of the room together, talking quietly as they went. Not even so much as a glance toward Paige to say goodbye. The sting of being alone grew and tears pricked her eyes.

Forcing herself to take a deep breath, she steadied her emotions. She wouldn't become a basket case because of them. She'd come too far during this show for that. She was stronger now than she'd ever been before and a little loneliness wasn't going to change her back to how she used to be.

The couch shifted beside her as Miles joined her.

She wouldn't let betrayal take away her confidence either.

"How's it going?" Miles asked, leaning back against the couch.

She didn't say anything. Instead she took a big bite of her food so she couldn't possibly say something. How was it going? That was as good as he could come up with? How did he think it was going when he'd dumped her for his buddy? Left her on the trail feeling like a puppy that had just been kicked.

I'm great! Awesome. Never been better.

"I wanted to come over earlier, but Ben needed to talk about a couple of things."

Of course, Ben comes first.

She forced another deep breath into her lungs forgetting that she still had a mouth full of food until some of it hit the back of her throat. She coughed into her napkin, her eyes watering. Miles sat forward, patting her on the back to help her catch her breath.

Paige put her plate on the coffee table, her appetite gone, and took a sip of water. When she finally stopped coughing, Miles continued to rub her back. She wanted more than anything to lean into his chest, bury her face in his neck, breathe in his manly scent.

She shifted on the couch, leaning away from Miles and propping herself up against the arm of the couch for support. She would not give in to temptation. Not after he'd made his real feelings about her clear.

"Paige," he said softly, stroking the side of her leg with his fingers, sending tingles of heat along her skin. She wished he'd stop touching her. It would make it easier to ignore him. "I know you don't understand why I decided to finish the cache with Ben, but I can explain if you'll listen to me. Ignoring me is childish and silly."

Oh, no. He did not.

Paige turned to face him. "You know what's childish and silly?" She didn't wait for his answer before continuing. "Choosing your hiking buddy over the girl you claim to like enough to take to bed. Or maybe that was all I was to you—a girl to take to bed while you were stuck on this stupid show. Just a way for you to fill the long boring evenings."

She got up from the couch and grabbed her plate before crossing the room to throw it in the garbage. Miles stood.

"Come back and talk to me about this."

Paige paused. "You made your choice, and now I've made mine. See you at the finale."

She walked out of the common room with her head held high, feeling every bit as confident as she did in her heels even though she was currently barefoot. She didn't need Miles to win this game. Hell, she didn't even need Zoe. All she needed was a few good caches to secure some points and she could win this whole game. That would show all of them just how strong and confident she was now.

Pulling open her bedroom door, she wasn't at all surprised to find Ben and Zoe talking. Ben looked pretty comfortable on Paige's bed, but he was going to have to get uncomfortable.

"Ben," she said, making them both jump since neither had paid her any attention when she'd walked in. "You're a nice guy and all, but I need you to get the hell out of my bed."

He raised his eyebrows at her questioningly, obviously surprised by this new Paige. "Okay. Sorry. I thought you'd be with Miles again tonight. He said he was going to talk to you once I left with Zoe."

"Oh, he did come talk to me. And I told him to get lost too."

Ben stood by the door while Paige fluffed her pillows. "Is everything okay with you and Miles?"

"Does it sound like everything's fine?" she snapped then regretted it. She lowered her voice as exhaustion set in. "No, Ben, it's not."

"Sorry to hear that," he said. "Maybe we can get it all sorted out tomorrow after a good night's sleep."

"I doubt that," she muttered, climbing into bed and pulling the blankets over her head. A moment later she heard the door close and Zoe turning out the light.

*

Paige peeled her eyes open to peer at the clock on the bedside table. One in the morning. It was inhuman to be awake in the middle of the night. Groaning, she reached out for her water bottle only to find it missing.

Damn it. It had been on the end table beside the couch in the common room. Probably it still sat there.

She rolled out of bed and slipped into the hall as quietly as she could so as not to wake up Zoe. It would take her approximately two minutes to walk down the hall to the common room to get her bottle and then she could be back to bed in another two. Sounded like a pretty good plan.

As she came up to the common room door, the quiet murmuring of voices from inside stopped her in her tracks. Who was up so late?

Holding her breath, she crept closer to the door, straining to hear who was inside. She didn't want to spy on anyone or eavesdrop, but she also didn't want to be seen by everyone in her thin pajamas in the cool night air. She'd done that once before, and all it had gotten her was a tumble in the sheets and a broken heart. No way would she risk that again.

She paused, listening.

Miles's voice drifted to her as if beckoning her to go to him. The sound of his voice in the dark made her long to feel his hands on her body. Made her belly turn to lava at the thought of forgiving him and going back to his bed for make-up sex.

Until she heard Eve's voice.

Then the lava in her belly thardened as fire sparked in her veins. They hadn't even been fighting one day and already he was chatting up Eve in the common room late at night. Alone. Next stop, Bedroomville, apparently.

She rested her forehead against the cold wall, trying to think of a valid reason why they were talking so late at night. Maybe they were forming a new alliance. Maybe they'd always been in an alliance. Maybe they were watching a movie on television.

Eve laughed. Giggled.

Or maybe Eve had finally succeeded in getting into Miles's pants like she'd hinted at wanting for this whole show. She wouldn't be surprised. Eve hadn't exactly hidden her attraction to Miles.

Maybe Miles had finally decided to stop pushing her away. Maybe he didn't like sleeping alone. He hadn't wasted any time. His feelings for Paige couldn't have been real.

Paige swiped at a tear that had broken free.

Damn him. She wasn't going to cry for him when he'd already moved on to sleeping with someone else. And she wasn't going to stand here in the hall like some jealous girlfriend and spy on them.

Nope. Miles could do whatever he wanted—whomever he wanted.

He wasn't her concern anymore. She wouldn't let him be.

Paige jogged back down the hallway on the balls of her feet trying to get away as quickly as she could without making any noise to draw them out of the common room to find her. The last thing she needed was a confrontation with Miles. She'd managed to keep her emotions in check earlier tonight, but she couldn't guarantee she'd be able to do it again now that she knew he was spending his free time with Eve instead of her. Not that it mattered anyway. She'd washed her hands of him the minute he'd chosen Ben over her. Hadn't she?

She climbed back into bed no longer thirsty and prayed Zoe hadn't heard her come back. She couldn't handle Zoe right now. Paige pulled the covers over her head.

Miles had made two choices today, both of them bad. And neither included her.

This time she didn't bother to stop the tears.

Chapter Twenty-Two

Miles knocked on the door to Zoe and Paige's room. With an hour left until they had to check out for the day, he hoped he'd have enough time to convince Paige he still wanted to be in an alliance with her.

And he still wanted to be with her in other ways too.

If only he could get her to talk to him for two seconds.

It had been a couple days since their argument at the cache when Paige ended up walking away from him—literally and figuratively. He'd tried a few more times to talk to her since the night by the fireplace, but he couldn't seem to get her to stay still long enough. Every time he approached her, she started a conversation with another team until he got tired of waiting around.

After completing the climbing cache with Ben, he'd realized how wrong he'd been to assume Ben couldn't do the harder caches. Miles also realized he'd probably been wrong about Paige and Zoe not being able to do the caches as well. And he planned to tell her as much when he finally got the chance to.

His last hope of getting his alliance back on track with her was coming to her room early in the morning before the day of racing started. Being that today was the last day of the race, he was out of options and time. He wanted to race with Zoe and Paige. He wanted to learn more about Paige before it was too late and the show ended and everyone went back to their own lives.

Damn it. He needed to spend time with her. It didn't seem to matter what he filled his time with each evening, not being with Paige made him lonelier than he cared to be. Lonelier than he'd ever been, even after Ben had stopped climbing and had gotten married.

He missed Paige.

Somehow she'd become a part of his life during the show and he hadn't felt the same since she'd walked away. It killed him knowing she thought so poorly of him. He had to change her mind.

He knocked on the door again, harder this time. They had to be in there. He'd checked all of the usual areas and he hadn't seen either of them yet. Therefore they had to still be getting ready. He had her trapped. There was nowhere for her to run off and hide… no one for her to start another conversation with except for Zoe and she didn't count. He wouldn't care if he had to interrupt her, not that he thought Zoe would actually bother to play along with Paige just to torment him.

Or maybe she would.

Come to think of it, Zoe had basically only spoken to Ben for the last couple of days. He was glad they'd connected. Ben needed someone in his life who actually understood what he was going through, since his wife and Miles were only so helpful.

The door cracked open. "What the hell? God, you're annoying," Zoe said through the door.

"Good morning to you too, sis. Is Paige here? Can I talk to her, please?"

She narrowed her eyes at him. "No."

He sighed. Dealing with Zoe first thing in the morning always required an incredible amount of patience. Far more than he ever had available. Today was no exception. "No she's not here, or no I can't talk to her?"

Zoe shrugged. "Either. Both."

"Come on, Zoe. Be a good sister and let me talk to her."

"I can't. She's in the shower right now, and there's no way I'm letting you in there."

"I'll wait in the room and you can let her know I'm here."

She shook her head. "She told me specifically, on many occasions I might add, that she doesn't want to talk to you again.

You lost your chance when you pulled that alpha male crap on her."

He closed his eyes and banged his head against the doorframe feeling defeated. "I didn't mean to."

"Well, you did. And now you have to deal." Zoe stepped back and moved to close the door.

He thrust his hand into the space, gabbing the side of the door, stopping her from closing it all the way. "Let me talk to her. If you have any heart, don't close the door on me."

"I think you should know me better than that by now." She smiled and he knew she wouldn't budge. When Zoe made up her mind about something, there was no changing it. One of the ways they were very alike. "Today's the last day of the show and our last chance to get caches. I can't let you talk to her or else instead of a capable partner, I'll have a distracted, sniffling mess to take care of like I have since you pulled jerk."

"That's exactly why I need to talk to her. I promise she'll be fine to compete today if you let me apologize."

"I thought you wanted Ben to win. Isn't that why you chose him over Paige to begin with?"

"I didn't mean to pick him over Paige. At least, I didn't think that was what I was doing when I did it. I only wanted to prove to him that he could climb and you're right, I want him to win."

Zoe nodded. "Yeah, I wanted him to win too."

"You did?" Miles asked unable to keep the shock from his tone. Zoe didn't do nice things for others especially not let them win a pile of money she could try to win herself.

"I thought winning would help Ben get his life back, just like you did," Zoe said. "But take a look at him now. He doesn't even need to win anymore. He doesn't need our help anymore. He can win all on his own merits if you let him. And so can I. I want to win too. So I'm keeping Paige away from you until after the check in tonight."

"So now you're out to get us?" Miles asked. Typical Zoe. Using someone until she got what she wanted then walking away without remorse.

Fuck. Just like Paige thought he'd done to her. Great. Another similarity to Zoe. No wonder Paige didn't want to talk to him again. Wow. They really were related after all. Paige was right. His actions did speak louder than his words. His stomach rolled. He was no better than Zoe.

"Fine," he said, sighing. "Can you give her a message for me?" Zoe nodded, so he continued. "Tell her that I'm coming to find her tonight at base camp and I want to apologize. And… I know she's strong and all that, but ask her to be careful. I hate that I'm not there to race with you girls today. Keep an eye on her for me, okay?"

Zoe's shoulders dropped a fraction at his words. If he could get through to her, maybe he still had a shot at saying something right to Paige to help make this all better too. Now he had to wait until tonight to get a chance to say it.

He stepped back from the door and turned away as Zoe closed it. Hopefully tonight wouldn't be too late.

*

"Who was at the door?" Paige asked, walking out of the bathroom with her hair wrapped in a towel and another around her body.

"It was Team Father Daughter checking to see if we're okay since we haven't made it to breakfast yet. I told them we were running late." Zoe crossed the room and slipped her feet into her sneakers, tying them. "I can't wait until I'm out of these stupid sneakers. How can I look cute on TV in these?"

"You look great as always. You could wear flippers on your feet and you'd still look awesome."

Zoe smiled. A genuine smile. "Thanks. You look pretty hot today too. I'd do you."

Paige laughed and blushed while she straightened her shirt. She did look pretty hot today in her yoga top, tight Capri pants, and heels. Too bad Miles wouldn't get to see it.

Not that his opinion mattered anymore.

"Well, thanks. I appreciate the compliment coming from you," Paige said. Maybe their last day racing would be an enjoyable one.

"Don't get used to it. I'm just being nice for the cameras."

"You remember there are no cameras in our rooms, right?" Paige asked.

"Damn. I guess I was nice for no reason then," Zoe said, the teasing tone in her voice unusual but welcomed.

"We should probably head out. I need to grab something for breakfast quickly and I want to make sure we leave right on time. We have to try and get as many caches as possible today since it's our last shot."

Zoe nodded. "Are you sure you don't want to work with the boys again today? We usually got a bunch of caches with them."

Paige shook her head. "No. I'm done with the boys. They don't want us around anyway. We'd probably get to a cache that's 'too hard for little girls' and then they'd leave us again to do it themselves. No way. Today I'm all about girl power."

"I think Miles feels bad about that."

"Good. He should feel bad." Paige squared her shoulders and looked directly at Zoe. "Today I want to go for the hard one."

"The firefighter's cache?"

"Yep. I know it's tricky, but they wouldn't open it again if it wasn't safe. And no one else has done it yet, so I really think we should do it. And we won't have Miles around to tell us we suck."

"I don't know about this," Zoe said, looking nervous for the first time Paige could remember. "I think there's a reason none of the other teams have gone for it."

"Yeah, because they're all scared like Miles. But I'm not scared.

I know we're strong enough to do that cache—now's our chance to prove it to everyone else. And we'll score an awesome prize too."

Paige held her breath waiting for Zoe to disagree with her. If she did, Paige had another few arguments in her arsenal to use. She wasn't going to give up until Zoe said yes.

"Okay. I'm in. But if it gets too scary or looks too dangerous once we get there, then we have to leave. I'm not going to risk being removed from the show because of an injury on the last day. We've been here way too long not to be in the finale. Deal?"

"Deal."

*

Paige and Zoe stood at the edge of the bluff peering over the side. Below, water splashed gently against the rocks. Somewhere on the side of these rocks the cache that had caused the firefighters to fall was hidden. But could they find it?

"I think we should go back to the truck and find another cache," Zoe said, her voice wavering.

"No way. We can totally do this." Paige did feel confident, sort of, but maybe not as confident as she made her voice sound. She didn't want to add to Zoe's already nervous state since both team members had to descend to find the cache.

"But it's so steep. And the water…" Zoe's voice trailed off as she took a step away from the edge. "I don't know."

Paige turned with her arms crossed. "Are you trying to tell me there's something in this world that Miss Zoe Oliver is too chicken to do? 'Cause I don't believe it. I might have to call the tabloids myself so they can get the inside scoop on the real Zoe."

"You wouldn't," Zoe said, trembling less and looking a lot more annoyed.

"I would—*if* you're too chicken to try. But it's okay, people love to know everyone is human and has weaknesses, even the people they see on TV." Paige shrugged and turned back to peer over the edge again.

Zoe huffed from behind her then came to stand at her side. "That's a dirty trick."

Paige grinned and nudged Zoe with her elbow. "I learned from the best."

Zoe rolled her eyes. "Let's get it over with."

They waved over the rappelling crew for a quick lesson. It didn't sound too hard, and this was apparently a fairly easy rappel, but Paige couldn't stop her hands from shaking.

"Okay, so you told us how to get down to the cache, but how are we supposed to get back up?" Zoe asked. Paige wondered the same thing.

"You don't," the instructor said. "This is a one-way trip. Once you get the cache, you rappel the rest of the way down. When you get close to the bottom of the lines, a boat will come over and you'll land in it."

"We have to rappel into a freakin' boat?" Zoe shrieked in an octave Paige thought only dogs would hear.

"That's right. Then the boat will bring you over to shore and you'll hike back up the path to where you parked."

"You make it sound so easy," Paige grumbled while another repelling crewmember fastened different belts and loops around her legs and waist.

"If it was easy, the other team wouldn't have fallen and we wouldn't be stationed out here to make sure you hook on right." The instructor shrugged. "Just take it slow, be careful, and yell if you need help."

"And what happens if we do need help?" Zoe asked.

"Then I climb down and help you and then you have to leave the game."

"What?" Paige and Zoe said together, turning on him as if he'd insulted their hairstyles.

He took step back. "If you have to be rescued, you have to leave the game. It's the rules."

"Those are stupid rules," Paige said.

Maybe coming to do this cache wasn't the best idea she'd ever had. But they'd spent so much time driving back out here that they probably wouldn't get too many more caches today. It seemed like a waste to come all this way and leave empty handed. Again.

No. They were staying and they were going to get this cache marked off their logbook.

Paige walked to the edge again, fully clipped to one of the four rappelling lines available. Zoe came up beside her and turned her back to the edge like the instructor told them. Paige did the same. Somehow, she'd expected it to be less scary if she didn't have to look over the edge anymore.

Turns out it was actually way more terrifying.

Paige's hands shook as she started down the side, leaning back as the instructor had told them. The first few steps were the worst, but once she was over the edge and on her way, her fear subsided as she focused on the task. Before she knew it, she was halfway down.

"How much further?" Zoe asked a couple of feet higher up the side from Paige.

Paige peeked at the GPS unit clipped to her chest. "Says just a few more feet. We should see the hiding spot soon. Come further down so we can find it together."

"Okay," Zoe called. "Wait for me."

Paige peeked over her shoulder and scanned the rock face below her trying to find anywhere there might be a nook to hide a cache. With Zoe on the farthest outside line on the left and Paige on the line beside her more to the middle, it made more sense that the cache would be somewhere below Paige. That way, the other two lines on Paige's right could reach the cache as well if another team happened to show up at the same time. It only made sense that the cache would be directly in the middle of the four lines so that two teams searching at the same time could have equal ability to reach the cache.

"It's gotta be near me and in the middle somewhere. It's the only thing that makes sense in this situation," Paige called back up to Zoe who was slowly making her way closer.

Paige continued to search until Zoe dropped down beside her. "See right there," Paige said, pointing to an outcropping of rock a few feet below them, directly between the middle two rappelling lines. "I think that could be where it is."

"It's as good a place as any to check," Zoe said. "Let's just find this thing and get the hell out of here. I don't feel good about this at all."

"We're doing great. Don't worry."

The girls made their way down a little further then Zoe stopped moving. Paige stopped where she was. "Why did you stop? Let's keep going if you want to get done and out of here."

"I'm trying," Zoe said, her voice shaking. "I can't go any further."

"Zoe, come on. I'm right here with you. You don't need to be afraid. We're totally safe here." Paige tried to make her voice sound as reassuring and calm as possible. But in her head, she yelled a string of obscenities. Hanging around being scared on the side of a cliff wasn't going to help their situation any, so Zoe needed to suck it up and keep moving.

Paige looked up to find tears brimming Zoe's eyes. She'd only ever seen Zoe cry once and that was at the finale of *The One*. And now the girl was tearing up again. This couldn't be as bad as being publically rejected on TV by Brad.

Paige needed to be even stronger for Zoe right now. "It's okay, try wiggling the thingy a little to see if you can get going again."

"No, really." Zoe breathed in a hitched breath. "I can't move. I think I'm stuck."

Chapter Twenty-Three

"I can't believe you hid this from me," Miles said, slamming his palm against the steering wheel again.

"I didn't think it was that big of a deal. They're their own team. They can do whatever they want to now that you broke our alliance with them."

"How did you know they were going for that cache today anyway?" Miles asked, annoyed with himself that he hadn't figured out the girls were on their way to getting themselves in trouble.

"I saw Zoe before we left and she looked a little worse for wear. When I asked her if anything she was wrong, she mentioned being nervous about attempting the cache that had landed the firefighters in the water, then in the hospital."

Miles cursed under his breath. This had accident written all over it. Damn it.

He skidded the truck to a stop on the side of the road next to what he assumed must be the girl's SUV and bolted out the door. He barely waited long enough for Ben to get out of the truck before heading off down the trail in the direction the arrow on the GPS unit pointed.

"I wish you'd told me sooner. Then we could have stopped them. I just hope we're not too late."

Ben kept pace with Miles but his breath came out a little harsher than it should. "Maybe you don't need to stop them. They're stronger than you think they are, you know? It wouldn't be the first time you'd underestimated someone recently."

Miles glanced over to his friend and saw the sheen of sweat already covering his forehead. Miles slowed his pace even though every fiber of his being told him to sprint as fast as he could. Ben was right. He'd underestimated what Ben could do the entire time on the show. Had he underestimated the girls too?

They walked in silence for a few minutes. The ground was rough with large boulders in some areas and potholes in others. Ben stumbled more than once but Miles resisted the urge to grab his arm and steady him, knowing Ben wouldn't want the help.

Please tell me Paige didn't hike this in heels today.

Finally they crested the top of the gradual slope they'd climbed. The view was outstanding. A large lake, surrounded by green hills and rock bluffs on every side. Simply a little slice of heaven.

Or hell if you made a stupid mistake and ended up hurting yourself.

Or worse.

The girls' cameraman Evan stood at the edge of the cliff, a safety rope tied around his waist. He leaned out precariously over the edge with his camera pointed down, a serious expression creasing his brow.

Shit. They'd done it.

"Are Paige and Zoe down there?" he asked one of the instructors milling around.

"Yep," answered the closest one without elaborating.

"Well, are they okay? Did they get the cache?"

"I can't tell you about the status of the cache or any other team."

Miles looked to the heavens for strength not to punch someone in the face. He just wanted answers and all he got was the run around. If they wouldn't tell him, then he'd damn well find out on his own.

He walked to the edge then dropped to his stomach before peering over the edge. Paige and Zoe dangled about halfway down. They didn't appear to be moving but they also didn't look as if they were searching for the cache. So what the hell were they doing? Having a picnic? Taking in the view?

He forced in a deep breath. His instinct was to tell them how silly they were for taking such a chance. But he couldn't do that.

Paige hated how overbearing he'd been with her the other day, telling her what she could or couldn't do. He wouldn't make that same mistake again. Nor did he want to. He wasn't overbearing like that normally. This whole process of filming the show and searching for caches constantly was really getting on his nerves. When he'd thought they'd put themselves in danger for a stupid show, he'd lost his better judgment for a minute. But he wouldn't do it again. He had to play this off the right way or he'd risk making his situation with Paige worse.

Of course, how it could get worse than her refusing to even speak to him, he didn't know. But he was confident there was a worse scenario.

"How's it going down there?" he called, forcing his voice to be casual and aloof. "Find any big prizes yet?"

"Miles?" Zoe asked.

She looked up at him, tears spilling down her cheeks. He'd only seen her cry a handful of times in his entire life and the sight of it brought back terrible, painful memories. Something was definitely wrong.

"I'm here, Zoe. Are you okay?"

Stupid question. She was hanging on the side of a rock cliff with only a rope and a few carabineer clips supporting her while she dangled over a large body of deep water. No, of course she wasn't all right.

"I've been better, actually." She laughed.

"I can see that." He paused while trying to decide whether or not he should attempt talking to Paige now. It wasn't like she could run away from him at least. "Hey, Paige. How's it going? Just taking a little break down there?"

Paige looked up at him with fire in her eyes, not fear. "I'm fine, but Zoe is stuck."

"What do you mean by stuck exactly?" Stuck while rappelling wasn't good.

"Something's wrong with the metal thingy. The rope won't go through it anymore." Paige touched Zoe's arm. "I can get down the rest of the way, but I don't think Zoe can without figuring this out."

Shit. No wonder Zoe was upset. She hated not being in control. She was terrified of being trapped.

"I'm coming down. Stay where you are," he called, getting to his feet.

"Where do you think we're going to go, smart ass?" Zoe snapped.

Miles stood and faced the instructors, anger bubbling to the surface now that he knew the full extent of the situation. "Why didn't you go get them yet?"

One of them shrugged. "They wouldn't let us."

"So go get them anyways. What are they supposed to do, dangle there forever until they magically get unstuck?" How could they be so stupid to just leave them there?

"If we rescue them, they're out of the game. That feisty dark-haired one threatened to stick her stiletto heel in a very inappropriate spot if I caused them to forfeit the game." He shook his head, his cheeks noticeably paler at the mention of the very long, pointy heels. "That's just not right, dude."

Paige and her heels. She knew she was trying this cache today and she still wore those shoes. When he got her back on solid ground, he was taking those heels and chucking them into the lake. Barefoot would be safer than rappelling in heels.

"You're the one who let her over the edge with those shoes on to begin with," Miles said as he stepped into one of the harnesses lying on the ground, securing it then hooking onto the rope.

"Where do you think you're going?" the other instructor asked.

"To rescue them." He paused. "Why? Am I going to get disqualified if I do?"

"No, you're free to rescue whoever you want, but your partner has to go too. Teammates must repel together to claim the cache."

"But I'm not claiming the cache. I'm rescuing them. I don't give a shit about the stupid cache."

The instructor shrugged. "Rules are rules."

Miles turned to face Ben only to find him already harnessed and lowering himself over the edge of the last line. "What are you doing?"

"Rappelling. Are you going to join me or get me disqualified?" Ben called up, disappearing over the edge as easy as he always did. No fear. No hesitation. No worry.

Miles grinned and double-checked his work to make sure he was fully clipped before following Ben. He couldn't help the swell of pride and satisfaction in his chest seeing Ben rappel again.

Easing his way over the edge, he glanced down to see Paige and Zoe looking back at him. Just waiting and dangling. He could see how this cache would be difficult for teams to reach if they'd never rappelled or done any kind of climbing before. The sheer vertical drop was enough to spook even the person most comfortable with heights.

Miles climbed down quickly, the cliff posing little problem to him after the others he'd climbed in his lifetime. Ben stayed to the side, out of the way and with an expression of pure happiness radiating out of him.

Miles stopped when he reached Paige's side. "Hey, you. So I've been trying to talk to you for days now and you just keep ignoring me."

"Really, Miles?" Zoe squeaked. "You're really trying to settle things with Paige now?"

He chuckled. "No, I'm only teasing her."

"It's not funny." Paige turned away, effectively ignoring him again.

Even on the side of a cliff, she put up a fight. She must be more pissed than he'd expected. But he'd have to worry about her later. Right now he had to figure out how to get Zoe down to the waiting boat.

"Wearing those shoes while rappelling isn't funny either. When we get down from here, I'm throwing them in the lake."

"The hell you are." The fire in Paige's eyes excited him, made him even more eager to get things sorted out with her so they could go back to the way they had been.

"We'll see." He turned his attention back to Zoe. As much as he wanted to deal with Paige now, he had to deal with Zoe's situation first. "Why didn't you let them help you?" he asked, evaluating Zoe's situation as well as he could from his spot a couple of feet away.

"Because then we wouldn't just lose this cache, we'd be off the whole show." Zoe met his gaze.

"It's only a game."

Zoe pleaded. "Can you get me down now? I don't care about the cache anymore."

Paige faced Miles. "Is that why you've been trying so hard to win, even at the expense of your relationships? Nice to know you care so little about people that they mean even less than some silly game."

"I could have explained that a couple of days ago if you'd let me." He focused on Zoe again. As much as he wanted to, he didn't have time to deal with Paige right now. "I want to talk to you about this, but I need to get Zoe down before she really freaks out. To do that, I could really use your help."

Paige sighed but nodded. "What do you need me to do?"

He gave Paige a few instructions and she started her descent again, stopping when she was a few feet lower—just enough space for him to cross her rope line to get to Zoe. He lowered himself another foot on his line then gripped the wall with his fingertips and dug his toes into the tiny spaces between rocks.

Miles climbed to Zoe and quickly saw the problem. The hem of her shirt had gotten caught in the rappel device, jamming it so the rope couldn't pass through.

"It's okay. I'm here now." He might get annoyed with Zoe on a regular basis, but it killed him to see her so upset. "I know how to get you down."

She nodded, biting her lower lip, which quivered uncontrollably. It was a rare occasion he'd seen her in this state and it deeply unsettled him. Best to get her down quickly.

Slipping one hand into the cargo pocket on his shorts, he removed the Swiss Army knife he always carried. "Hold still." He sliced through the material of her blouse, carefully avoiding touching the rope with his blade. When her shirt was free, he fiddled with the device until he could pull the cut section from inside it and the rope could once again slide through.

"My poor shirt," Zoe said softly.

"It was either your shirt or learning to live on the side of a rock."

"I can buy a new shirt." She smiled and swiped away her tears.

He smiled back reassuringly. "Let's get you down."

Miles talked Zoe into moving from where she'd been dangling for far too long. She slowly started making her way down the rock face. When they got to where Paige waited, he paused while Zoe carried on.

"Where are you going?" Paige asked Zoe. "The cache is right around here."

"I give up," Zoe said, shaking her head. "I'm done with this one. I just want down."

"You can't give up. We're right here. This could win us the show—and what about the prize that could be inside waiting for us?"

Zoe shrugged. "It doesn't seem so important anymore," she said, her eyes tearing up again. "I want to be done, okay? Please? I'm asking as nicely as I know how."

Miles watched as Paige clearly debated about whether or not she was going to put up another fight. He sighed with relief when she nodded and started down the rocks again.

"Thank you," Zoe whispered.

*

Paige's feet tingled as they landed on the boat's small deck. After hanging in the rappelling harness for so long, all the blood had pooled in them and putting her body weight on them again didn't feel so great.

She couldn't say the same about Miles's hands as he massaged them for her.

Zoe had insisted her feet were fine in her sneakers and she just looked relieved to be sitting in the boat and headed for shore. She sat next to Ben, discussing something so quietly Paige couldn't overhear them. When Paige had tried to insist her feet were fine too, Miles completely ignored her, then took her feet into his lap and slipped off her shoes.

Then he'd thrown her brand new, sexy-as-hell stilettos into the lake.

She sighed as they sank below the surface, gone forever. Just like her hope of winning the game. Just like her hope of ever proving she was strong enough to conquer anything the show could throw at her.

Now she'd have no choice but to go back to her hiking boots or sneakers for the finale. And no choice but to go back to being plain, pathetic Paige.

If she was really being honest with herself, she wasn't that heart-broken over losing the shoes. Those things were torture devices. Her feet had never been so sore for so long in all her life. But she was sad about everything else.

"You didn't have to do that," she said to Miles, referring to the shoes. "They didn't do anything to you."

He met her gaze, his eyes holding a spark of familiar heat. The same heat she'd seen when staring up at him as he hovered over her in bed. Heat she wasn't sure she'd ever see in his eyes again.

"That's not true," he said, his voice huskier than it should have been. "Those shoes did more to me than you'll ever know."

If she weren't so mad at him, she'd jump into his lap and kiss him until that twinkle in his eyes became all out, unstoppable desire.

But she was mad and she wasn't going to let him get away with things because he was cute. And sexy. And—*oh my God!*—expertly massaged the spot on her arch that had been hurting for weeks.

The boat docked. Zoe and Ben were off of it and onto the shore before Paige had even tried to retrieve her foot back from Miles. He didn't give her a chance. Once the boat was secured, he scooped her into his arms and stepped out of the boat, starting on the climb back up the path to the vehicles. Zoe and Ben were already so far ahead of them Paige couldn't see them.

"Put me down and I'll walk," she said, wiggling in his arms.

"On bare feet? On a rough, rocky trail?"

Sure. Why not? It was her best chance at maintaining a clear head with Miles around. Doing that while he carried her was a lost cause. Especially when her hand was pressed against his flexed pectoral muscle. "I'll be fine. It'll be too hard for you to climb and carry me at the same time."

"You really want to walk barefoot on a trail in the wilderness where there might be bugs, spiders, and snakes?" He raised his eyebrow at her.

She tightened her arm around his shoulders. "Maybe this is okay."

He laughed. "That's what I thought you might say. So, since we're finally talking, tell me why you really insisted on wearing those ridiculous heels all the time because after the massage, I know it wasn't for comfort."

"They looked cute." She didn't offer any more explanation and she knew he wasn't going to accept her lame excuse. But she didn't want to tell him the truth. Certainly she didn't want to tell him while she was in such a compromising position.

He nodded. "That they do. They're damned sexy too. I spent many nights in the last week dreaming of you wearing those heels… and nothing else."

She swallowed.

"And now the real reason?" he asked.

"I wanted you to notice me," she said quietly, hating that it was the truth. Hating that she was so weak and unsure of herself. Or at least she used to be. Lately she'd been feeling pretty strong and determined. Confident even. But now she wasn't so sure it had anything to do with the shoes.

"You didn't need fancy shoes for that," he whispered.

"No?" she questioned, holding her breath.

"Nope. I haven't stopped noticing you since day one."

"Really? I'm not sure I believe that. I think you're just saying that so I'll stop being mad."

He shook his head. "I've noticed a lot of things. Seems no matter how hard I tried, I couldn't get you out of my head when I wasn't around you. And when I was around you… well, I couldn't pull my eyes away."

Really? What had he noticed exactly? Did he notice her staring at him all the time when she thought he hadn't been watching? Oh God, had he noticed that time she'd dropped her water bottle by accident and had checked out his ass on the way back up after retrieving it from the floor? Had he noticed all the times she'd undressed him with her eyes even after they'd been together?

Her cheeks burned at the thought of being caught by him. "Notice any other interesting things during your studies?"

"Only that you look great with a messy ponytail, prefer yoga tops over T-shirts, and drink hot chocolate every night. With three marshmallows. I know you prefer minty lip balm because you like the way it tingles, unless you think I'm going to kiss you and then you put on cherry instead because you think I like it better."

Those were some pretty detailed observations he'd been keeping track of.

"And that you like to check out my ass when you think I'm not looking," he added with a smug grin. "I noticed every time."

She licked her lips while she thought of something witty to reply, suddenly wishing she had some readily available cherry lip balm to apply. Sadly, she'd left it in the truck. Probably for the better since she didn't want to encourage him. She wanted to stay mad at him, not kiss him.

Which would totally be easier if she could walk. His strong arms wrapped around her made her feel protected and safe. The muscles of his chest flexing as he carried her made her all hot and bothered. His labored breathing made her wish he was breathing heavy because of another activity that involved a lot less wilderness and a lot fewer clothes.

Until she thought about the things she'd noticed about him. Like how he seemed all too happy to talk with Eve whenever he thought Paige wasn't around. Or like how he'd chosen Ben instead of her at the cache.

The familiar anger overrode the desire in her body. "And what about Eve? Do you know how she likes her coffee? How about what she eats for breakfast? Or maybe even the type of underwear she wears?"

He stopped walking and set her down so she stood on a rock. "What are you talking about?"

As if he didn't know. "You and Eve. Don't think I didn't notice things too. Like you talking to her every chance you got. Cuddling on the couch late at night when you thought no one else was around. Don't think I didn't notice how quickly you moved on once you couldn't get in my pants anymore."

He shook his head, frowning at her. "I can't believe you think I'd be with Eve. Especially after I'd been with you."

"I can't believe you think I'm stupid enough not to see what was so clearly going on between the two of you."

"What went on was her trying to help me figure out a way to win you back." He rubbed his hands across his face, then leveled his gaze on hers again. "Sure, at the beginning of the show, she'd hinted pretty strongly about having feelings for me. But once you and I were together, I told her it was never going to happen. And then she became just a friend, and nothing more."

Oh.

"I didn't… I thought…"

He cupped his hands along her jaw, tilting her head up toward him. "You thought wrong. But that's okay because I happen to think you're pretty damn cute when you're wrong. And when you're right. And when you're tucked into my bed."

"What about Ben?" she asked. She had to know before she could give in to her desire to kiss him. To forgive him.

"I'm not interested in Ben either," he said, inching closer, a smile playing on his lips. "I didn't realize you were jealous of him too."

"That's not what I meant." She fought to control her thoughts, which were quickly becoming more and more clouded every moment, pushing her hands against his chest to force a little more space between them. "You chose him over me at the cache. That doesn't make me feel very good about where we stand."

"I didn't choose him over you. I came on this show to help Ben get his life back. When he wanted to prove to me that he could climb that rock wall, I couldn't say no. And I would have happily gone climbing with you too if I'd managed to get rid of your silly shoes sooner. I wanted you there with us, but I couldn't keep you safe while climbing in those shoes, not when I also had to keep Zoe and Ben out of trouble too."

"You don't have to keep everyone safe. We're not all your responsibility."

"I know that now. Trust me. Ben ripped me a new one after you guys left. I'd been short-changing him and treating him with kid gloves for too long. He's so much stronger than I gave him credit for." He ran his thumb along her cheek. "You're a lot stronger than I thought too."

"I am?"

"You are. The way you tackled every cache and tried things like rappelling today, without fear, is inspiring. I didn't realize how confident and amazing you really are until I thought I'd lost you for good."

"Honestly, I didn't realize how confident I could be either." She glanced down to her bare feet, embarrassed about her action. "I thought I had to wear those unbearable and uncomfortable shoes and this silly push-up bra to feel confident and for you to see me that way. I couldn't be more embarrassed. Well, until I have to watch it all play on TV again and then I'll surely feel worse."

"You are one of the most amazing women I've ever met. I don't think you need anything extra to make you more incredible than you already are."

"Not even the push-up bra?" She smiled. "You gonna throw it in the lake next?"

He smirked and cocked an eyebrow at her. "The bra can stay." His gaze flickered down to her chest, her nipples beading in response. "At least until I get you back to the lodge."

His lips were on hers in a heartbeat at which point her brain leaked out her ears, leaving behind a mess of swirly lights and a cloud of fog. She shivered as his mouth pressed against the pulse point in her neck. He kissed her on the mouth again, harder this time, filled with need that matched what she felt coursing through her own body, pooling low in her belly. She clung to his chest, pulling him closer.

"Maybe until I get you to the truck," he said against her lips then pulled back to look at her.

"What about the rest of the day? There's still a chance one of our teams could win if we find a few more caches today before the show ends."

He tangled his hand in her hair. "I don't know about you, but I've already won. I love you, Paige. I think maybe I have since that very first day of taping when I saw you standing alone waiting for your partner to show up. I've never been so drawn to anyone before."

She wrapped her arms around him, her body melting into his. "I love you too, Miles." She kissed him again, softly, sweetly. This was the only man she could ever imagine being with. The only man who'd ever seen her for who she really was, even when she didn't see it herself.

Epilogue

Zoe stood beside Paige while they waited for the finale to wrap up. They'd already filmed all the lead up stuff, and all the filler, and all the flashbacks from the season. If they didn't get on with announcing the winner soon, she might actually start hurting people.

She already knew her team hadn't won. She and Paige had compared notes with the other teams and even if their caches had a ton of points each, they still wouldn't have enough points to win. Their cache number had simply fallen too short.

The same went for Ben and Miles.

As much as she'd hoped to see them win, she just couldn't see how that would happen with the amount of caches they had, which ended up being only a handful more than her team. Nope. Some other team would win. Most likely Team Frat Boy since Team Firefighter was out. Too bad. She'd rather have seen the firefighters win it instead of two spoiled rich boys who really needed to grow up and graduate from college.

Paige giggled while cuddling into Miles's side. The giggling could stop anytime. Their lovey-dovey bullshit was enough to make cupid feel like hurling.

"So does this mean you two are together now?" Zoe asked.

Paige nodded. "Looks that way."

"Yep, better get used to the idea, sis. I don't plan on letting her go anytime soon."

"Oh, goody. It wasn't bad enough that I was stuck with Paige on the show, now I'm going to be stuck with her in real life too. Thank God we only see each other for major holidays, weddings, and funerals."

"I'm looking forward to spending time with you too, Zoe." Paige smiled.

Spencer walked back to his spot in front of them before Zoe could say anything else. There would be plenty of chances to say something later if Paige really was going to be a part of her brother's life.

"Now for the part we've all been waiting for," Spencer began, speaking directly to the camera. Since there wasn't a live audience for this finale, Spencer spent most of his time talking to the camera instead of the contestants.

Zoe couldn't care less who he looked at as long as he hurried up and got the filming finished. They'd been at it for two hours already because of retakes, which was way longer than necessary in her opinion.

"Time to find out which team is our big winner," Spencer said with so much enthusiasm even she couldn't help but cheer with everyone else. "But first, I have one last surprise."

Zoe's stomach dropped. She glanced over to where Chip stood watching the final production, a huge grin on his face. After participating in three shows for Chip she knew surprises from him were never good.

"We have a little secret that we didn't tell you at the start of the show." Spencer paused as if for dramatic effect and arched his eyebrows. "We aren't just naming one team the winners tonight, we're naming three!"

Everyone in the room appeared shocked. Even Zoe. She hadn't guessed this was coming at all and she was usually pretty good at predicting the twists in the game.

She glanced past Miles and Paige to where Ben stood. He'd been smiling the entire two hours already, apparently enjoying every moment of his last television experience. But now his grin was huge.

Zoe and Ben spoke briefly before they'd started filming tonight. Ben had been happy to feel like himself again, no longer needing to win the whole game to be successful. He'd rediscovered his love for climbing and being outdoors, just as Miles hoped he would. And all without winning the actual game. She took a little bit of pride in being part of the reason he felt that way. Their long talks during the show had really made a difference to how he saw his physical challenges.

They'd made a difference in how she'd seen her own too.

She blinked away the sting of her tears and focused on Spencer again.

"I know you're all excited, so let's get on with it, shall we?" he asked, not really pausing long enough for a response. "Our third place team is, Team Everest. Come on up here for a minute, guys."

The teams clapped as Ben and Miles walked to Spencer's side, the disbelief clearly evident on their faces.

Zoe couldn't help but smile and laugh with Paige as they watched the two boys jokingly fist pump the air. She was thrilled for Ben to receive some token of recognition for his achievement. And she was happy for Miles too. He'd come a long way during the filming. Realizing he couldn't control every situation in life and that it wasn't his responsibility to protect everyone was huge. Maybe now he'd finally feel free and less weighed down by his own expectations for himself.

"As our third place team, we'd like to award you with fifty thousand dollars."

What? Holy shit.

Spencer sent the boys back to their spots. They were too shocked to say anything for the cameras anyway.

"Our second place team is…"

Zoe held her breath. She hadn't expected to win, but now that she knew there was money involved for the other place prizes, she hoped they would.

"Team Father Daughter." Spencer clapped and waved them to his side where he awarded them a one hundred thousand dollar prize.

Damn. She really could have used that money.

"Finally," Spencer said, "our first place winners are... Team Frat Boy."

The boys ran around the stage area acting like they were at a football game instead of filming a TV show. When they finally settled down enough to join Spencer, he named them the winners of the half a million dollar grand prize.

Confetti rained down from the ceiling covering everyone in flakes of silver and gold. *Tacky.*

"So close again," Chip said coming up beside her. Spencer had already moved on to the makeup trailer now that filming was officially complete. "You want to come on another show and give it one last try to win?"

She took in Chip's sharp features and completely put together look. Some girls might not like a guy so stylish, but she'd always thought there was something sexy about a guy who took care of himself.

"I don't think so, Chip. I'm afraid I've hit my reality show limit at three losses."

He smiled. He was cute when he smiled. "Maybe the fourth time's a charm."

"Or maybe the forth time's another humiliating loss on national television and a wasted effort."

Chip stroked his hand along her jaw. She flinched, not used to people touching her there. Ever. He pulled his hand back but stepped closer, dropping his voice. "Or maybe the world hasn't gotten to see the real you. They haven't seen what you're really capable of yet. I can help you change that, Zoe. Say the word and I can make it happen for you. And I could guarantee a payday too. No more leaving empty handed."

He didn't wait for her to respond before walking away to congratulate the winners, which was good since she didn't know what the hell to say to him anyway. What did he know about who she really was?

And what was with the sudden touchy-feely stuff?

Her fingers traced the patch of skin still blazing from the warmth of his touch. Along her jaw she felt the familiar ridge of raised skin—scars that had faded with time but were still so painful and carefully hidden beneath her makeup. She'd never told anyone about the car wreck that had nearly killed her and the years of painful recovery she'd suffered through.

She glanced over to where Ben celebrated. Now he had a way to finish paying off his medical bills.

Been there, done that. Still doing it, actually. But the bills were worth every penny... every sacrifice.

She'd convinced him his physical disability was actually a trophy, and yet she couldn't say the same about her own scars. She couldn't let them go. Couldn't share the truth with anyone. She'd worked too hard to forget the past—to change her life, to protect her future—to share her secrets with anyone.

Chip was wrong. No one could ever see the real her. If they did, they'd think she was weak and that wasn't something she could stomach. Not after everything she'd been through.

She'd spent the last ten years making sure no one would ever find out. She wasn't about to throw that all away now.

But if he could offer her a "guaranteed payday" as he called it, could she afford to turn him down? The stack of overdue envelopes in her mail had probably doubled while she'd been on the show and all she had to go toward them was a shopping spree at Macy's.

She needed the money and Chip made a compelling offer.

Maybe finding out the details couldn't hurt...

About the Author

Heather Thurmeier was born and raised in the Canadian prairies, but now she lives in upstate New York with her own personal romance hero (aka her husband) and their two little princesses. When she's not busy taking care of the kids and an adventurous puppy named Indy, Heather's hard at work on her next romance novel. She loves to hear from her readers.

~Heart, humor, and a happily ever after.

Website: *http://heatherthurmeier.com*
Email: *heatherthurmeier@gmail.com*
Twitter: *https://twitter.com/#!/hthurmeier*
Facebook: *www.facebook.com/HeatherThurmeierAuthor*

In the mood for more Crimson Romance? Check out *Edie and the CEO* by Mary Hughes at CrimsonRomance.com.